For Jan

TREASURE of SAINT-LAZARE

This is a work of fiction. Other than easily recognizable historical figures, no character is intended to represent any person, living or dead.

Published by:
Alesia Press
PO Box 51004
Sarasota, FL 34232
(941) 315-8304
info@alesiapress.com
www.alesiapress.com
ISBN: 978-0-9859626-1-6

CHAPTER ONE

Sudden Death

Sarasota, June 2008

There was only one witness, and he was not a good one — the busboy at a new restaurant in the nearby arts colony walking back from the bank. He heard a sudden shout and wheeled just in time to see a large black car accelerate around the corner – "kind of a big SUV, but not as big as a Hummer, maybe a Lincoln" was what he told the patrol cop who first responded to his 9-1-1 call. "It hit the old man right in the center of the front end and sent him flying."

The old man, Roy Castor, had not been thrown far and with luck he might have survived if he'd been thrown the same direction as his hat, which flew left onto the grassy median. But the impact tossed him to the right like a broken stuffed toy and his head hit the curb with a sickening hollow thud.

"Man, I dropped a melon on the kitchen floor last week and it sounded just like that," Arturo said, adding his view that the old man was dead when he hit the curb. In fact Roy didn't draw his final breath for another hour, in the cold and remarkably empty emergency room of Sarasota Memorial Hospital.

"The dude went by real slow and looked at me, " Arturo told the detective who arrived later. "I don't think he saw me until after he hit the old man, then he just floored it and screamed around the corner to the right and he was gone. That's when I ran down to the old man and called you guys."

Thom Anderson, the Sarasota police detective who had drawn the case, thought it a straightforward hit-and-run. An overpaid and overeducated punk kid, Thom figured, with a job selling insurance or houses or stocks, had run over an old man crossing in the middle of the block, panicked, and fled. He would probably turn himself in the next morning, ashamed and completely lawyered up, maybe with his equally overpaid father beside him. His moment of panic would cost him a fine and a few months of probation and might cost him the fancy job. Thom had seen it more and more often as Sarasota had gentrified, and he didn't like it any better this time than the last.

CHAPTER TWO

The Young Fellow

Paris, Ten Days Later

Eddie turned away from the window of the first-class TGV car and put down the glass of Bordeaux he'd been nursing since Le Mans. The train curved around an old concrete water tower that disappeared as quickly as it had come into view, his signal that Gare Montparnasse was only a few minutes away. With luck, he'd be in his office near the old opera house in an hour, which would allow more than enough time to catch up on the day's business and get ready for dinner with his mother. His seventy-five-year-old mother, he reminded himself. His seventy-five-year-old mother and her lover.

He stood to take his blue blazer from the hook behind him just as the conductor announced the train's arrival at Gare Montparnasse in ten minutes. As she clicked off the microphone the iPhone chimed in his shirt pocket.

"Margaux. Nice to hear from you. Are we still on for dinner?" They spoke French, as always.

"Of course, Charles Edward. But that's not why I called. I need your help."

"Anything. Well, anything reasonable."

"I — we — have a surprise visitor. Does the name Jennifer Wetzmuller ring a bell?"

His smile faded. He sat in silence for a moment. "I haven't seen her for twenty years. Exactly twenty years, I think, when I got out of college. Artie wanted to see her father and I went to Florida with him."

"Hmmm. Sadly, Jennifer's father is dead. He was killed in an auto accident ten days ago, and in going through his things she found a letter from him to your father, with instructions to deliver it personally and immediately. She got on an airplane and arrived at my front door less than an hour ago."

"Margaux, can you give me some idea of what the hell this is all about?"

"The work Artie and Roy Castor did just after the war, when they were hunting down looted artwork, but I don't know any more than that. You must handle this, not me. I can't go through that door again."

Margaux had spent the war living on the run with her father, a Resistance leader, and as a result she feared nothing. But she did not want to reopen the story of her much-loved husband's life. "What would you like me to do?"

"I'm giving a fund-raising reception for Senator Obama here in an hour and a half, and I have to get ready. Can you pick up Jennifer and talk to her at your place? You can bring her to dinner tonight. Paul can pick you up. He's already on the way to Gare Montparnasse."

"Confident, weren't you? And why is it you're raising money for American politicians? You can't even vote."

"I can't even donate, but I give any help I can, and it seems my American friends like coming here for the view. Things aren't in good shape over there. I hope you're watching our money closely."

Eddie thought for a few seconds as the train started to slow. "OK. I'll come up to get her then we'll go to my place while you politick. And yes, I'm watching out for us. We have almost no positions left in the American market, and zero in the housing or banking industries. Our real estate in Le Mans is doing well. We should be fine unless the entire world goes to hell."

The best-known face of Gare Montparnasse is the north end, which opens onto the hulking brown Montparnasse Tower — one of the best vantage points for an inspiring city view despite the Parisians' distaste for its dissonant presence in the harmonious skyline.

Most TGV passengers exit the other end of the station, near the striking Place de Catalogne and its modern fountain, an immense stone disk precisely engineered to allow an unbroken sheet of water to flow smoothly over it.

Eddie looked briefly at the fountain as he emerged blinking into the strong afternoon sunlight. Then he spotted his mother's prized black Peugeot 607, the same model sometimes used by the French president, with his army buddy Paul Fitzhugh standing at the open driver's door.

"Ça va?" Paul asked as Eddie settled into the passenger seat.

"Ça va," Eddie responded, ending the only French exchange they would have. Paul was sensitive about his pronounced accent — he said if he was going to be taken for an American anyway he'd rather do it in English and be understood. He refused to speak French with anyone who spoke good English, which included just about everybody Margaux and Eddie knew.

"What do you know about our visitor?" Eddie asked as Paul took advantage of the Peugeot's power to merge smoothly between a bus and a small delivery van. He was surprised to realize he was reluctant to use her name. Damned big mistake, he told himself. I'm sure Margaux knows all about the trip to Sarasota but I'd like it better if it doesn't go much farther than that, so I'll have to act normal.

"Only saw her for a minute," Paul responded. "She's about your age, blonde, nice looking, I can see she's your type. A little taller than Margaux, long legs, good figure. A stunner.

"Margaux stepped right up and said her capable son Charles Edward would take care of the matter. That was the only time I saw her smile."

I hope she did, Eddie said to himself. They had spent three luxurious days in bed together and then he left without another word and married his fiancée. It wasn't his proudest memory.

"Well, let's pick her up, then you can take us to my place. She can rest before dinner, then we'll walk to the restaurant and I can show her a few of the sights around the opera. Will you and Margaux pick up Philippe?"

"Margaux says he'll drive himself. He's invited his daughter the history professor. You'll be surrounded by your past."

"Never mind that. Looks like you'll be eating alone again."

"Not a problem. I can keep a closer watch on the room, and Philippe sometimes brings a young officer along. Helps me practice my French, except these days they always want to practice their English."

Paul's role in the Grants' world was vague by design. His business card said he was in charge of buildings and facilities for Eddie's business, a chain of schools devoted mainly to teaching commercial English to the French and French to the Americans. Unofficially he was the family's chief of security and trusted bodyguard, driver and confidential friend, a role that had assumed more importance after the mysterious deaths of Eddie's father, and then his wife and son, seven years before. The police were never able to assemble enough evidence to file charges, and Paul had volunteered to spend more time on personal security.

Eddie had known Paul since 1991, when they served together in an infantry company during the first Gulf war. Eddie was a green company commander and Paul, the company's senior sergeant, had proved to be a valuable source of fatherly advice. After Paul was badly wounded and his wife divorced him, Eddie followed his recovery and offered him the job in Paris. Within two years he had married the concierge in Margaux's apartment building, a widow Eddie's age, and settled comfortably into daily Parisian life. He'd even become a fair pétanque player, and met a group of men every Sunday afternoon to roll the boules and drink pastis. There he had no choice but to speak French.

"How does it feel to come from West Virginia to Paris?" Eddie had asked him one Saturday afternoon as they shared a drink down the street from Margaux's home.

"I come from generations of Appalachian men, most of them farmers and almost all of them soldiers. But if my Scots ancestors had come here instead of to West Virginia, I guarantee every one of us would have been happy. I'm completely at home here, and here's where I intend to stay."

CHAPTER THREE

Together at the Luxor

Paris

For more than a hundred years, the Hôtel Luxor had stood imperiously on the narrow sidewalk of Rue Saint-Roch. Its cut-stone façade and wrought-iron balconies reflected to perfection the austere design dictated by Baron Haussmann when he razed and then rebuilt whole sections of the city for his patron, Emperor Napoleon III. Its sole distinguishing feature, other than a discreet brass plaque bearing the hotel's name over four stars, was an immense revolving door made of dark-stained oak highlighted with brass, which the hotel staff polished every day to a mirror finish. The single doors on either side of it stood open in the glorious late-spring weather that often settles over the city in mid June. Spring turning to summer is the time all the other Parisian seasons envy, and this June day was one of the best.

Late afternoon was a slow time for the reception manager — he was born to the hotel world and would stay at the Luxor until he died. His name was Monsieur Duval, and he believed he was at least partly responsible when the hotel received its coveted fourth star the year before. Monsieur Duval arrived at work each morning in casual dress — that is, he wore no tie with his starched white shirt, which his wife had carefully ironed that morning. In the small cloakroom behind the reception desk he changed to a dove-gray suit, adding a silk tie a few shades darker. Only Eddie and the payroll clerk knew his first name, so complete was his devotion to both his and his guests' privacy.

He was peering suspiciously at a slightly loose button on the left sleeve of his jacket just as Eddie's tall silhouette filled the open door. Jen Wetzmuller entered the lobby and Eddie followed, pulling her wheeled suitcase.

"Bonjour, Madame, bonjour, Monsieur Grant. Welcome back." Monsieur Duval said seriously, no smile. His hand came from beneath the counter holding two envelopes, which he handed to Eddie. "You have a little mail today. Not much."

"Thank you. Allow me to present Madame Wetzmuller, who is visiting me and my mother for a few days. Her father and mine were close associates during the war."

"The Luxor is very pleased to have you as its guest, Madame," Monsieur Duval said gravely. "Please ask for anything you need." Surprised by his formality, she muttered a barely audible "merci," then managed a tight smile and a dip of her head.

Eddie bypassed the large winding staircase he normally took to his apartment on the top floor, instead leading Jen toward the elevators to its left. He pressed the button marked 7 but the elevator did not move until he entered a code into the keypad above. "Remember the code, 6161," he told her.

As they rose, he reflected that Jen had retained the fresh air of youth he'd admired in 1988. She wore a traveler's outfit of white blouse and pleated blue skirt, and had coaxed her hair into a shape he had not seen in Paris for several years. With difficulty, he brought it back from his very small store of fashion knowledge — *coupe à la Jeanne d'Arc* — Pageboy cut, that had been its name, and it had been popular in the U.S. twenty years before. Despite the June warmth she had a sweater over her shoulders. The skirt fell precisely to the top of her knees, and her legs were as attractive as he remembered. She wore a delicate perfume he couldn't identify, except to remember that it was different from the one she'd worn in 1988. Under the perfume there was the delicious woman smell he'd immersed himself in during their three days together.

She looked up at him and said gently, "It's been a very long time. I never expected to see you again."

"Nor did I. But I could never forget those three days in Sarasota."

"They were memorable, weren't they?" She smiled at him for the first time, a generous open smile that lighted her deep blue eyes and told him his disappearance was forgiven, if not forgotten. The weight of mortal sin lifted from him.

She broke the silence as they passed the fifth floor. "What happened after?"

"Pretty much as planned. I went into the Army, served in Desert Storm, then came home to Paris."

"Did you ever marry?"

"Yes, once. You? My wife died."

"That is sad. I married once, for three years. A big-time cardiologist who wanted a younger wife. It lasted until he found another blonde trophy."

"Then you've stayed in Sarasota?"

"God knows why. It's a beautiful town but no place for a single woman my age. It's a huge, deep pool of blue-collar men looking for college-educated women and, surprisingly, finding them. I'm almost too old for that group now. I suppose I'll sign up for the club of unhappy middle-aged divorcées and widows who understand deep down they'll spend nights alone for the rest of their lives.

"You're selling yourself short. We're only forty and you still look like the girl I knew back then. It's far too early to start wearing black and sitting in a rocker on your front porch."

"Thanks for that. You haven't done badly yourself. You still have all that black black hair I admired. And you still carry yourself like a West Pointer." She smiled again.

They stood in silence until the elevator stopped. The door opened and she stepped out into a small lobby decorated in Second Empire style. A marble table held a large bouquet of yellow flowers, which complemented the blue walls.

"Just one door?"

"This floor was an afterthought some time after the building was built. It's a little smaller than the others, which is the reason the city has winked at it. The French are pragmatic about that sort of thing. If it pushes a little over the edge of the law but doesn't hurt anything, they generally close their eyes. It was a little risky, but I decided to turn the entire floor into my own apartment."

"How did you work that?"

"I needed a place to live seven years ago. This old hotel needed a lot of work but the owners didn't have the money to do it, so I bought it."

He opened the door and with a sweep of his arm invited her inside, following with the suitcase. They walked down an entrancc hall hung with bright oil paintings. She recognized one of them, a streetscape at dusk showing an early twentieth-century trolley passing the square of Châtelet, and stopped to look at it.

"Is that an Éduardo Cortès? I had one of them in my gallery. I hated to sell it."

"I remember that painting, and this is one almost like it. My father gave it to mc as a wedding present. It's the only thing I kept from that part of my life."

"Will you tell me about it?"

"Later. It's not a pretty story."

They continued into the living room, where he invited her to sit in a gray leather armchair to one side of a fireplace. He sat in its twin opposite her. A glass wall faced southeast over the city, with the spires of Notre Dame in the distance.

All the furniture was upholstered in muted shades of gray and beige except for one armchair on the opposite wall, which was a brilliant cardinal red. Jen first thought it was an error, but with a second look realized it was the bridge between the low-key furniture and the two dozen striking oil paintings that lined the wall from floor to ceiling.

"What a beautiful room. And you have a lovely view, like your mother's."

"Thanks. At Place Vauban she has Les Invalides and Napoleon's Tomb across the street, I have Notre Dame on one side and the Champs-Elysées on the other. I'll show you more of the sights a little later, but I think we should get business out of the way first."

"You're right." A sigh. "Roy is dead. Killed ten days ago by a hit-and-run driver just a couple of blocks from home."

"I was sorry to hear that. I remember him as a kind and interesting man."

"The police think it may not have been an accident, but aren't sure yet. I'm here because of something that was important to him. When I went to find his will, there was one other envelope in the bank vault – addressed to your father. It looks pretty old."

She paused and took a deep breath, then drew a heavy beige envelope from her purse and handed it to Eddie. On it was written in blue ink, in a European script, "For Artie Grant. Please hand deliver to him as soon as possible." It listed his mother's address on the Place Vauban, where his parents had bought the penthouse apartment shortly after they were married in 1952. Eddie was born 16 years later and grew up there.

"I caught a flight from Tampa as soon as I could. I had only the address on the envelope, no telephone number, so when my plane arrived I took a taxi straight there and met your mother. She asked me to pass the letter directly on to you. She handled like it was radioactive."

"Margaux believes in letting the past stay in the past."

And in this case I agree with her, Eddie said to himself. Anything that involved Roy Castor was bound to deal ultimately with the immense quantities of art and other treasure the Nazis stole during the war, much of which had never been found. For a time it had been Artie's holy grail as well, but he'd eventually turned his attention elsewhere.

Eddie dropped the envelope on his lap, willing it to disappear. When it did not, he picked it up like something distasteful he'd found on the street, touching it only with his thumb and forefinger.

"Was it sealed?"

"I wasn't about to fly all night to deliver a dirty joke."

"Tell me what's in it."

"A short letter, very cryptic, one paragraph. I don't understand it, but I can tell it refers back to their work at the end of the war. It's not exactly a code, but an outsider would have a hard time getting it – I certainly didn't. I don't know a lot of details about my father's war duties, but I know that after the Germans surrendered he and your father worked in Munich helping find stolen paintings. I know there was one special painting that interested him more than any other. Maybe you'll understand it better."

"Or maybe Mother will." Eddie unfolded the single sheet of rich beige stationery, heavy and stiff as though Roy had chosen it to last a long time. There was no date, but the paper had American dimensions, not European, so Eddie knew it had been written while Roy was in Florida. Just great, he thought. That narrows it down to the last thirty years or so.

"Dear Artie:

"The young fellow has disappeared into a dead end. I think the long-necked bastard planned to wind up in Paris and sent him there but he may also have used the underground railroad. Ask your round-heeled contact. Maybe you can find more than I could.

"Roy"

"What the hell does that mean?" Eddie asked, puzzled.

"I don't know. But he thought it was important enough to make sure I'd find it and get it to you. And he didn't want to give up the chase during his lifetime — otherwise he would have mailed it, maybe years ago. We have to find out."

"We need to get on it right now. If your father was murdered there may be other things going on we need to know about. We'll start with my mother. She's the best one to fill you in on what your father and mine did together during the war, and she knows a lot more about the history of the time than I do. After all, she lived through it."

He read the letter again from start to finish. "I'd like to look at this more closely and think about what it might mean. Would you like to rest before we talk about it? You've been traveling a long time. And we'd like it if you would join us tonight. There's a long-standing dinner with my mother on the schedule."

"We?"

"Margaux, of course. Then there's our friend Philippe Cabillaud, a semi-retired executive in the Paris police. When you arrived Margaux told him about it and he offered to bring his daughter, who's a history professor at the Sorbonne. She should know something about the lost art.

"My mother is bound to have more insights than either of us. And Aurélie, Philippe's daughter, has solid connections in the intellectual world here. Even though it has a really high BS level, it is very intellectual."

"I won't say it sounds like fun, but thank you for inviting me."

"You can use the guest room to get ready for dinner. I'll show you a sight or two on the way to the restaurant."

As she followed him down the wide central hall past the formal dining room, Jen glimpsed exercise equipment behind a half-open door. "You're still a weight lifter?" she asked.

"A casual one. I walk a lot and do some lifting a couple times a week, play some tennis. Not as much as I used to."

"It seems to be working."

He pushed open the door to an elegant bedroom, classically decorated except that the heavy brocades and mahogany popular in old Paris had been updated to light fabrics and woods, accented with brass. He twisted the handle of a wide double window and opened both panels into the room.

"In Sarasota we'd call that a French door. It's far too big for a window," Jen said with a little laugh. She leaned out over a waist-high protective bar set firmly into the thick stone walls, all that separated her from an eight-story drop to the tree-shaded courtyard below.

"There's almost no air conditioning in Paris," Eddie said. "With windows like this, we don't regret it more than two or three days a year. And we're too far north for many bugs, so no screens."

She looked across the courtyard and asked, "How many people have this view of Notre Dame?"

"Not many. It's beautiful this time of day, with the sun shining from behind us on the towers and the spire. From the front of the building you can look up the Champs Elysées to the Arc de Triomphe." He turned toward the door.

"We need to leave in an hour and a half. Please make yourself comfortable, and plan on staying here while you're in Paris."

As he closed the door, Jen tried to sort out what she knew about Eddie Grant. For one, he looked much like the pictures of his father Roy had shown her. Artie had been tall and Eddie was a bit shorter, a touch under six feet. Like his father, he had a large head topped by carefully cut and brushed black hair, so black its highlights appeared purple, long by American standards but fashionable in Paris. His hands were large, like those of a basketball player or a pianist -- Jen hoped he was a pianist but they hadn't talked about either music or sports during their three days together. It was the end of the day, but his navy blazer showed little wear. Neither did his gray slacks or checked shirt. Even the tie was still tightly knotted. It was, she thought, a man's outfit of the sort she hardly ever saw any more in Sarasota, and missed.

The apartment's high ceilings, ornate plaster decoration and designer furnishings reminded her that Eddie's father had been the last member of the founding family to work at Norway Steel, which had been an industrial giant from the Civil War until U.S. corporations became multinationals and moved their jobs offshore in search of cheaper and more docile workers. The company had disappeared in the wave of mergers that had swept over American business in the 70s and 80s ("stupid financial engineering by mental defectives," Roy had called it), but Artie had known when to sell and as a result his widow and son were among the wealthiest Americans in Europe. The apartment showed it.

CHAPTER FOUR

Family History

Eddie walked back to his office, leaving the door ajar in case Jen called him. He read Roy's letter again, then began turning over in his mind some of the wartime stories his father had told him. As he always did during the rare times he allowed himself to think back over his father's accomplishments, he pondered the unusual mix of circumstances and abilities that had put Artie in position to achieve big things – scion of American industrial royalty but reared in Paris, a Harvard Law graduate persuaded to turn his back on a lucrative but boring career at the family firm and join Army intelligence a full year before Pearl Harbor. Military officers weren't the public heroes they became after the war started, so his decision appeared bizarre to his friends and family.

He rejoined Norway Steel after the war, only to abandon an almost certain chance to become its president. He was repelled by McCarthy and thought he could contribute more to helping Europe rebuild if he lived in Paris, where he had spent happy childhood years with his mother. And his marriage was failing.

The Grants were part of the Dutch burgher community that had settled in and around the wealthy unprepossessing town of Hyde Park in a scenic part of the Hudson River valley less than 100 miles north of Times Square. Eddie's great-great-grandfather and a few other farsighted businessmen pooled their resources just as the American railroads accelerated their historic expansion to the West. His distant cousin the Civil War hero and president had added an unquantifiable but tangible strength to his efforts to line up buyers for the fledgling company's products. He had a nodding acquaintance with the most famous son of Hyde Park, Franklin D. Roosevelt, which had ultimately led him down an unexpected career path.

His grandfather had been born in 1890 and fathered Artie in 1917, shortly before he went off to die of pneumonia at Château-Thierry. Artie had never known him, and his French mother had abandoned Hyde Park as soon as the war ended and taken her young son to Paris, where he had lived until it was time to go to college and law school. Eddie's experience had been almost the same, except that he had chosen to join the Army instead of go to law school. The Grant men had always been drawn to military service.

Artie married a Hyde Park debutante as soon as he returned from the war in 1947, but the marriage wasn't a success and they divorced when he returned to Paris four years later to become European president of Norway Steel. He lived for a while with his wartime friend Alain d'Amboise, a genuine Resistance hero and rising political star in the Gaullist government, and daughter Margaux, no longer the child he'd met once in 1943 but a rigorously educated dark-eyed beauty of 19. In a week they were lovers, in a month they were engaged and three months later they were married. They ignored the malicious society chatter about their twenty-year age difference and short courtship, and for the next 16 years Margaux worked alongside Artie to turn Norway Steel into the largest of the companies furnishing basic materials to Marshall Plan projects. Their fortune, already large, grew to mammoth proportions.

After Eddie was born she turned her attention to him. Neither she nor Artie let him forget that she had been an important part of the family business, never mind that French women didn't get the vote until the end of the war. Her attitudes had shaped Eddie's.

Eddie forced his attention back to the letter, which he had let fall to his desk as he reminisced. He tried to avoid random walks down the gnarly paths of family memory because they led to dark comparisons between his life and his father's. He shook off the thought. He was getting better at that.

There was a certain rootlessness and self-doubt about him, a feeling of not being fully involved in his own life. He hid it well, except from his mother, who thought it had no merit and thus ignored it. During his youth in Paris he had been fully and unconsciously French; during his college years in the United States he had worked very hard at becoming American. Then came his experience of war in Kuwait and Iraq, the first time he had felt completely at home outside of Paris.

His return to Paris was partly an effort to ground himself somewhere — anywhere — and he believed as the years went by that it had worked. That is, he believed it until the terrible year 2001, when his American wife and son were murdered, his father died under suspicious circumstances, and his ancestral country was attacked. For the next two years he was lost, wandering in the wilderness of his own confused mind. He went through a series of short-term relationships, always with French women, but the ghosts of his unhappy year were stronger and each of them wandered away confused and disappointed. After three or four years his doubts lessened but even after seven years he wondered almost daily how so much could have gone so wrong in that one year. The police had never found good suspects for the murder of his family, and remained uncertain that his father's death had been anything other than an old man's loss of control just long enough to run into a tree.

Eddie looked again at the letter. Roy's clues pointed back to his and Artie's war, of that he was certain. It seemed clear that "wind up in Paris" meant the art — whatever it was — was supposed to be somewhere in his city, or at least was supposed to have been there at the end of the war. The "long-necked bastard" baffled him, as did the reference to a "round-heeled contact." He knew it told him to seek out a woman, and one for whom Roy had little respect, but it didn't remind him of anyone his father had mentioned. He tucked that clue into the back of his mind for later. Then he ran the page through his scanner, printed six copies and folded them into an inside pocket of his jacket, and locked the original in his safe. He showered quickly and changed to a blue suit with a maroon tie.

Jen opened the door before he had time to knock twice. She had changed to a trimly cut dark-gray silk blouse with black slacks, just the right color for Paris, and added a black-and-red Hermès scarf that fell from her neck to a loose knot at her waist, the fashion currently popular among chic Parisian women. The contrast of the dark ensemble against her blonde hair was dazzling, and Eddie remembered that twenty years before he had thought her a lovely girl. He forced into the background a picture of how she had looked naked.

"Do you think your mother will like it?" she asked, spinning to give Eddie the full effect. "She was wearing a scarf like this. I got the idea from her and from women I saw on the street on the way over here. Roy gave me the scarf during our last trip to Paris."

"She will," he replied. "I certainly do. Are you up to a short walk? That is, short by Paris standards. We could get a cab but the walk will only take 15 minutes, and the city views are terrific, especially the Opéra."

"Then we'll walk."

The elevator door opened immediately. Her perfume was more mature than twenty years before but it suited her just as well, he thought as they descended to the lobby. He nodded goodnight to the night clerk, who responded with a sober "Bonsoir, Monsieur Grant, Madame" then together they pushed the revolving door and walked out into Rue Saint-Roch to hear the sound of piano music filling the air.

"What is that?" she asked, surprised.

"Our regular concert. One of my neighbors across the street is a famous for her Chopin." He stopped a moment to listen. "That's one of the Études, I think. Sometimes I move a chair to the window and listen to her entire practice session.

"That's lovely. I guess my equivalent would be country music on a car radio.

"But tell me about yourself. What do you do now? I should have asked your mother."

"Business. I moved back as soon as I could after I got out of the Army and bought a little school where we teach business English. I've expanded into a few other cities. The French officers I met in Kuwait all told me they needed better English, because even then it was just about everyone's second language. Our office is just a block from here, in fact." He pointed up Avenue de l'Opéra toward the Palais Garnier. It had recently been refurbished, and what appeared to be acres of gold leaf gleamed in the setting sun.

Jen stopped to stare. "That's absolutely magnificent."

Eddie quickly took her elbow. "Let's get out of traffic first."

They turned right, crossed in front of the fortresslike Bourse, then left up a two-lane street with little traffic.

In a few minutes they reached the front of Pierre-Victor, whose glass windows were filled with elaborate displays of its wares – it was famous for oysters, and seemed to have dozens of different types.

The headwaiter recognized Eddie immediately. "Bonsoir, Madame. Monsieur Grant, bonsoir. Votre mère vous attend au fond du restaurant." He turned to lead them to a large table, set off from others at the rear.

The table had clearly been set aside for dignitaries, celebrities, or lovers — anyone who wanted space to talk without being overheard. To Eddie's practiced eye, the other customers settling themselves into the comfortable chairs appeared to be an even mix of couples and groups of three or four men out for business meetings. In the front corner of the room, with their backs to the wall so they could see everyone in the room, he spotted Paul with Gabriel Domingue, the tall police officer assigned to drive Philippe. Both had the ramrod posture of military men who would have been more comfortable with their jackets off in a bar in the 19th arrondissement than in a white-tablecloth restaurant in the 2nd.

The waiter was middle-aged, a man clearly at home in his work, polite without being obsequious. As she followed him, Jen surveyed the small group waiting at the round table. Margaux, clearly in command, watched expectantly as they approached. Eddie had told her his father first met Margaux when he was smuggled into southern France by submarine to coordinate D-Day preparations with her father. She was 11 at the time, which meant she had to be 75 or 76 years old now, although to Jen she looked closer to 60. She had dark eyes and hair of a deep chestnut, with reddish highlights that shimmered under the restaurant's flattering lights. Jen wondered briefly how long she had spent that afternoon having it done into a perfect chignon, and decided she was a Frenchwoman of the old school, the ones who get dressed and made up to take out the trash, for whom the time invested would always take second place to the result. At her right sat an older version of the policeman sitting with Paul, whom she took to be Philippe Cabillaud. Philippe's daughter Aurélie, a striking blonde about 30 years old, sat across from Margaux.

Eddie said a quick hello to his mother, then introduced Jen to Aurélie, who looked up with a friendly and open smile, her green eyes sparkling. He and Philippe shook hands warmly. Philippe kissed Jen gravely on both cheeks and told her in quiet French that Margaux had explained her trip and he was enchanted to meet her although it was unfortunate it had to be at such a sad time for her. She thought he was wonderful.

Aurélie had already heard the story of Jen's surprise visit and of Margaux's certainty that it had something to do with her husband's wartime work.

Even though Aurélie wasn't born until a generation after the war, she grew up in its shadow. She had watched as the large American military presence in Europe was dismantled during her childhood, and her doctoral studies in French history had required her to spend a great deal of time examining the mangled relations between France and its European neighbors that led up to the two brutal 20th-century wars. To her it seemed completely natural that the theft of Europe's patrimony could reverberate for seven decades and fire the imagination of men like Roy Castor and Artie Grant. European countries had been stealing each other's art treasures for centuries — to wait decades to avenge a theft or settle a grudge was nothing.

“Hello again,” Margaux said to Jen with a smile. “I'm glad to see you again. Were you able to divine the meaning of your father's letter?" She spoke English fluently but with the tinge of formality common to French speakers who learn English as adults.

"Unfortunately, it is still a mystery to us, Madame Grant. Eddie thinks you might be able to help decipher it." She heard herself mirror Margaux's formal language and thought it sounded very strange coming from an Americanized German.

"We can talk about that after everyone's had a glass of champagne. I think a trans-Atlantic flight on short notice deserves an apéritif a little more elegant than a kir, and Aurélie and I have already started. Philippe just arrived." Margaux signaled to the waiter.

Jen told herself it was a good thing she'd remembered to bring the stylish scarf. Without it, she would have been underdressed next to Margaux and Aurélie, who radiated the understated elegance of Parisian women out for a fine summer evening. Margaux, her fashionable chignon set off by simple gold earrings, wore a slim black skirt with a silk blouse of tiny multicolored stripes -- the effect was somewhere near the red end of the spectrum.

Aurélie, on the other hand, would have been just as comfortable in New York as in Paris. She looked like what she was, an affluent young professional approaching the peak of her beauty. Her shoulder-length ash-blond hair contrasted starkly with an all-black outfit of slacks and a trim short-sleeved sweater cut low enough to emphasize her figure. She wore only one piece of jewelry, a wide choker the distinctive brilliant color of high-carat gold.

Margaux had the olive complexion of her Mediterranean origin. She and Jen were a few inches over five feet tall, much shorter than anyone else at the table, with Jen and inch or two taller.

"I think the *langue du soir* should be English," Eddie said to the entire table after the champagne arrived. "I heard Jen speak good French when I first met her years ago, but it's been a long time and she's tired. So English it will be?"

Jen said with relief, "I appreciate that. I learned French in school but I'm shaky now. We don't speak a lot of French in Sarasota. Or German, for that matter, so I've pretty much become a monoglot American."

The waiter came and went. As they waited, Aurélie turned to Eddie with a smile and said, "Édouard. I haven't seen you in a while."

He was Eddie to his friends and Charles Edward to his mother, but to Aurélie Cabillaud — and only Aurélie — he was Édouard, with its silky drawn-out syllables that always made him think of languid afternoon romance. He was christened with the name on just such an afternoon five years before, the day before he bought her the necklace.

"I've stayed busy with the usual. You?"

"Much the same. New students, different classes, but I still like my work, and I'm going to start a new book soon, one about the Revolution as it was seen in the distant provinces. It should be fun to do the research."

Eddie and Aurélie's friends had been disappointed when they broke up. His closest friends weren't as surprised as hers because they'd seen his dark moods and flashes of sharp, unexpected anger. Hers, on the other hand, saw none of that because he hid it behind the veneer of bonhomie he had first erected for his clients. Aurélie did not enlighten them. She said only that both had wanted a permanent marriage and had simply decided the time was not right.

As they chatted, Margaux turned to Jen and said, "I was very sorry to hear of your father's death. He was a very important part of my late husband's early life, before we married, but for one reason or another I never met him. Would you mind telling us about him and your life in Florida? It may help us figure out what's happening."

Everyone else fell silent.

Jen thought for a few seconds, then lowered her voice.

"I'll do my best. You should know about it." She paused and took a deep breath.

"You know Roy owned an antique and art business in Frankfurt. It was successful – after the war many new fortunes were built, and all of those people wanted to flaunt their new wealth, and Roy was always there to sell to them. He also was one of the first dealers to sell in great quantity to American dealers.

"My mother worked as Roy's office manager and accountant, in a converted house across the street from a wonderful park. Her name was Gutrud Wetzmuller, and she had been born in Berlin during the war. Her mother didn't want either of them to be captured by the Russians, so in the chaos near the end she found a way to escape toward the west with a German officer. She wound up in Frankfurt, in the American zone of occupation.

"My grandmother raised my mother in poverty but paid close attention to her education, and by the time she finished what we call high school in the States she was a pretty good accountant, so she had no problem finding jobs. She was also very attractive, which didn't hurt.

"We never lived with Roy, but he paid my mother a far larger salary than he had to, and she told me he also paid my school fees. I actually spent two of my middle-school years in Lyons, which is where I learned my French. That was while she was married to a very odd man, an older Frenchman who had been a collaborator during the war and found it more comfortable to live in Germany afterward. He hit her from time to time, he drank too much, and he had a nasty son about my age. She divorced him and brought me home from France the year before she died.

"As I grew older I became less certain Roy was my father. He and my mother didn't socialize, and I never knew him to be involved with another woman, either in Frankfurt or Sarasota. I think he was just one of those people who are a little confused about their sexual identity and deal with it by doing nothing. But none of that matters now. In Sarasota he treated me like his daughter.

"My mother asked him to take me when she found out she was dying. Roy had moved to Florida when he sold his business a few years before. She'd already had one bout with breast cancer before she was 30, and the doctors just couldn't handle the second one. When she died she was just a little younger than I am now.

"I remember he came to Frankfurt to get me. He arrived the day my mother was buried.

"Ten years or so ago, only when I asked him directly, he told me he thought he was my father. He and my mother had a short affair on a buying trip to the East. She was living with someone else at the time, so neither of them could ever be sure, but I was happy to think so, and I believe he was, too."

Aurélie could see Jen was having more and more difficulty talking about her father, so as the appetizers arrived she tried to move the conversation back to safe ground. "Did he talk to you much about what he and Mr. Grant did during the war?" she asked in a gentle voice.

Jen was relieved to change the subject. "He said they first met in Paris just after the Liberation in 1944. Roy was a sergeant in the

Signal Corps and Artie was a major in intelligence who was very much involved with the Resistance in the last year before the Normandy invasion. After Paris was liberated he was recruited by the Monuments Men.

"When Major Grant was ordered to Munich to help look for looted art treasures he asked for Roy as his assistant. Roy always said it was Major Grant who picked him out of the Signal Corps and set him on the way to such an interesting life. There was quite a difference in their ages, and Major Grant was an officer and a very educated man while Roy was a sergeant with a high-school education, but they became friends. He always told me it was because they were both very curious."

Margaux jumped in. "That was Artie, curious about anything and everything. He told me he was surprised to be invited into the Monuments Men, because most of them were highly educated in their field, while he was a lawyer and a spy.

"And I'm curious right now about this letter from Roy you found. May we take a look at it before dinner arrives?"

Eddie took the copies from his pocket and passed them around the table.

"I have part of the answer," Margaux announced after only a few seconds. "Artie once used the same words. Hans Frank was governor general of Poland and a thoroughly brutal man. Artie met him and never could understand how a trained lawyer could bring himself to act the way Frank did. And he was known for his stolen art collection. In fact, behind Hitler and Göring he was one of the worst of the art thieves.

"Artie called him the long-necked bastard because he was hanged after the Nuremberg trials."

Aurélie asked, "So the young fellow is someone or something Hans Frank wanted to send to Paris so he could find it later?"

"More than likely he thought he'd get a prison sentence and wanted to keep it safe until he got out," Eddie said. "I doubt he thought he'd be hanged, and in fact the allies only executed about half of the Nazis they tried, and that was a pretty small group to start with – too small for my taste. Frank knew he would need money to start a new life, and by the end of the war it must have been clear the allies were going to occupy Germany and not repeat the mistake they had made after the First War. He probably figured the French would have no stomach for a military government once the war ended, which would make it easier to pick up his loot in Paris than in occupied Munich.

"It's most likely some sort of valuable art that Frank wanted to hide until he and his friends could resurrect the Fourth Reich. Hundreds — maybe thousands — of pieces of treasure the Nazis stole are still missing. The Jews were the easiest marks. They were sometimes offered exit visas in exchange for all their valuables. Other times they were just shipped off to Auschwitz and the property was stolen outright. The same thing happened in all the occupied countries. Poland under Hans Frank was one of the worst."

The waiter arrived with their main courses. Jen discovered she was hungrier than she thought, and wished she had ordered more than a salad.

Long seconds passed until Aurélie broke the silence. "So we have a couple of questions for which we have no answers. Who or what is the young fellow — it's probably art, maybe gold or jewels, but we don't know — and who is this round-heeled person? And then there's the underground railroad angle."

Margaux said, "That name was a sadistic play on the Underground Railroad that smuggled American slaves north. The old Nazis set up their own version.

"It flourished for a couple of years after the war, and there was some activity until the early 50s. Its main purpose was to take Nazi fugitives to South America, but there's no reason it couldn't have been used to move looted treasure as well. One of its main relay points was a small town near Munich called Memmingen. As I recall, the local priests were very active. And Artie told me he suspected some of the Americans in his unit knew about it but did nothing to stop the traffic. It was called Die Spinne — The Web."

"So the mysterious young fellow is our key," Aurélie said. "We know Hans Frank was an art thief, and that he was in charge of Poland. I know a little bit about art history of that period, but this doesn't ring a bell. I have some friends who teach nothing else. I'll ask them tomorrow."

Eddie signaled to Paul that Margaux was ready to go. While they waited for him to bring the car, they finished their small cups of dark, aromatic expresso. Margaux and Eddie argued good-naturedly over the bill, but in the end she paid. Eddie invited Aurélie to walk part of the way with him and Jen and she accepted, curious to know more about this American woman who, she suspected, also had a history with Eddie. Philippe waited on the sidewalk while his driver got the car.

Paul stopped the Peugeot at the restaurant door. Eddie bussed his mother on both cheeks and told her, "We'll walk. It's not far, and Jen — all of us — will love passing the Opéra while it's all lighted. Call me first thing if you think of anything else about the letter, and we'll work on it in the morning as well. We'll come to Place Vauban."

CHAPTER FIVE

Too Close For Comfort

Paris

Eddie stepped into the street to close the car door for Margaux and noticed two men who had left the restaurant just ahead of them waiting on the sidewalk a hundred yards away. An image of Mutt and Jeff, from the American comic strip his father read faithfully for years, flew through his mind as he turned to watch them climb hurriedly into the back of a large black Mercedes sedan as soon as it glided to a stop.

"Odd," he said to himself as his mother's car disappeared up the street and turned left.

The smile Aurélie had worn through the dinner changed to a look of concern. "We can figure out Roy's letter. Margaux got us partway there tonight, and I'm confident my friends at the Sorbonne will help tomorrow. But we haven't even started to think about what it really means.

"It could be the musings of an old man who had decided to give up, or it could have been a serious warning to Mr. Grant. And that probably means to you and Jen as well."

Jen replied, "The police in Sarasota say officially Roy's death was an accident, but the detective in charge thinks there's something fishy about it, and so do I. It's very unlike Roy to cut across a street in the middle of the block.

"The police are out looking for the car. They think it'll turn up in a repair shop sooner or later."

The black Mercedes pulled away from the curb and turned behind Paul and Margaux. The boulevard was brightly lighted and bustling with pedestrians and theatergoers as they crossed at a few minutes before 10:30.

Eddie reached for his telephone, intending to alert Paul to the possible tail, when the Mercedes stopped in front of the wax museum, Musée Grévin, a hundred yards from the corner. The right rear door opened and tall Mutt stepped out, followed by short Jeff, and then a city bus pulled out to avoid them, blocking his view. When the bus passed the two men had disappeared.

Aurélie was pleased to show off her Paris to a fascinated visitor and kept up a running commentary. Jen, no longer tired, asked question after question and suggested they stop for a last cup of coffee along the walk to Rue Saint-Roch.

Eddie half listened because his attention was focused on the Mercedes. It stood idling in a no-parking lane, rear door fully open. That wasn't uncommon in this part of the city, where drivers often had to wait for their passengers to finish dinner or the theater, but to leave a door open in the June heat struck him as odd. The two men had disappeared, either into the alcove entrance of the Musée Grévin or Passage Jouffroy, one of the most charming of the city's many covered shopping arcades.

He interrupted Aurélie's explanation of the wax museum. "This whole thing feels strange. The two men who got out of that Mercedes up ahead were in the restaurant with us, and they left just as Margaux was paying the check -- but they were only there a half-hour, not nearly enough time to have even a quick dinner. And now they're parked where we have to pass them.

"Just ahead of us is one of the old passages, a 19th-century mall where people could shop out of the weather, and halfway down it there is a hotel called the Chopin. My family lived there for a month while our apartment was being renovated. I was about 13 years old then, and bored, so I explored every inch of it. If they're waiting for us now, we'll go there."

As they neared the Mercedes the two passengers walked briskly out of the museum alcove and stopped facing them. The taller one pulled his jacket open just enough to show the leather-wrapped hilt of a large knife protruding above his belt. A prominent scar on his left cheek showed he was no stranger to knives.

He lifted it partway out of the scabbard, just enough for Eddie to identify it as a World War II American Army bayonet – his father had told him it was the sharpest knife he had ever seen.

Mutt spoke roughly in hesitant French, with a strong German accent. "We want the painting, and you are going to tell us where it is. Now. Get in." He gestured with his head toward the Mercedes.

He reached with his left hand for Aurélie's shoulder, keeping his right on the hilt of the sheathed knife, but a sharp blast of the Mercedes's horn distracted him for an instant. Without thinking, Eddie called on the close-combat training he'd received two decades before and grabbed the man's right wrist with his left hand, preventing him from drawing the knife. With his right, he reached for the man's other elbow and pulled it sharply to force him off balance. Turning to the left like a dancer leading a clumsy and untrained partner, Eddie pushed him forcefully toward the car. Off balance, he staggered drunkenly across the curb, hit his head on the top of the car, and slumped into the back seat. The bayonet clattered to the pavement.

The smaller man tried to reach for Eddie just as he pushed Mutt away. Aurélie shouted a warning and kicked him hard in the shin. He didn't appear to have a weapon, but Eddie took no chances. He hit the man hard in the jaw, backhand with his closed fist, then grasped both of his shoulders and spun him around to face the street. Taking him in a bear hug to immobilize his arms, Eddie pushed him toward the Mercedes and watched as he bounced off the rear fender and fell into the street, just missing the bumper of a city bus that missed him by inches as its driver furiously sounded his plangent warning chimes.

Eddie ran back to the two women and whispered, "Hotel Chopin. They'll be closing the gate any minute."

They sprinted the remaining few yards to the Passage Jouffroy entrance, arriving just as the night porter prepared to close the ornate iron gate, a 10:30 p.m. tradition. Aurélie told him quickly they were guests of the Chopin, and then they ran for its entrance fifty yards away, at a corner where the passage jogged to the left between two antique-book stores. Halfway there, they heard the night porter argue with the Germans, then give an angry shout as they pushed him roughly out of the way. "That guy's gonna be pissed. Cops will be here before long," Eddie said as the three approached the door.

The lobby was empty, as Eddie had hoped. They pushed the door open, then as it closed Eddie said, "Help me put this sofa against it. It'll give us a little more time." He piled two large green leather armchairs atop the sofa for good measure, then the three turned and dashed up the half-flight of stairs to the level of the breakfast room. They froze momentarily as the sound of a man's scream came from the passage. A second scream, then the only sound was the Germans' footsteps on the marble floor.

"I hope you know where we're going." Jen had been surprised at the quick burst of activity because she hadn't seen the knife.

"This is where my misspent youth will work for us," Eddie said with a lopsided grin. "I hope the goons will look for us upstairs. But we're going down below. The back door leads into the service area for all the buildings around here. If we're lucky, we'll come out a long way from where they expect to find us. If not, we'll have to think of something else. This way."

They ran to the end of the hall and Eddie pulled an ornately painted door, which led to a gloomy utility stair. At the bottom they pushed open a gray metal door to reveal a service alley. Eddie found a wedge the hotel staff used to keep the door open and forced it tightly under the outside of the closed door. The doorstop should give them enough time to escape even if their followers figured out where they had gone.

All three stood with their backs against the old stone wall to catch their breath. "Well," Aurélie said. "At least we know now what we're chasing. And we know these salauds will stop at nothing to get it. Let's go find the young fellow."

Suddenly they were in the gritty 19th century backstage inhabited by the city's immigrant service workers. Above them, a pair of dim yellow bulbs struggled in vain to illuminate the hotel's back door, aided ineffectively by the glow from a few curtained rooms higher on the wall. Down the alley a dozen yards to their right, a single bright window high in the back wall of a Japanese restaurant threw a checkerboard pattern on the cobbled pavement.

It wasn't really an alley. There are almost no true alleys in Paris because every square inch of space is used for buildings or for the elaborate and parklike courtyards found in the center of almost every block.

To the left was a double steel door – the main exit to the street. Eddie ignored the pungent smell and pushed aside two overflowing garbage cans, dislodging a black cat sleeping behind them, and tried the door. Locked. He turned and signaled in the other direction. The cat let out a single angry hiss and ran ahead of them toward the lighted kitchen window, tail standing straight up.

As they passed under the bright kitchen window an argument broke out, the harsh sound of voices raised in several oriental languages sharpening the hot smell of soy sauce and sizzling meat. The clang of steel against steel faded and after a few steps they reached Eddie's backup goal, a short, dark passageway that branched left to a fire exit of the Théâtre du Nord-Ouest. A thread of light at the side of the door hinted it was ajar, but he and Jen stood at the corner to watch for pursuers while Aurélie tiptoed ahead to pull carefully on the handle.

"Voila!" They slipped through to join the departing audience as it flowed through the lobby and deposited them on a busy side street, the Japanese restaurant to their left. A hundred yards to their right the first police car arrived, a single blue light flashing on its rooftop. An ambulance followed.

"Let's get out of here." Eddie's tone did not invite questions.

The crowd thinned as they followed it away from the police lights. Aurélie set a rapid pace down a side street lined with restaurants, while Eddie lagged behind to answer his telephone.

He hurried to keep up, phone to his ear, anxious. "Can you call Philippe? I know it's late, but I'd rather talk to him than meet the local flics in the basement of the police station. Tell him I need to see him about the Hôtel Chopin, and we think they're connected. He'll understand. We're on the way."

He put the phone back into his pocket and said, “Not good news. Someone broke into her apartment -- lots of damage to the door but they were gone when she got back and she's OK. She doesn't know yet what was taken but they went through my father's office. It was probably the guys we just met.”

Aurélie turned and said, "Don't slow down now. We can catch a cab at a Best Western hotel just two streets ahead. We need to get to her fast.”

The taxi took them across the Seine on the Pont de la Concorde, then a few minutes later stopped under a row of plane trees whose dense leaves blocked the streetlights, making them almost invisible.

They huddled next to the old stone wall of the military academy as Eddie outlined the next step.

"Jen, we're going to Mother's through the back way. If the Germans left watchers for us they'll be on the other side guarding the entrance. Please stay close.”

They would meet inside a parking garage. “Go down the ramp to the left and wait around the corner. Remember, we're tourists, so let's try to act relaxed. And no English. It's too easy to pick out of the background noise.”

He dispatched Aurélie down one side of the street while he and Jen took the other. “A small thing, but it might gain us an extra step if they don't see a group of three,” he said.

Aurélie waited for a car to pass then crossed to a Moroccan restaurant where a few customers remained on the sidewalk, chatting over their coffee and paying no attention to her. Eddie and Jen crossed at the end of the block then passed a closed newsstand, a grocery, a stationery store and a brasserie where a few tipsy drinkers remained. At the end of the block they turned left to pass a Thai restaurant and a row of large and genteel private townhouses.

"Cross now!” Eddie whispered. “Aurélie is waiting for us to move. She'll hang back to be sure we're alone." She held tight to his arm.

The garage entrance was a gaping black square in the face of the dimly lit office building. They ducked in, feeling their way down the railing of a narrow ramp that led to a landing out of sight of the street. In less than a minute, Aurélie joined them. "No signs of life on the block, so I think we're in the clear," she said. A pause as her eyes adjusted. "I bet you did this as a boy," she said softly to Eddie.

"Almost," he replied. "I watched it go up during my visits home from college. It's handy now because it's a shortcut to mother's car."

He told them the pedestrian walkway ended just a few feet further into the garage, and at that point they would cut across the main driveway to reach the rear exit. The automatic lights would come on, but they were so dim they were hardly visible from the street.

They crossed the driveway to a short corridor with machinery-room doors on each side, its smell announcing that it was a frequent rest stop for the city's homeless, then stepped into a tree-shaded courtyard much like the one Jen had seen from Eddie's apartment window.

"That's Margaux's building across the courtyard."

He hoped they looked like three friends returning from a neighborhood party as they sauntered under the trees then down a short flight of stairs to a small landing. He tested the door, then keyed in its digicode and pulled it open to reveal a brightly lighted service corridor curving down the full length of the building, whose shape mimicked the half-circle of Place Vauban.

A short walk to the left and they stopped at an elevator. "This is three buildings in one," he said. "There are three elevators, each opening onto a lobby between two apartments. The exception is my mother's floor at the top, where there is only one apartment."

The elevator rose smoothly. They stepped out into a small lobby furnished with a gleaming antique mahogany table. A spray of roses stood wilting in a crystal vase neatly centered on its marble top. The apartment's main entrance door had been jimmied violently and stood ajar.

"Eddie, look at that," Aurélie exclaimed when she saw the bent steel of the doorframe. "They just used brute force. These weren't experienced burglars."

Eddie called to his mother around the damaged door. They heard her reply from inside, "I'll let you in the service door."

The service door was to their left, its face blank so it could be used only for exit. After a brief wait it opened slowly, its seldom-used hinges squealing in complaint. Inside stood Margaux, still dressed for dinner, her shoulders slumped. The sad expression on her face gave Eddie the impression, just for an instant, that she had been crying. A surprise.

Eddie put his arm around her and led her to an upholstered chair facing the living room fireplace. "Aurélie and Jen will stay with you while I find out what happened here," he told her.

"Thank you, dear. I don't think they took anything valuable, and they didn't even do much damage, except for the door. They mainly went through your father's study.

"Philippe just called me back. He will be here in a half-hour, and we're not to touch anything in the meantime. He wants to find out more about the Hôtel Chopin on the way." Eddie nodded and walked down the hall to his father's study. Initially, Margaux had kept it just as it was when Artie died. After a few years she began to use it herself, giving up the Regency desk in the corner of her bedroom, but to anyone who visited it was still "Artie's office." Eddie saw no sign that would ever change. It resembled his own home office, down to the dark wood of the heavy desk.

The room was ransacked in a way that suggested the burglars had been looking for something specific. The desk drawers had been pulled out and turned over, and several books lay on the floor below the library shelves. He remembered his own visits to Iraqi households and thought that he had left much more wreckage than this in his search for weapons or telltale documents. These burglars were obviously looking only for documents that could lead them to a painting, or for the painting itself.

He feared he would find the same thing when he returned to his own study. He kept a small gray document safe in a closet, and when he opened the door to his father's closet there stood its twin, empty.

Back in the dining room he asked his mother what was in the safe. "Whatever was there is gone now, and I don't think I ever knew what Father kept there."

"It was empty. The deed to this apartment and a few other documents used to be there, but a few years ago I wasn't able to get into it and I had to call a locksmith to open it. He said the safe was so old it was bound to cause more trouble, and that the papers would be much safer in a bank vault. I took them to my box at HSBC and never relocked the safe."

"Good decision on your part. Tomorrow we'll go to the bank and see what they were looking for."

Margaux had regained her composure. "It's possible they went into your apartment, too, Charles Edward," she said. "I think all of you should stay here tonight and you can check on that tomorrow."

Once she saw there was nothing more to be done about the burglary until the police arrived, the hostess in her took over. "There's a nice bottle of Graves in the refrigerator. Why don't you bring it out to the end terrace while we wait for Philippe and we'll show Jennifer what Paris looks like from here."

Margaux's building, constructed only five years after the end of the war, was one of the last of the cut-stone luxury residences. At seven stories it was the same height as the older buildings designed in the 1850s, but it was larger than most, curving around half of the semi-circular Place Vauban. Margaux and Artie had bought their grand penthouse shortly after they married in 1952.

She led the way toward the end of the building, where a large open terrace offered views in three directions. As soon as she opened the door, Aurélie exclaimed, "I could never tire of this view."

To their left stood the Eiffel Tower, majestic in its late-night dress of golden light. "It looks so close I feel like I could reach out and touch it," Jen said excitedly. Aurélie said, "I felt the same way the first time I saw it from here. It's actually a mile away, but it's so large it just seems close."

Jen turned to take in the views -- the new Branly Museum, close by the tower, then the Invalides across the street, with its broad lawn stretching to the Seine a half-mile away, barely visible behind the gilded dome. Further to the right she picked out Place de la Concorde and beyond it the long Tuileries Gardens, dark at night, leading to the magnificent Louvre stretching a half-mile along the river. By peering around the corner of the dining room she could just make out the grand Cathedral of Notre Dame, far beyond the thousands of buildings that made up the affluent sixth and seventh arrondissements.

"When Artie and I first moved in we loved this view so much we sometimes spent all night on this terrace, frequently with a bottle or two of wine just like this one," Margaux told them. "But not tonight. Jennifer, you come with me and I'll show you your room, then you can come back out here and wait for Philippe and his men. Charles Edward and Aurélie know their way."

"I believe I'll go home, Margaux," Aurélie said. "There's no reason the burglars should know about me, and Father can deliver me and take a look through my apartment, just in case."

Jen followed as they retraced their steps down the long corridor they had taken from the living room. "We have a guest bedroom -- two of them, actually -- at the other end of the apartment. When Artie was in business we had a lot of overnight visitors, so I just always kept them ready. Sometimes people stayed overnight when they didn't plan for it, so you'll find everything from a bathrobe to a toothbrush." She opened the second door on the right.

"Margaux, it's lovely," Jen said.

"I hope you will like it. The bedrooms are on the back of the building where it's quieter, so if you'll look out the window to the left you'll see the area around Rue de Sèvres where Aurélie has her apartment, on Rue Oudinot."

"She's not married?"

"No. She was married, but it ended badly and Philippe tells me she's very reluctant to get involved with anyone else right now. Her husband turned out to be a gambler, and dishonest as well. The smallest of her problems was his infidelity."

CHAPTER SIX

Philippe

Paris

"We caught the two men who attacked you at the hotel. They had a confederate, the driver, who seems to be the boss. Unfortunately he got away, but not before the good citizens of Paris beat him quite thoroughly after he stabbed the hotel clerk. It seems some of the pedestrians were the right age to remember the war."

Everyone's eyes were fixed on Philippe, who sat at the head of the dining table. The women, especially, gave him their rapt attention. At two inches shorter than Eddie and reed thin, he looked like an actor playing a French aristocrat, down to the tonsured bullet head fringed with short gray hair. In fact, he was the son of a small-town policeman and a schoolteacher, and had risen to the upper ranks of the Paris police on the strength of a strong performance in school, keen investigative skills, and his political sense, which included his friendship with Margaux's father. Gabriel, tall and trim in his working uniform of starched white shirt and blue trousers, sat at his left to take notes. Margaux had placed his kepi carefully on a sideboard.

"They were in fact Germans, and they made the very serious mistake of nearly killing the night porter. He was cut up very badly with a large knife that the driver picked up in the street. I believe he will live, but it will be a long time before those Germans are released.

"I saw the knife," Eddie said. "It was an old American Army bayonet. Very sharp and very dangerous, and if its main purpose was to threaten us it succeeded. The tall one dropped it when I pushed him off the sidewalk into his car."

"I recall that you have some experience with weapons like this one," Philippe said drily. "Please tell me how it first came to your attention." He was ready to hear the full story.

Jen interjected, "The German who threatened us with the knife made it clear he was looking for a valuable painting, and he thought we knew something about it. Do you know anything about them, other than their identities?"

"I don't think we even know that. Their papers are almost certainly false. We are checking the two we arrested through the German police. We don't have anything on the driver, other than his odd appearance. One of the citizens who saw him stab the porter said the bottom half of his right ear was missing."

Jen looked up quickly with a sharp intake of breath. "Oh. They are from the East, which frightens me."

"We don't know that," Philippe responded. "How can you be sure?"

"From their accents -- definitely eastern. I haven't heard that accent since I moved to Florida with Roy, but it brings back bad memories. It's the way my stepfather sounded, and we only found out later he was an old Stasi agent."

Philippe reassured her. "We will be careful. If they do have connections with the old East German government we'll need to take special care. They seem to be interested mainly in one painting, but their friends the Russians looted many more artworks and treasures that the Nazis had already stolen. Who knows what else they might be after?"

Eddie recounted how the Germans had followed Margaux's car around the corner, then stopped in front of the wax museum. He summarized the brief fight and their escape through the Hôtel Chopin, then the call from Margaux when she had discovered the burglary.

After an hour of questions, Philippe stood up to leave. He agreed with Margaux that Eddie and Jen should stay with her that night, and offered to survey Eddie's home later in the morning. "Give me time for a little sleep. Can we meet at 10:30? I can pick you up here and we'll drive over together."

Promptly at 8:30, Jen heard a sharp rap on her door then a few seconds later a knock on the next one down the hall. She opened the door and saw Eddie leave the room to her left.

He smiled at her. "Today's the day the real work begins. Aurélie said she has a class at 10, but as soon as that's finished she'll start on this project. There are several art historians with offices near hers, so she'll see what they know about the missing painting. They may have heard about other cases like this one, too."

Jen followed them into the dining room and came face to face with Martine, thin, unsmiling, and wearing a black dress trimmed with white lace, very unlike the blue smock Jen had seen the day before. It was all she could do to keep from laughing out loud. She had no idea French maids still wore French maid uniforms — the last one she'd seen was laid out on the bed of an older lover ten years before. She'd refused to wear it.

"Oh, Madame, I am so sorry to hear of your father. And now all of this ..." She did not finish the sentence.

Margaux jumped in to fill the uncomfortable silence. "This is all unpleasant, but we'll get it cleaned up. The concierge has already called a contractor who does work in the building and in two or three days everything will be back the way it was."

They ate quickly, a classic French breakfast of café au lait and croissants, with ham added. Then they moved into the living room. Jen took in the postcard view of the Invalides through the long windows that had been covered with heavy drapes the night before.

Even though the sun had been up for four hours it was far from overhead and the dome still cast a strong shadow to her right. The gold leaf on it shone brilliantly, much brighter than it had under the floodlights. Jen thought it must be spectacular to live in a city with such views whose summer days were three hours longer than hers.

"Margaux," she asked, "do these views ever bore you?"

"Never, my dear. I could spend all day every day just moving from this chair to the terrace and having Martine bring me lunch. This is where I plan to be until the day I die."

Eddie pulled a wooden chair close and said, "Time to work. As I see it, somebody thinks we have something valuable dating from the war, or at least know where it is. It's almost certain the 'something' is a painting, because that's what the Nazis stole the most of, and that's what the Germans wanted last night. It must be something that was well known at the time -- I suspect one of Aurélie's colleagues will be able to tell us off the top of his head what we're dealing with, especially now that we know, from Mother, that Hans Frank was involved."

His iPhone chirped. He looked at the screen and said, “Philippe.” He listened a few seconds and then said, “I'll be right down.”

“Philippe will be downstairs in a couple of minutes. I'll go meet him so we can survey my place. If nothing's out of line I'll come back here at once and we can go check the bank box. Is that OK with both of you?”

“That's a good plan,” Margaux told him. “It will give me a chance to learn a little more about Jen and her father.”

“Well, my dear,” Margaux said after Eddie had left through the service door. “We'll have some time together before Charles Edward comes back. Let's learn a little more about each other. Nothing in this world is ever as simple as it seems on the surface.

“For instance, have you and Charles Edward kept up with each other since your dalliance in Sarasota? For that matter, is dalliance still a word in America?”

Jen's face reddened but she looked Margaux in the eyes without flinching. “Not once. If he'd come back I would have left with him, and things might have been different. I still don't know anything about his life since then, and he doesn't seem anxious to tell me about it.”

“No, I don't imagine he is. He was ashamed of the way he acted, because he was engaged to Lauren at the time. He swore he would never do anything like that again, and as far as I know he hasn't. But

I do know you enchanted him and it tortured him to think he'd made the wrong choice."

"Please tell me what happened to his wife."

"You need to know, because it still affects Charles Edward. Our family had a terrible year in 2001. I lost Artie and Charles Edward lost both Lauren and their son. It isn't something I ever want to live through again."

"Eddie had a son?"

"His name was Sam, and he was born the year after they moved back to Paris, so he was nine years old. They lived across the river in the 16th, in a lovely old apartment they had renovated.

"That was the year Artie died. He normally went to Rennes once a month to talk to the managers of a commercial property we own there. He would go over on the train in the evening, rent a car and stay in the hotel next door to the shopping center, then meet with the property manager the next morning and take an early-afternoon train back to Paris.

"One day in the Spring the manager called me to say Artie hadn't arrived for their meeting. Artie was never late, so this worried me a lot. He didn't have a portable telephone then. He said he didn't need one in Paris, and at that time there wasn't widespread coverage in the smaller cities, much less the country. So I called Philippe and he asked the Rennes police if they knew anything.

"They found Artie's body in the rental car in a grove of trees. The gasoline had caught fire…" Margaux stopped and Jen stepped closer to put her arm around her shoulders. "I'm very sorry you had to tell me that," she said.

"Philippe had to go to Rennes to identify the body," Margaux said. "I've always appreciated that he did that."

Jen said, "That was in the Spring. Then Lauren and Sam died the same year?"

"Just a couple of months after 9/11, so the year was pretty bad already. Charles Edward was in Rennes on the same inspection tour Artie used to make. He came back in the afternoon and called Lauren but there was no answer and he figured she was out shopping.

"But earlier Philippe had called me to say Lauren and Sam's bodies had been found in their apartment. They'd been murdered quite brutally, and the apartment was set on fire."

Jen stood back, horrified. "That's absolutely terrible. Poor Eddie."

"He did not take it well. Philippe and I went together to his office to deliver the news. He knew it was something bad when we came through the door together, and when we told him he did not say a word. In fact, he said almost nothing until the the funeral was complete and they were buried, then he went to the Hotel Negresco in Nice for a week. I understand he was drunk the entire time.

"When he returned he refused to discuss Lauren or Sam. He didn't mention her name for five years. He was very seriously depressed, although he has so much personal discipline it didn't show in his work."

Margaux stood. "I'll show you a picture. We don't leave it out any more because it makes Charles Edward very sad, so I moved it to my bedroom."

She returned and handed Jen a gold frame containing a family portrait of Eddie and Lauren seated, with a handsome boy standing between them. All three looked at the camera, the boy with an impish grin on his face. "This was made the year before Lauren and Sam were killed."

"I didn't realize Lauren was black," Jen said in surprise. "Wasn't she pretty."

"She was a lovely woman and a very good mother, although I'm afraid Paris turned out to be a disappointment to her," Margaux said.

"Charles Edward is the best of France where race is concerned. It doesn't matter to him at all. I think he took some grief about it at college, even though Lauren was the daughter of the campus military commander — ROTC, I think they call it. He was a decorated Army officer and Charles Edward looked up to him. I believe he's still living, although I haven't seen him since the funeral. His wife, interestingly enough, is French, with a Vietnamese grandfather. She worked at the American Embassy here when he was a young attaché.

"The police never made any arrests. They were pretty sure Artie's death was an accident, but the fires in both cases made them suspicious. Philippe says they never even got any good leads."

Margaux took the picture back to her bedroom and, as she returned, Eddie knocked on the service door, and Martine went to admit him.

"That didn't take long," he said. "There was no sign anyone had been in the house. Anyway, it would be tough for a burglar to get in without the desk clerk seeing him.

"Why don't we go to the bank now?"

Jen asked, "Would you mind if I stay here? I'm still exhausted from the flight and an hour's nap would help me a lot."

Margaux and Eddie took the elevator to the ground floor and walked out onto Avenue de Breteuil. At the gate a policeman touched his cap and wished them bonjour. "Philippe said he'd have someone watch for a day or two," Eddie told Margaux. "He thinks only one of the Germans is still free and is unlikely to try anything by himself, but he doesn't want to take the chance they might be able to call on local help."

They walked in silence down the shell walkway bordering the first long block of the broad green esplanade, passing a homeless man dozing on a green bench, then a few yards further along a couple nuzzling in the sun, the remains of a picnic spread on their blanket. A plastic wine glass had tipped over, spilling its red stain dangerously near his trousers, but they were oblivious to it.

They turned down the narrow street leading to the HSBC Bank branch where Margaux kept her accounts, just a few yards from the ornate church of St. François-Xavier, where the establishment of Paris goes to preen on Sunday mornings.

The bank manager brought a locked steel box large enough to hold a stack of file folders and placed it on a small desk in the corner.

Margaux tried to insert her small key into the box's lock but fumbled. "Nerves," she said, then turned and handed it to Eddie, who opened the lock and raised the lid of the box. Inside were two large envelopes, one marked "Place Vauban," the other blank.

"We want the blank one," Margaux said. "That's where I put everything except the deed for the house. There were some letters and papers in the safe and some on Artie's desk, so I put them all together in the second envelope. I tried to keep them more or less in the same order I found them."

Eddie said, "Let's look quickly at them here, just in case there's something we don't want Jen to see just now."

Margaux was surprised. "Are you concerned?"

"I just don't know much about her, and I'd rather avoid a problem now than try to make it go away later."

Artie and Roy had communicated almost entirely by mail, and Artie had clipped their correspondence together with the latest on the top, mixing the originals of Roy's letters with carbon copies, then photocopies during the later years, of his own. The only exception appeared to be the last one, which was two handwritten pages dated only a few days before his death.

"It doesn't look like he mailed that one," Eddie said.

"I found it in a desk drawer and just put it on the stack without thinking."

Eddie looked at the next one in the stack, dated several weeks before Artie's unsent reply. It appeared to have been printed on a laser printer.

"Damn," he said under his breath. Then, louder, "Roy was onto something and he wanted Artie to follow it up. This talks about a dinner party he attended down in the Loire Valley, at some chateau near Tours. There was an art dealer there who said some interesting things about old Nazi treasure — like he knew where some of it was hidden. But Roy couldn't get any more information out of him, and asked Artie to go talk to him."

"I remember that," Margaux said, showing more interest than she had before. "He did go see someone near Tours just the month before he died. It was his next-to-last trip. He took the train back as far as LeMans and rented a car to drive down to the chateau country. He had to stay an extra night there, but he told me when he came back that he didn't get anything worthwhile because the old man wouldn't open up to him. And he said he was tired of Roy's wild goose chases."

Eddie looked back at the first page on the stack. "This says he didn't find out anything but was suspicious the man was hiding something. It's not much, but it's something and it's apparent he intended to pursue it further. I wonder if he ever asked Philippe about it?

"Anyway, this is the first semi-solid lead we have, so maybe there's something real here, and not just the imagination of some old Nazi who moved back to Germany. The Germans who met us outside the museum last night seemed convinced there really is something to be found, and here we find a story about an art dealer who might still be alive saying he knows where it might be. It's all vague, but there obviously are forces at work out there we need to know about, if only for self-protection."

"Jen asked me today if you'd be willing to go back to Sarasota with her. Would you do that?"

"I suppose so, for a few days. I'd like to find out if the police there think her father's death is anything more than a tragic accident. It's just too coincidental that the Germans came after us last night just a few days after Roy's death. It could be an accident…"

"But you don't think so."

"I don't know what I think. What I fear is that something evil, something that Artie thought was dead history, has come back to life, like desert flowers that bloom every twenty years."

CHAPTER SEVEN

Old Times

Sarasota

Jen and Eddie had carried their second glasses of wine to the covered deck that overlooked the cool, green garden spread under two ancient live oak trees.

"We don't have Martine or your mother's crystal, so you'll have to make do with the Wetzmuller special," Jen said with a smile.

She seemed more relaxed than she had been in Paris, which Eddie thought meant she was more comfortable back on her home ground. He had wanted to stay at a hotel and at first she hadn't resisted, but then she suggested that after all the problems they'd had in Paris she would be more comfortable with him in the downstairs guest room. She would stay in her upstairs apartment, as usual. He yielded to her logic, secretly pleased.

They had flown to Tampa via New York on a Delta flight that gave them time to drive to Jen's home before 7 p.m. "Neither of us will feel like going out," she told him. "We'll have steak and a baked potato, which is something I've never seen in Paris."

"You could probably get it somewhere, maybe Hippopotamus, but it wouldn't be the same. That's also where Americans go to get a Coke, but they aren't the same, either. Steak and baked potato sounds good."

She had changed to a thin light blue blouse and matching slacks. Eddie had put on a red golf shirt and Dockers khakis. They sat side by side in deck chairs, shoeless feet stretched toward the garden.

"Roy bought this old cracker house right after he moved here from Frankfurt, then he renovated it from the top down," she told him. "He wanted something in the classic Florida style, with wide porches all around to catch the breeze, and a metal roof because he liked the sound of the rain on it. I think he was captivated by Sarasota when he came here on vacation a couple of times, and this is certainly the best part of the state. A lot of the rest is a little rough."

"So you've lived here since your mother died?" Eddie asked her.

"I was just 13 when I came here, and I wasn't a happy teen-ager. I was a handful for Roy the first few years. I had a European attitude toward sex, which was heaven for the high-school boys I dated but wasn't really a good way to grow up. I think Roy sent me away to college mainly to get me out of his hair. And I matured a lot there. When you and I met I was just about to finish my art history degree, which seemed to come naturally, maybe because both Roy and my mother were interested in the same thing. I was here mainly because I was trying to decide what to do when I graduated, come back to Roy or go to New York. I finally decided to come back and I've only regretted it occasionally. Roy really was my family, and he didn't have a lot of friends, so we became each other's best friend."

She told Eddie more details of how she had started working in her downtown art gallery when it was much smaller. Summers, she was a showroom assistant to an owner who mainly wanted to cut a swath through the town's embryonic black-tie scene. She started to work full time when she graduated, then three years later she bought it at a very good price from his Michigan family after he died of a heart attack during the finale of a concert in the city's purple symphony hall. "His heirs couldn't get rid of it fast enough, which was great for me.

"The gallery took a lot of work at first and Roy was a big help to me. At the time it handled a lot of local art, which tended — still does — toward seagull sculptures and paintings of old Florida houses under the waving palms. I wanted to make it something more classic, and that was what he was good at.

"I had learned the academic side of art but he had been immersed in it for forty years and had developed a fine sense of what was good and what was not. And believe me, some of what's still sold as good around here is not."

"That sounds like a good reason to stay here with Roy."

"While I was away at college he rebuilt the second floor into a nice two-bedroom suite with its own entrance and kitchen and told me I should live my own life there the way I wanted. He never went back on that, even when men lived with me for months at a time, or when I disappeared to live with them, once for quite a while, and once again when I was married three years to the society doctor. We usually found time to see each other several times a week, either at lunch downtown or for a drink on this porch. It was important to both of us. He was the reason I am whatever I am today. Sometimes I look around me at what's become of some of my contemporaries and I think that could have been me. Not a happy thought."

"It must have been a pretty good life. And by the way, what's a cracker house?"

"Cracker is a cultural icon in Florida. Shakespeare used it to mean a windbag or braggart, and in the Florida frontier days it came to refer to the cowboys who herded cattle by cracking whips around them. But if you had to define it in one word today it would probably be redneck."

Eddie tilted his head and looked at her for a moment, then said, "Redneck I understand. Lauren told me her father talked about all the redneck kids he had to supervise at college, and he didn't mean it as a compliment."

"It wouldn't be. And they would have called him much worse behind his back."

"A black man in the South, even an Army officer? I'll say they would. The hardest lesson I had to learn was how much racial prejudice there was. Is it better now?"

"That depends on who you ask."

As they talked the shadows in the garden lengthened, then it turned dark, illuminated only by a street light outside the privacy fence and small white lights Roy had installed to mark the garden path. Jen got and went into the kitchen to serve the steak, potato and a small green salad. Through the screen door she called to him.

“Why don’t you come in and open another pinot noir? Then we can eat on the porch, at least until the bugs drive us in.”

At 9:30 they had finished dinner and had coffee. Jen said, “That’s it for me. It’s after 3 a.m. on my rundown body clock, and I’m going up to bed. Come in when you’re ready. And please lock the back door, just in case.”

The streetlight outside the fence turned the live oak trees a subtle gray. He poured the last glass of burgundy and sat back, his feet on the bench that ran along the edge of the deck. The light from Jen’s bedroom window shone into the garden, then went out. He remembered that twenty years before she had enjoyed the last minute before bed by standing naked in the window gazing out on the garden, and he thought briefly about turning around to see. The thought caused a not entirely unwelcome tightness. He forced his thoughts back to Roy Castor.

What was the nexus between his death in Sarasota and the Germans in Paris? It had to be Jen. That was the conclusion he and Philippe had reached two days before when they checked his apartment. The driver of the car had to be the only one of the three who knew what Jen looked like — Mutt and Jeff were hired muscle, and to them both blondes looked the same, so they had tried to seize Aurélie and had changed their target only when the driver sounded his horn.

So Jen was the target. But why that particular moment in Paris? Wouldn’t it have been more logical to kidnap her in Sarasota before she left, or to wait until she returned? Or had the Germans simply been caught flatfooted when she left town suddenly? Were they afraid she'd found something that needed to be intercepted? He smiled in the dark -- she had found something, but so far it had contributed nothing but more questions.

"Oh, well," he muttered under his breath as he stood up. "Time for bed. Tomorrow's when the fun really begins." He gathered the glasses and the now-empty bottle and took them through the into the kitchen.

He locked the door, went to the guest room's small bathroom to brush his teeth, hung his clothes carefully in the closet and climbed under a single sheet.

In five minutes he was sound asleep and dreaming of his last visit to Sarasota and his first meeting with Jen. She was working that summer in the art gallery and Roy had called her to say he and Artie needed to have a private dinner. Would she take on Eddie for the evening? She had nothing else planned so agreed to entertain him. "Just this once," she'd told Roy. “I’m really not that fond of military men.”

Eddie had gone to meet her at the gallery. She gave him a quick tour but soon realized he was bored by everything but one street scene of Paris at the turn of the 20th century. A streetcar, its headlight and windows brightly lighted, passed by the theaters at Châtelet. He had recognized the location immediately.

They had walked down sleepy Palm Avenue to a Spanish restaurant on Main Street. The dinner had been lively. Eddie told her of the changes in France since she'd been a student in Lyon and she told him of her life in Frankfurt before her mother had died, then of her life in Sarasota.

At 10:30 she looked at her watch and said, "We're going to close this place. We've been here more than two hours and Sarasota's not a late-night town. We can have a nightcap back at the gallery by the light of the pictures."

She took his arm as they crossed the deserted street, holding it tight against her breast. They stopped once under a tree for a long kiss, and after Jen locked the front door behind them she took his hand and led him toward the back of the store.

“The previous owner lived in Orlando, and when he came here he didn’t want to go to a hotel, so …” She opened a door to reveal a small efficiency apartment with its own bathroom and kitchen and a large double bed. “My boss won’t be back for several days.”

His dream replayed in slow motion as they slowly undressed each other. He dreamt of sliding under the cool white sheet, and of Jen climbing in beside him, pressing herself close.

He awakened slowly to the realization that it was no longer a dream. Then he was fully conscious of her naked body pressed close to his, her breast resting on his chest.

Without a word, he put his arm around her and pulled her astride him. After an hour they tried to sleep, but soon Eddie felt her hand caress him as she put her leg over his.

"My turn this time," he said as she rolled onto her back and clamped her legs around him. "Sleep is for later." As he entered her he heard her murmur, "Old times."

CHAPTER EIGHT

Monuments Men

Sarasota

"I want to help Thom Anderson solve this case. He seemed bright and determined, but I'm not sure he's convinced yet it was murder." Jen said.

She had been reviewing her conversations with the detective over the remains of a fried-egg-and-bacon breakfast. "I'm not used to this much breakfast," Eddie told her. "I will have to watch my weight here."

"I'll do all I can to help you get exercise," she said with a mischievous grin.

Eddie smiled but changed the subject.

"We need to be careful in case it goes beyond one murder. Tell me about the detective."

"Thom's a long-time Sarasota cop, and the force here is pretty good, based on the few experiences I've had with them at the gallery. Why don't I call him and ask him to see you today?"

"Ask him to meet me at the site. That will make it easier for both of us to re-imagine what happened."

Jen went into the kitchen to call the detective and Eddie took his iPhone from his pocket. A text message from Aurélie said she would call him later in the day, before midnight Paris time. As he returned the phone to his pocket, Jen came back carrying a note. "I reached Thom," she said. "He'll meet us in half an hour. I told him I will stay just long enough to introduce you and then I have to go to the gallery and be make sure everything is still working there. Here's his number."

As they walked through the house toward the front door, Eddie said to her, "When we come back later today I want to go through the house carefully just in case there's something that might help us."

"I think you should. I looked it over carefully, but I didn't know what we know now. I think it's possible he left other clues for us."

She locked the door as they left, then handed Eddie a key. "Keep this, in case you come back when I'm not here. You can use Roy's study. There's a wired internet connection there. He didn't trust wifi."

They turned to walk the block and a half to their rendezvous point, and as they approached the spot they saw a black Crown Victoria turn into the parking lot of a small apartment building. "That's Thom," Jen said. "The police think their unmarked cars make them anonymous, but who else drives a black Crown Vic?"

The detective stepped out of the car as they approached and stuck out his hand, first to Jen then to Eddie. As she and Thom exchanged pleasantries Eddie sized him up. He saw a man about his age but an inch or two shorter and twenty pounds heavier, with sandy hair behind a receding hairline. He was wearing beige slacks and a blue blazer, neither of them expensive, and a white short-sleeved shirt with a thin black tie. Eddie picked him for a former military man, probably an Army sergeant who had served a few years after high school and then gone to college, which he might not have finished. His eyes were active and curious, a good sign.

"Sorry," Eddie said when he realized Thom was speaking to him. "I was thinking about what happened here."

"It wasn't important. The only real news I have for you is that we found the car. The airport police checked the surveillance pictures and it came in the same day Mr. Castor was killed. It was a pretty smart plan -- the owner left it to catch his flight and the thieves drove it out within 15 minutes. Then, a couple hours later, they brought it back and left it in the same spot. We didn't hear about it until the owner came back and found the damage to the front end. They had run it through a car wash to remove the blood, but we found enough inside the grill to match it to Mr. Castor, so we know it was the murder weapon.

"There's no longer any doubt this was a crime, not an accident. We've upgraded it to a murder investigation and I've been told to focus most of my time on it. Unfortunately, we still don't have much to go on."

Eddie asked if he would walk them through the events, and Jen interrupted to say, "I think I'd rather skip this part, and I need to go downtown to the shop. Call me there if you need me."

Thom gave Eddie some of the background. "As far as we can tell, Mr. Castor was walking home from a Greek restaurant downtown, where he and a half-dozen friends have gathered every Wednesday afternoon since forever to talk about things. You know that he went back to Germany after the war. His friends tell us he accumulated considerable assets there and sold his business to move here. One member of this Wednesday group was his commanding officer in Germany."

Eddie asked if he had their names and addresses.

"That will be no problem. Nothing we've found in this case so far needs to be kept confidential, mainly because we haven't found much.

"He walked up Main Street to this north-south cross street, where we're standing now, which is Osprey. He turned onto Osprey for a block, and when he got to Ringling he crossed and continued down Osprey, although normally he would turn and walk further up Ringling so he could cross through the art colony, which is shady. We don't know why he chose this route that day, but it probably didn't make much difference. These guys were waiting for him wherever he went."

The day was hot and humid, as coastal summers in Florida tend to be, and Eddie noted that the sidewalk opposite where he and the detective stood was a cool green oasis that smelled deliciously of honeysuckle. It would have been inviting on a June day to avoid traffic-clogged Ringling and walk down a pastoral residential street. Thom's voice recaptured his attention.

"Did Ms. Wetzmuller tell you about the witness? He's a busboy in one of the Towles Court restaurants — I think it's the only one —

and he was on the way back from the bank when the killing happened behind him. We're pretty sure one or more people came out of the parking lot behind this apartment building, grabbed Mr. Castor, and pushed him into the path of the car they'd stolen, or that he was trying to escape from them. We estimate the car was moving just under 20 miles an hour when it hit him, which doesn't sound like much unless the thing that's moving weighs almost two tons. This was a big Lincoln Navigator.

"The busboy told us he was walking this way to his job, so his back was turned and he didn't see much. He said he heard someone call out, then turned to see the impact. I think he's mostly telling the truth. He seems to be a good kid, twenty years old, lives with his wife and baby daughter just on the edge of Newtown, our black area, and has been working steady since he got out of high school a couple of years ago."

"May I have his name and address?" Eddie asked.

"I presume you'd rather go by yourself?"

Eddie just nodded.

Thom offered to show Eddie the damaged Navigator. Although it was the blow to his head when it hit the curb that killed him, the impact of the car had been strong enough to leave blood on the damaged grill. Its DNA had matched Roy's.

"The final test results just came back from the state lab," Thom told Eddie as they drove toward the garage, which was in the center of a dreary suburban industrial park on the east side of town. "I didn't have any doubt, but we've settled it for certain now.

"We also got some fingerprints and a little DNA material from inside the car, but there weren't any hits from either of them, either in the state or FBI databases."

"You won't find any," Eddie responded. "I'm pretty certain the killers were the Germans Jen and I met, to our unhappy surprise, on a Paris sidewalk two nights ago. One of them was carrying a nasty-looking knife, a bayonet."

"He tried to kill you, too?" Thom asked, surprised.

"No, I don't think so. They were looking for something, and they thought at one time Roy knew where it was. They obviously decided he didn't, so they killed him. Either that, or it was an ugly accident. Maybe he was trying to escape."

Thom asked, "Pardon me if I'm being too inquisitive, but how are you involved in this? Don't you live overseas?"

Eddie told Thom about his father's association with Roy during the war and how they had stayed in touch for several decades after it ended, and how his father had brought him to Sarasota in the late 1980s, which was where he had met Jen for the first time. "But I think Roy's interest flagged in recent years. He left a letter for my father that looks a lot like he'd reached the end of the line and given up on the project. It wasn't dated, but it appeared to be several years old. It was marked for hand delivery to my father, so Jen got on a plane and delivered it."

"So you think he may have been killed because of something out of the distant past?"

"It's beginning to look that way. Someone is very interested in it. The two men who tried to attack us the other night in Paris were from the eastern part of Germany. That happened less than two weeks after Roy was killed, so I'm betting it was the same people."

"How could you tell they were from the east?"

"The police in Paris arrested them after we got away. And, Jen heard them talking to each other and recognized the accent."

"She speaks German?"

"She moved here when she was 13 years old. She doesn't use it much but you don't forget your mother tongue."

"That's interesting. She's a very well-known businesswoman in Sarasota, so much so that my chief asked me to keep him up to date. I haven't had much to tell him yet, but he was very interested in the Paris connection.

"How did they attack you, and how did you get away?"

Eddie told him about the two men waiting in the museum's front door, then how he had fought them off and escaped through the hotel, where the police had arrested the Germans.

"That's impressive. Where did you learn close combat like that?"

"Special Forces. I hadn't even thought about it in years, but it really came in handy."

Thom said, "That's what I wanted to do in the Army, but there was nothing going on while I was in and I couldn't find a slot."

"You must have been a few years behind me," Eddie told him. "I was in Kuwait and Iraq, and mustered out shortly after that, then moved back to Paris."

"Paris is without a doubt my favorite place in the world. My wife and I went there on our honeymoon, traveling on a dime, but we loved it. Have you lived there long?"

"I was born there and have lived there my entire life except for college, when my American father wanted me to come back to the States, and my time in the military. I wouldn't live anywhere else now, although your town is pretty nice. I know Jen loves it here."

Thom steered the Crown Victoria behind a nondescript beige steel building that could have been in any industrial park, then opened the door with a passcard. The gloom of the interior was relieved by pools of bright light cast by fluorescent fixtures hanging on chains from the high ceiling. A row of fans turned quietly high in the opposite wall, reducing a strong smell of gasoline and chemicals.

In one of the circles of light stood a large black Lincoln Navigator, its front grill pushed in. The heavy bumper was undamaged.

"The technical types have been over it carefully," Thom said. "We think they ran it through a gas-station car wash to get off any obvious signs, but they didn't get the blood behind the grill."

Eddie asked if Thom could send the DNA and fingerprint information from the interior to the French police for comparison. "If they match, we'll know we're dealing with something international and even if the French have to release them you can ask for extradition."

"I've already asked the state's attorney for permission and it's under way," Thom replied. "It can't hurt us and it might really help, because otherwise I don't have any real clues to go on."

Thom drove Eddie back to Jen's house and pointed out the restaurant across the street where Arturo Ruiz worked. "Most restaurants are closed on Monday, so he's probably not working today," Thom told him. "He lives on the edge of Newtown. It's safe so long as you don't go there at two in the morning looking for drugs."

Eddie nodded as he wrote Arturo Ruiz's name and address in the thin black Moleskine notebook he always carried. “And the one who was in the Wednesday group?”

“Sommers,” Thom replied. “Al Sommers. He lives on five acres outside of town to the east. He’s pretty prominent. He used to be in local politics and he owned part of a bank, which is a big deal here.”

As he walked back to Jen’s house his iPhone beeped and he found a text from Aurélie asking him to call. She answered immediately with "Édouard, mon cher. I am glad you called, because my friends and I have solved a big part of the problem."

“Dis-moi.”

"We know from the two men who tried to attack us that they're looking for a painting, and we know from Roy's note to your father that it was associated with Hans Frank. I put those two facts to a friend down the hall, and he's pretty certain it can only be one thing -- a very famous old-master painting by Raphael called "Portrait of a Young Man," which may be a self-portrait.

“It was stolen from one of the major Polish museums, the Czartoryski, right after the Nazis invaded. They earmarked it for the big museum Hitler planned to build in Austria after the war. Several Nazi bigwigs fought over who should have custody in the meantime, but it spent most of the war on Hans Frank's wall in Cracow. As the Russians closed in near the end of the war he supposedly sent it to his home in southern Germany, near Munich, along with two other famous paintings he had looted and a bunch of smaller stuff. The other two arrived and were recovered by American soldiers, probably including your father. The Raphael hasn't been seen since. I can see why those two Germans want it, because it would be an incredibly valuable piece of art today. More then ten years ago its value was estimated at perhaps a hundred million dollars.”

“Wow. That has to be the connection between the painting and Roy, and maybe my father as well. They handled the other two paintings, and someone thinks they know where the Raphael is hidden. Or thinks they stole it themselves."

"Maybe, but Frank's son wrote a bitter memoir after the war and said Frank had one of his assistants steal it. That might agree with

Roy's letter about the painting going to Paris, but it's impossible to be certain. My colleague is talking to some of his contacts right now. The big problem is that all the principal actors are either dead or very old."

"It's a good start," Eddie responded. I've spent the morning with the police detective, and he's now certain Roy was murdered. He's given me the name of the only witness, and I'll try to interview him this afternoon."

"So both of us are making progress. Maybe you can come back soon. I'll send you more information by e-mail as I receive it. And how are you getting along with your old friend Jen?"

Damn, he thought. Margaux told her. There was an edge hidden in her question, but he decided to ignore it. "She's fine. She's at her gallery and I'm about to search her house. Then I'm going to see the witness."

"My father wants me to stay with your mother tonight, which is probably a good idea, although I have no idea why he doesn't do it himself. Call me anytime before midnight or so. I'll probably be on the terrace looking at the tower and enjoying some of Margaux's Chablis."

Eddie put the phone slowly back into his pocket as he replayed the call in his mind. The relationship between her family and his went back before either of them had been born. Their ten-year age difference had meant they were never childhood buddies, but they had clicked in 2003 and lived together for a few months before Eddie realized he still could not commit to another woman. Desperately unhappy, she had left him for a fellow Sorbonne professor only to learn a year after their marriage that he was a gambler who had lost all of his money and a great deal of hers. She had been divorced more than a year and they had run into each other several times since but he'd never sensed any rekindling of her romantic feelings for him. At least until today, when he'd heard a definite warmth under the factual presentation about the painting. It was mystery to him, but a welcome one.

Eddie went further into the house to look for places Roy might have hidden more information about his search for the painting. He was certain Roy had more documents than just the letter Jen had found — he had spent more than 50 years chasing his evanescent dream, so his records might be bulky.

He looked first for hidden compartments inside closets or above the ceiling. More than once Artie and Roy had located them behind wall panels or above loose boards in the ceiling of old German houses. But after an hour of knocking on walls he came up empty and concluded that Roy must have hidden the files as he had hidden the letter to Artie, somewhere safe that he knew Jen could, with work, discover. The most likely choice was a bank vault, where the papers would be protected from fire as well as theft, and he suspected the Germans had come to the same conclusion so had tried to kidnap Roy rather than burgle his house. Or maybe after burgling his house and coming up empty.

He looked for an entrance to the basement before he realized that almost no Florida homes have basements. The water table is too high and they would be wet all the time. "Dumb of me," he muttered.

When in doubt go for the simplest explanation, he thought, and papers are usually kept in offices. He returned to look closely at the bedroom Roy had turned into a study and office, with a simple wooden desk and an easy chair with a reading light next to it. A table on the other side held an old Macintosh computer and a small laser printer. He'd look into the computer later but he didn't expect to find anything there, it would be too obvious. If anything came through the computer he would have printed it and kept it somewhere safe. Jen had told him Roy was an old-fashioned man who considered the computer a fancy electric typewriter, nothing more.

A bookcase was built solidly into the entire 15-foot wall behind Roy's desk. The shelves were permanent, not adjustable, and made of inch-thick oak. One shelf at a time, Eddie removed each book, flipped through it for secret cavities, examined the wall behind it, and replaced it. After an hour he was almost half finished. As he replaced the second volume of the Oxford English Dictionary on the lowest shelf it caught briefly on something. Puzzled, he removed it again and under the shelf above it he felt a small flat object firmly attached with tape. He worried a corner of the tape loose, then pulled the entire piece off and held in his hand a large round-headed brass key marked "Do Not Duplicate." It was unmistakably the key to a bank safety-deposit box.

As he finished replacing the other books he heard Jen's key turn in the lock. When she appeared in the study door as he held the key out to her.

"Did Roy have a bank box?" he asked.

"Just the one that contained his will. Its key didn't look like that one, though. It was shorter, and the head was a different shape."

"Then this may be where his files are hidden. All we have to do is match it to a bank. That could be like finding a needle in a haystack -- I've never seen a town this size with so many banks."

"It might not even be in Sarasota. He liked to drive out to different small towns from time to time, and I'd go with him when I could. We would usually stop for lunch, and sometimes he'd leave me waiting in the restaurant while he ran an errand or took a walk. I learned after the first time to take a book whenever we made one of these excursions."

"Did he have a favorite?"

"Not really. Victor Coulson might know. He has clients in a lot of the little towns around Sarasota, and he did all of Roy's legal work. Mine, too. He did the paperwork when I bought the gallery and he helps me out from time to time."

"Then he'll be our first stop tomorrow. Meanwhile I have a lot of ground to cover today. See you tonight. Think of a nice place for dinner."

Eddie walked across the street to verify that the restaurant was closed, then walked back to his rented Ford and set a GPS course through downtown and out North Washington to a short street not far from Martin Luther King.

The number of small wooden churches surprised him. Most of them represented Pentecostal denominations he had never seen in France, much less Paris, where the churches were built long ago in massive cut stone and many are no longer used for their original purpose. The vacant lots and convenience stores seemed full of idle black men, the young ones standing in small groups, the older sitting around tables playing cards and dominoes.

These are working churches, he told himself, whereas ours are tourist destinations. But these unemployed boys and men don't look particularly dangerous, just dispirited and poor.

He passed his turn and continued another dozen blocks to explore the neighborhood. He made a U-turn through the parking lot of a grocery store, then backtracked and turned right onto the narrow street where Thom said Arturo’s home would be found, passing the warehouse of an air conditioning company, the razor wire atop its fence glittering in the sun. A block further, almost at the entrance of a chocolate-colored concrete-block apartment complex, he spotted Arturo's house number to his right. Behind a sagging and rusted chain-link fence stood a neat white cottage with blue shutters, painted during the last couple of years. Most of the houses on the block were neatly kept, although one across the street stood abandoned and boarded up. The plywood covering a window was pulled half off, which meant it was now a refuge for the homeless or a drug house. Lawns were beginning to green as the June rains broke the drought that settled in every winter.

He parked the car and pushed open the gates. A dog barked as he knocked on the door, and in a minute a young woman came to the door carrying a baby girl.

"Excuse me for disturbing you, madam," Eddie said, "but I'm looking for Arturo Ruiz. He was a witness to an auto accident a couple of weeks ago where a friend of mine was killed, and the police said it would be OK if I talk to him."

"He's at work now, mister," she replied after a few seconds of thought. Eddie heard a Caribbean accent.

"His restaurant is closed today, so I thought I might find him at home," Eddie replied, keeping his voice level and friendly.

"Mondays he works for Labor Force. With a new baby we need everything we can get, and the restaurant doesn't pay that much."

"When do you expect him to be home?"

"Pretty soon," she said. "He gets off at 3 and it's almost that now. You can wait if you want, but I'm not supposed to let anybody in the house."

"I'll just sit out here if that's OK."

Eddie went to his car for a Sarasota guidebook he had bought at the Tampa airport. Then he found an old and deteriorating garden bench in a little shade on the side of the house and sat down to read.

He looked up as he heard the gate open. "My wife called and told me you wanted to talk about poor Mr. Castor," said a slim young man as he came through and closed it behind him. "I've already told the police everything I know." The sound of the Caribbean was there, too, but less pronounced. Eddie suspected they had been in the United States since they were children.

"That's what Detective Anderson told me, but Roy Castor was a very old friend of my father's and I thought I should do everything I can to help his daughter find out exactly what happened. Can you take a few minutes to talk to me?"

"Sure. Come inside and let me wash up, then we can talk." Eddie offered his hand and Arturo shook it.

Arturo introduced him to Lil -- "Her real name is something long and very Jamaican, so here she goes by Lil" -- and their daughter Sophie, a bright-eyed one-year-old with pigtails and pink ribbons who sat in a playpen happily fitting together colored alphabet blocks. A small black-and-white dog sat contentedly at Lil's feet, licking its chops. It put its head on its forepaws and closed its eyes.

In a few minutes Arturo came back into the living room wearing different clothes and a blue baseball cap instead of the yellow one he'd worn when he arrived. Eddie explained his father's long relationship with Roy Castor and how Jen had found the letter and brought it to him.

He added, "It's possible that there is some pretty valuable stuff involved — a very old painting and maybe some gold. But frankly I'm not interested in those. I'm just interested in knowing about my father and wrapping up the loose ends, mainly for the sake of Roy's daughter Jen, who lives here, and my mother."

Arturo nodded and looked at Lil, who smiled. "Family's the most important thing," she said.

Eddie then asked Arturo to recount all the events that he saw or heard. "I know it's boring for you, but going through a story from start to finish sometimes helps find facts that weren't obvious the first time."

"Sure," he told Eddie, "I was walking back to the restaurant after I'd been to the bank when I heard a shout behind me. I turned around just in time to see that car hit Mr. Castor. I knew he was dead when his head hit the curb."

"Did you hear him say anything?" Eddie asked.

"Not after he was hit, but just before. I didn't know what to make of it at first. But as I think about it, I'm sure somebody shouted 'You!'"

"'You!' That doesn't sound quite right. That sounds more like he recognized someone he didn't expect to see."

"That's what I think now. Do you think I should call the detective?"

"Not quite yet. Would you mind going over the whole sequence once again?"

"Sure. I walked to the bank on Main Street on my break. I usually go after work because it's a pretty long walk to make in a 15-minute break, but we needed the money and my boss said I could have a few extra minutes if I needed them. Lil had to pay a couple of bills."

Lil had moved across the room to an armchair, covered with an old blue blanket that either Sophie or the dog had been abusing. She looked up and said, "Yeah. The phone was about to get cut off."

"Anyway, I was moving as fast as I could. I must have passed Mr. Castor just before I crossed Ringling. I was moving pretty fast, so by the time the car hit him I was more than halfway down the block. I heard the shout, then I turned around."

"How fast was the car moving, do you think?"

"Pretty slow. I guess he had just turned the corner and hadn't speeded up much because he wasn't moving fast at all when he hit the old man. When he passed me he really speeded up."

"Can you describe the man who was driving?"

The tinted passenger window was rolled up so the view wasn't good, but Arturo had the impression that the driver was around 40 years old, with light hair, wearing a brown jacket. "I thought the jacket was weird because it was almost 90 degrees out, but maybe he was cold in the air conditioning. And he was short. He could barely see over the steering wheel."

"Did you see anyone else other than Mr. Castor? I'm trying to figure out who shouted. For instance, was there anyone nearby on the sidewalk?"

Arturo paused and glanced at his wife. "I think there must have been because I heard someone running away. But I didn't see them."

"Did you tell Detective Anderson about that? It might be important."

"No, sir, I didn't." Arturo's tone had changed. He was no longer confident.

Lil interrupted. "You need to tell Mr. Grant everything you know. It's not fair to let those men get away if you can help catch them."

Arturo turned to Eddie. "She's right, but I can't take chances with my job. They're hard to get this year – I was out of work for three months and we got into debt. Lil did need money for the phone bill, but when Mr. Castor was killed I was making a payment to a man we owe. He was looking the other way over my shoulder and saw the whole thing."

"Why didn't he wait for the police?"

"He don't talk to the police if he can help it. He's been known to sell some things that aren't completely legal, know what I mean? But he's not really a bad guy. I think he'll talk to you if you explain things to him the way you did to me."

He gave Eddie the name Deus Lewis. "We call him D because nobody on the street knows what Deus means. He's about 25, nearly as tall as you are, but skinny, and really black. He has short hair but he usually wears a cap, and in weather like this he'll be wearing a muscle shirt to show off. He's a strong guy and wants everyone to know it."

"Where can I find him?"

"Not far. Go down to MLK and Osprey. There's a grocery store there where he usually hangs out. He should be there this time of day."

"OK. Why don't you let me tell Detective Anderson what you saw? I'm sure he'll have to talk to you again, but it might help if I approach him first, particularly if I can get some information from Deus." Arturo nodded as Eddie left.

The GPS told him MLK and Osprey was only three or four blocks away, so he slowed down to get a feel for the neighborhood. Everywhere he looked there were black men sitting on benches and standing on the street corners. Some of them were clustered in the timeless tradition of old men everywhere.

The others were young and stood in groups. As he turned the corner two of them broke apart and ran down an alley. Eddie figured he'd done his duty by breaking up a drug deal, which would certainly regroup and get completed in a few minutes. So goes the war on drugs, he told himself wryly.

He spotted the grocery store and pulled into its parking lot. A knot of four young men, all wearing baseball caps with the bills turned in different directions, looked at him with mild interest but no real hostility. He got out, locked his jacket in the back seat, and walked over to them.

"I'm looking for D – Deus Lewis – and I'm told he might be around here this afternoon," he said to none of them in particular.

"Lemme see yo' badge, man," said one, who appeared to be the oldest.

"I'm not a cop. I'm looking for information about a traffic accident D saw. Not for the police, but for me. The man who was killed was a good friend of mine.

"You," he said, pointing at a tall man leaning against a light pole wearing the telltale muscle shirt. "Are you D? I think you are. I'd like to talk to you."

"What's in it for me, man?" D retorted.

"You get to do a good deed and maybe earn a merit badge for it. Also, you won't have nearly as much trouble with the cops if you talk to me as you will if they send a bunch of cruisers down here to talk to you about the drugs you sell."

"We don't know nothin' 'bout drugs," the oldest one said. He appeared to be about 30, old for a druggie, but he wasn't much of a physical specimen, more like a car driven hard for a lot of miles. The other two shifted around, unable to decide whether to fight or run.

“Look, guys, I'm not here to make trouble for you or get into a fight. That wouldn't be smart for any of us. You might win, but three of you would get hurt bad in the process and then you'd really be involved with the police. All I'm looking for is some information that will help me solve the murder of a friend. It will come out whether you tell me or not, but it'll be easier for all of us if you tell me.”

D thought for a few seconds about his choices and decided going with this guy was better than risking the police. “OK, man. I'll talk to you a little bit.”

“That's the right choice. Now let's get in the car and go talk about it.”

“I ain't goin' out of the 'hood,” D responded.

“I tell you what,” Eddie said. “I made a U-turn at a big grocery store a few blocks up. We'll go there, your friends will know where you are, and if you decide not to come back with me, you won't be so far away you can't walk back here. How about that?”

“I guess that's OK.” D went to the right side of Eddie's car and waited for the door to unlock. Eddie let him in and locked the door, then turned and said, “It's not that I don't trust you, D, but please put both your hands on the dashboard.” Eddie frisked him quickly. Nothing.

They drove north to the Winn Dixie store on the right. Eddie parked in the lot as far from the building as he could.

“Let me tell you what's up. My name is Eddie Grant, and my friend Roy Castor was killed a couple of weeks ago. You saw it, and I think you can tell me something about who was involved. It'll be better if you don't lie to me. I questioned a lot of tougher guys than you when I was in charge of a Special Forces company during the first Gulf War, and I understand pretty well when a man is lying or when he's telling the truth. And if you have any thoughts at all of getting physical with me, I learned a lot about that at the same time, so I don't recommend it.”

“Shit, man. I was just trying to make a living. I was collecting some money from one of my good customers when two guys came out from a parking lot on Osprey and grabbed that old man. He really fought with them, for an old guy, because he obviously recognized them."

"How do you know that?"

"When the first one grabbed him, he said real loud, 'You!'. Then he said something else. It sounded like, 'You bastard! You're no better than your father.'"

"And then what happened?"

"I thought he was going to get away. He wiggled out of their grip and he ran, but he ran right in front of the car. The car came along and hit him, and that's when I left."

"You don't think they pushed him in front of the car?"

"No way, man. They was holding him tight and the car was slowing down. They were going to take him with them."

Eddie asked, "But you think he might have escaped from them?"

"Maybe so, if he'd run the other way. But the guy holding him was really big – almost your size. It would have been tough to get away from him."

"And how about the other guy. What did he look like?"

"He was almost as tall, but skinny. Dressed sort of the same. They were both 40, 45 years old."

"What were they wearing?"

"Man, it happened awful fast. But it looked they were wearing brown leather jackets, the kind with elastic around the bottom. God knows why. It was hot."

"Would you recognize them if you saw them again?"

"Maybe the biggest one. He had something wrong with one of his ears, like part was missing." He reached up to touch first his left ear then his right. "It was his right ear."

"Was it the bottom or top of his ear?"

"Definitely the bottom," Deus responded. It was sort of like a big bite was taken out of it. I could see it when the light was behind it."

Eddie asked, "Did you see the driver?"

"He speeded up after he hit the man and I lit out. I hadn't gone twenty steps when he came squealing around the corner and passed me. He didn't even slow down."

"Did you see where he went after that?"

"He turned right at the next corner. I figured he was going to stop and pick up the other two. They lit out down a little alley that leads to a vacant lot and could have met him the next street over. I've walked through it a lot of times."

"How did you come to be in that block right then? It's a long way from home."

"I had some business to do, that's all"

"What kind of business? I heard you were collecting on a past-due loan."

D chuckled. "You might say that. I was selling that bro some weed and he hadn't paid me yet for last week's. That's all."

"Just ganja?"

"Far as I know that's all he's ever done, and not much of it at that."

Eddie thought back over the conversation and decided he had about as much as he could expect to get, maybe all D knew. He said, "D, you've done me a great favor. I'm ready to take you home now if you want."

"This is just as good as down there. I'll walk from here. I'd buy a few groceries for my mom if I had any money."

"I can help a little with that." Eddie reached into a pocket and took out a $50 bill he had put there earlier, clipped to a small slip of paper on which he'd written his name and U.S. cell phone number. "You've helped me understand what happened."

Deus walked toward the front door of the supermarket. He touched the pocket of his jeans occasionally, to remind himself the money was still there. When he reached the door he paused, turned and raised his right hand in a signal that was half thanks and half goodbye. Eddie put his left hand out the window of the Taurus and returned the wave, then took his telephone from his pocket and dialed the cell number Thom Anderson had written on the back of his business card that morning.

Thom's voice mail answered. He dictated a summary of his day, including finding Deus, and ended by asking Thom to meet with him before going to see either of the witnesses.

Eddie waited briefly while a large white sedan passed behind him. Somebody looking for a parking place, he thought briefly, then wondered why they were so far from the store when there were many free places closer. The car was almost as large as the one that killed Roy, which made Eddie puzzle, not for the first time, about the strange affinity of Americans for their very large cars. Must be something like supersized fast food, he thought before turning onto the oddly named Tamiami Trail in the direction of Albert Sommers's country home. Jen had called it his "ranchette." She did not mean it as a compliment.

The GPS led him under the Interstate on Bee Ridge Road, then down a series of two-lane paved roads. The homes along them were widely spaced, and some appeared to be the original farmhouses that dated back a hundred years to Sarasota's beginning as an agricultural community. The last turn took him into a nameless narrow track that had once been paved.

He stopped in front of a heavy gate made of welded steel pipe. Behind it, a winding gravel lane led to a ranch-style house a hundred yards away. A two-story barn stood behind the house, the caretakers' bungalow to its left. Eddie pressed the button marked "talk" on the intercom mounted next to the gate, then waited as it hummed gently. As he was about to press the button a second time, a voice scratched through the speaker. It was the voice of a younger man, not one in his eighties, and it did not sound friendly.

"... help you?" it asked.

Eddie told him quickly that he would like to ask the colonel about his friend Roy Castor and wouldn't take too long. "Wait a minute," the voice said again, more curt than before.

Another long wait, then the speaker said "he's not feeling too well today but he'll see you for a few minutes. Drive down the lane to the house and park on the side. The gate'll close itself behind you." Eddie tried to place the voice. It was definitely southern, but there was no magnolia in it -- more of a twang, like a bad country music song. The southwest, he thought.

Two horses ignored him as they grazed slowly in the burgeoning rain-fed grass at the edge of a pond. He parked next to a sidewalk that led to the front door through a small garden of thick-stemmed Florida plants crowding around a fountain that gurgled merrily in the shade. As he entered the garden the front door opened.

"The colonel feels kind of bad today," said the face behind the voice, a tall, thin man with a prominent Adam's apple dressed more for golf than – Eddie thought with an private grin — ranchetting. "He was really sorry about Roy's death and wants to help all he can but I know he'll run out of energy in just a few minutes. Follow me."

Eddie followed him through a small dining room whose walls were lined with paintings. He saw the outline of an automatic pistol tucked into his belt at the small of his back and wondered why a retired banker needed an armed bodyguard. In the living room, a very old man in a wheelchair watched a large TV mounted on the wall. A panel of heavily made-up young people dressed in similar blue suits, serious expressions on their faces, appeared to be trying to decide if the leading Democratic presidential candidate was a "real American" or some sort of Muslim secret agent. Below it, an electric fireplace flickered helplessly. The old man muted the TV with his remote and turned his wheelchair to face Eddie. A beam of sunlight escaped from the window's dark shades and flashed across his clouded and watery blue eyes and the corona of his thin gray hair.

"I'm Al Sommers," he said, in a voice that sounded much stronger than he looked, extending his hand. "I understand you're asking about Roy Castor. Tell me what's your interest in him?"

Eddie told him briefly about his father's relation with Roy, which Sommers cut off. "I know about that. They both worked for me in Munich. But Roy hadn't mentioned Artie in years. They were off on some wild-goose chase for a painting that disappeared at the end of the war. I thought they'd decided the Russians got it or it was destroyed."

"I don't know much about the painting, colonel, and it doesn't really interest me much. Roy left a letter for my father, which Jen brought to me. It may be that the whole affair is dead, but the police have decided Roy was murdered so I think we — all of his friends — need to help solve that if we can."

"Murdered! I thought it was a hit-and-run." Eddie sensed the attendant moving closer to Sommers and glanced at him in time to see a flash of surprise cross his face, then turn quickly back to the practiced blank gaze of an underling unsure his boss is going to say the right thing and fearing he won't. The Adam's apple bobbed vigorously.

"That's what they first thought, but they found the car. It was stolen and returned in a really devious way, and if the grille hadn't been damaged it probably never would have been found."

"That sure changes the picture, don't it?" Sommers said.

"By the way, this here is Mark Perry — Sonny to his friends. He comes up the coast from Naples to give my caretakers a day off now and then. They're Germans and nice folks, but I'll take a Texan any day. Sonny's father knew Artie and Roy." He turned to Sonny. "Remind me to find out what Woody knows."

To Eddie, "You said Jen brought you the letter, not Artie?"

"Artie was killed several years ago in a car wreck. He ran off a road at night into a tree and the car caught fire."

"I am damned sorry to hear that. He was a good officer and a brave man, to have spent all the time he did behind the lines. Finding paintings wasn't really his first choice for a job, but he pitched in and did some good work. He left a little before I did. I think he came back to get married."

"Yes, sir, that's right. He married a woman from Connecticut but it didn't last, then he moved back to Paris and married my mother. She is the daughter of a Resistance leader who went into politics with De Gaulle."

"So which are you, American or French?"

"Both. I grew up in France but went to college in the States, then joined the Army. I was in Desert Storm, then moved back to Paris. That's where I'll stay."

Eddie could tell Sommers didn't approve, but said nothing more about it. He knew he had only a short time to find out if Sommers had any useful information about Roy's background that might help crack the murder, so he asked if they had been in touch after the war.

"Not that I was ever able to recall. I met him again almost by accident ten years ago, after I sold my business in Midland and retired to Sarasota. We ran into each other at a veterans' ceremony. Pretty soon he asked me to join his Wednesday afternoon discussion group, which I did when I could, but I was also starting up and then running my bank. When I retired from that last year I started going more often. Once in a while we'd tell each other war stories, me about my days as a fighter jock, him about his time in Signals and then chasing Nazi art. Never understood that myself, since it was mainly for the benefit of the Jews, but it wasn't my call." His index finger wagged in disapproval.

"You were a fighter pilot?"

"Good one, too. I flew P-51s toward the end of the war and had a lot of kills, which is why I was a lieutenant colonel at 28. They sent me to Munich to run administration after I was shot down and hurt. Shot off my cock and balls, nothing else much damaged. They wouldn't send me home."

"Tough injury."

"Like anything else you learn to live with it. Anyway, I became a paper pusher. I looked for a chance to send some of this artwork home for my retirement fund, but it was guarded real well so I never got anything of real value. I think Sonny's dad may have done a little better."

Eddie turned to Sonny. "Your father worked with Roy and Artie?"

"He was an MP in Nuremberg. He was the guard when they did interviews with some of the prisoners, trying to find out more about where all the missing artwork went. He was lucky, too. He was able to send quite a few nice pieces home. He worked for the colonel here for a lot of years after the war." They spoke of their thefts like a trip to the supermarket.

Eddie turned back to the colonel. "It doesn't sound like Roy told you anything that might lead to his killers. If this painting is gone, or in Russia, I wonder why he was killed now?"

"That puzzles me, too," Sommers said. "He kept to himself, or with that daughter of his, and wasn't active in any new business deals or much of anything, as far as I know. The last time we talked about the missing painting was six or seven years ago, when he got back from helping make some French TV show about it. He said then he'd met some new people but they didn't seem to know anything concrete. One of them was an art dealer, as I recall. I think he might have been an Arab. Or maybe he was a German. I don't really remember."

Sommers glanced at the TV and Eddie could tell he was getting tired, so he stood up to leave. At the door, Sonny stopped him and asked, "How long will you be in town?"

"Not long. I'm here only because Roy wrote my father about the painting, and it looks now like both of them had already dropped the subject. I don't see that there's much for me to do here, and I don't want to get in the way of a police investigation. And I have a business to run back home in Paris."

He said goodbye to Sommers and Sonny escorted him to the front door. "The gate will open when you get close," he said.

Eddie walked to the gravel parking area and, as he unlocked the car, looked quickly toward the back of the property. To the right stood a small barn, big as a triple garage and two stories tall. Directly behind the house was an earthen mound that he would have recognized as a fallout shelter even without its rusty steel door. The property appeared to end fifty feet behind the barn at a solid wood fence seven feet tall, weathered but substantial. A trail was worn in the grass from the house to the barn.

The horses were still munching the grass as he left.

He used his key to go through the front door and found Jen in Roy's study, reading in a bathrobe at the desk. Eddie's laptop, a first-edition super-lightweight MacBook Air, sat on the corner of the desk.

She looked up and told him, "Jump in the shower pretty quickly if you're going to. I've made dinner reservations at the Columbia, a really good Cuban restaurant. We need to be there in an hour."

A half-hour later they backed out of Jen's driveway in her black BMW 335i. She had opened the hardtop and the evening breeze was warm on their skin as she drove across the brilliant blue-green of Sarasota Bay. The view from the high bridge both up and down the barrier island was the magnet for thousands of wealthy retirees who choose the city for their homes. For the first time, he understood the appeal of its escape from Midwestern winters.

"This bridge is pretty new," Jen told Eddie as they passed its crest. "The old drawbridge was far out of date, but when the state proposed replacing it there was a huge hue and cry. Now that the deed is done, we're happy with it. It's a beautiful bridge."

She drove once around the full circumference of St. Armand's Circle, bright and clean-looking home to expensive shops and restaurants, then stopped at the valet space in front of the restaurant and handed her key to the attendant.

The restaurant was all Jen had promised. They started with its famous garlicky salad and went on to paella and flan, all accompanied by a strong Rioja Gran Reserva from northern Spain.

"Eddie, do you drink white wine at all?" Jen asked.

"Not really. France has some good whites, as does Germany, but I'm pretty faithful to the French reds. Some people could spin a long line about the finish and mouthfeel and a lot of other BS, but I just like the taste. If I'm just going to have a glass or two I'll generally pick a Bordeaux, but if I want to drink a lot of it I go for Burgundy, a Pinot Noir or a Beaujolais, more like the one we had last night. I even have a little cellar in the basement of the hotel, but I'm not an expert by any means. I thought we'd like this Spanish wine with Spanish dinner, and it did turn out to be pretty good."

After the flan, she said, "Let's skip coffee here. I can make better at home."

They were silent during most of the drive back over the bridge and through town. He rested his hand lightly on her thigh, and she held it tightly until she had to take hers away to shift the six-speed manual transmission. "If I'd thought more about this problem I'd have bought an automatic," she said with a laugh, as she took his hand once again and pressed it between her legs.

They left the car in the driveway near the rear of the house and went in through the kitchen door. As he closed and locked it, and Jen reached into a cabinet to find her coffee press, he said, "Maybe we don't need coffee after all."

"You're so right," she said, taking his hand and leading him toward the bedroom.

CHAPTER NINE

The Bank Vault

Arcadia

"Roy trusted me with all his business problems -- or at least I think he did. No lawyer is ever certain his client is telling the whole truth."

Victor Coulson looked at them across a large glass-topped wooden desk where Eddie counted eight stacks of files, plus a random assortment of legal pads and single sheets of paper. Around him on the floor were more stacks. Through the window behind him, Eddie and Jen could see the vacant lot where Roy's killers had made their escape.

Jen asked, "Did he ever indicate where he kept private papers, other than his will?"

"Just the one bank where you and I went to find the letter that started all this complication. That's where we keep private client files, so he put his will there, too."

"What I don't understand is why Roy would go to so much trouble to hide the key," Eddie said. "Why didn't he just leave it for you with his will?"

"Flexibility," Jen said. "He always wanted to be able to change his mind. This way it was out of sight but he could always change his mind about who got access to his files. He just couldn't plan on being run down in the street."

"I think you may be right," Victor said. "He wanted to have a way out of every document he signed. Said he learned that from leaving too much money behind him when he sold his business in Germany."

Victor leaned back in his oversized chair, rubbing his forehead. Eddie could see he was trying to recall something, so didn't interrupt but looked at the picture of the basketball player on the wall to his left and wondered how that athletic younger man had turned into the overweight lawyer.

"If you have to go to every bank in Southwest Florida it will take days. Maybe -- just maybe -- I can help.

"When Roy came to me all those years ago he asked for a bank recommendation. Because my practice is contracts I get a lot of requests like that, so I have a list. He might have stored his records in one of them."

He pulled a single sheet of paper from a drawer and handed it across the desk. "Jen, do any of these look familiar to you?"

She ran her carefully manicured fingertip down the page. "Here's a possible. Arcadia. He went there more than anywhere else I remember. I went with him sometimes but it's been a couple of years."

"Is that very far away?" Eddie asked. "I didn't know there was an Arcadia in Florida."

"It's an old farming town out near the middle of the state. Its main claim to fame is a rodeo once a year. I never understood why Roy liked it. He would only say it reminded him of when he was poor."

"Looks like you get one more lunch in Arcadia. Do you have your estate papers?"

"Two copies. I'll drive."

"Jesus, that was a ride," Eddie said as Jen slowed the black convertible under a canopy of trees lining Magnolia Street. "Where did you learn to drive like that?"

"Like a told you, I had a wild youth. It cost Roy some money, but I learned you can drive pretty much any way you want as long as you don't speed over hills or around curves. I'm a pretty dowdy middle-aged driver most times, but it's still fun to push the limits."

On the way they had passed miles of pasture and low scruffy palms, the original landscaping of old Florida. But once past the ring of RV parks and auto dealers guarding Arcadia they saw the unmistakable signs of faded affluence side by side with swaybacked frame houses that long ago had been visited by shingle-siding salesmen.

Jen turned into a downtown area that still showed the signs of early-twentieth-century prosperity. The stone pediments bore construction dates a hundred years before, and many had been partially covered by new facades that appeared to date from the sixties and seventies. Once they had housed department stores and cattle feed suppliers but those had given way to antique stores and tea rooms, and the upstairs floors were mostly vacant. Jen pointed to a café on the left. "That's where we usually went for lunch. Great chicken-salad sandwiches."

She parked and Eddie took out the list of banks, which held only one name for Arcadia -- a big chain bank. "It's probably just around the corner. That's the direction Roy always took when he left the café," she said.

A cheerful receptionist greeted them in the lobby. She heaved herself up to lead them to a small conference room, her three hundred pounds unconcealed and unrestricted by her loose dress. Jen saw the look of surprise on Eddie's face as she closed the door and said, "That's what more and more of us look like. Some of it's poverty, but mostly it's McDonald's."

"We don't have it in Paris yet. Never, I hope, but we do have McDonald's."

The door opened and a balding man well into his sixties entered. He introduced himself as William Maxwell — "call me Billy Joe" — and said he had been the manager through three owners, for almost forty years.

Jen told him briefly that she was the executor of her father's estate and believed he had kept a safety deposit box at Jim's bank. "This is the key," she said, holding up the one Eddie had found in Roy's library.

He looked carefully at her driver's license and the state letter of administration naming her personal representative.

"I hate to be so picky but we've had to be a lot more careful since 9/11. Yes, Roy opened a box here more than thirty years ago. He also kept a checking account, which he used only to pay the rent on the box, as far as I can tell."

"Funny. I haven't seen any statements," Jen replied.

"That's because Roy didn't want anyone to know. He had me send all the mail to Jimmy Dean, a lawyer here in town. Once a year he made a cash deposit to cover the rent. But you've already talked to Jimmy, haven't you?"

Eddie looked at Jen, who had a puzzled expression on her face.

"I haven't heard his name until today," she said.

"Well, he called me and said he'd read of Roy's death in the Sarasota paper. He said he had your number and would call you."

"I haven't heard from him. We probably should go ask him what happened."

"Jimmy's getting on, a few years older than Roy. He's pretty sharp, but forgets things from time to time. He doesn't really practice much law anymore, but you'll find him either at the courthouse or his office most days. Would you like to see what's in the box first?"

He handed Jen an index card to sign. She pointed out Roy's last use of the box, almost a year before. Until then, his visits had been more frequent, about every three months. "Bet that's when he gave up," she said.

The three went into the vault. Billy Joe took the key Jen had brought and knelt to insert it into one of the locks on a box near floor level. He took the bank's key from an envelope and slid it into the other lock, then turned both and swung open the door. Eddie and Jen watched silently as he pulled a long, dark-green steel box from the wall, then stood and carried it into an inspection room just outside the vault door. Placing it on a counter, he said, "come out and call me when you're finished."

Jen looked up at Eddie as she opened the box. Inside they found a Leitz file binder, its labels brown with age, and under it a large brown envelope.

"Roy always was organized," she said. "This is the type of binder the Germans use for their files, which probably means he brought it with him from Frankfurt."

She opened it to find a two-inch stack of paper, each sheet neatly punched in the center of its left margin to fit the two binder posts of the heavy cardboard notebook.

Eddie felt a chill as he lifted the cover page from the little stack and saw his father's neat script in a note at the bottom. He took a sharp breath.

“What is it?”

“My father really was in this. That's his note.”

The paper was thin onionskin of the kind once used for carbon copies. It had started as bright pink but had faded and become brittle over the years. It was a report from Maj. Arthur Grant to his superior, Lt. Col. Albert Sommers, and was dated Sept. 25, 1946. It began:

"SUMMARY: The undersigned interviewed HANS FRANK, formerly Nazi governor general of the part of Poland not incorporated into Germany, for four hours over two days, 23 and 24 September. Also present were SSGT Roy Castor, assistant to the undersigned, and SGT Mark Perry, Military Police, present as guard. SGT Perry did not participate in the questioning.

"The purpose of this interview was to determine the extent of FRANK's knowledge of the current location of certain works of art, taken from the civilian institutions of Poland, whose locations are unknown as of the time of this writing. Most of what FRANK told us was known previously, but he did indicate that some valuable items may have been sent out of Poland before the main shipment of goods to his personal home near Munich early in 1945. He refused to be more specific about a painting known as “Portrait of a Young Man,” attributed to the Old Master Raphael, which was listed on the manifest but was missing when the shipment arrived and was intercepted.

"The time allotted to this interview was limited because of FRANK's pending sentence of death. Numerous agencies of the Allied governments wish to question him before his hanging, which is expected to take place within the next several days. FRANK indicated his awareness of this schedule and appeared willing to discuss any matter we brought before him, other than the matter listed above." A half-dozen pages giving more detail of the interview were attached.

Artie's handwritten note was brief:

"Roy:

"I checked the files in Sommers's office when I left Munich and the original wasn't there. Be very careful with this as it may be the only copy.

"Artie 6 Jun 88"

"June 1988. That's when you and your father visited us in Sarasota, isn't it?"

Eddie responded, "It was -- that was right after I graduated from college. He must have come here to bring this. It's like he was handing off the case."

Jen said, "This is really odd because Al Sommers is part of his Wednesday group. He was walking home from their meeting when he was killed. You met him, didn't you?"

"I went out to see him yesterday. He seemed harmless enough, but this gives a different spin to that conversation. We'll need to read this very carefully before I go see him again. Artie obviously didn't trust him."

"I never understood exactly what they were doing, and Roy wouldn't tell me much. Can you fill me in?"

"Sure. My father started out in Army intelligence. He'd grown up in Paris and knew both the language and culture, so he volunteered to work behind the German lines, mainly during the preparations for D Day. That's how he met my mother – her father was in the Resistance in Southern France and Father landed from a submarine to help coordinate sabotage.

"At that point the priority objective was to slow down German troop movements, to keep fresh troops from getting to the invasion beaches. Margaux was a child at the time, living in hiding with a farm family when she wasn't on the move with her father. Her own mother, my grandmother, secretly went back to Paris early in '44 and was killed during the Liberation battles that August.

"Father met Roy in Paris after the Liberation, in late August or early September of '44. Roy was a sergeant in signals at the time, and handled some of Father's communications back to London. They became friends, and when Father was asked to work with the Monuments Men he asked Roy to go along as his assistant."

"Monuments Men?" Jen was puzzled.

"They were a special group of mostly officers who were looking for the historic and valuable art the Nazis stole, most of it from Jews in France. But every museum in occupied Europe was stripped to the walls. The best pieces were earmarked for the grand museum Hitler planned to build in Linz, his birthplace, and many others wound up on the home and office walls of Nazi bigwigs. They even had their own set of corrupt dealers and agents to bring artworks to them. Those were always appraised very low so they could be bought cheaply with overvalued Reichsmarks. The dealers got rich and the big Nazis built great art collections. They fought with each other for the right to steal the best pieces.

"Hans Frank was a special case. Aurélie's told me something about him, and I Googled him as well – he didn't even pretend to buy many of the most valuable works. He just appropriated them from a big family museum in Krakow and put them on his walls for the duration.

"At one time he had a Leonardo, a Rembrandt and a Raphael. The Raphael is still missing. It would be priceless today but it disappeared while Frank was scurrying back to his home in Bavaria, trying to stay ahead of the Russians. At least it was on the manifest for that trip. It could have been stolen earlier, if I read my father's memo correctly. Aurélie and her colleagues are just about one hundred per cent sure the Raphael is the painting that's at the root of this whole business."

Jen asked, "Isn't sixty years long enough for most of it to be found?"

"Probably, but there are still some important works missing, and Frank's Raphael is the most valuable of all. Of course, it may have been destroyed or lost, or still be sitting in a bank vault in Switzerland or Houston."

"Houston? How would that be?"

"The Nazis weren't the only looters. Just a few years ago some very fancy Old Testament panels showed up in the hands of a former soldier in Texas. He had just mailed them home through the Army's own post office. Other pieces have been resold to museums, who generally bought in good faith. Some were returned to their owners by shady representatives of unknown sellers, most of them lawyers, who generally receive a generous finder's fee.

"The whole affair started out corrupt and it will end that way. People are willing to kill to preserve either their secrets or their fortunes. This affair combines both. Roy found that out the hard way."

Eddie turned another page in the Leitz binder, looked at the page for a minute and whistled. “Wait a minute. Look at what we have here.”

He pointed at the first of a series of letters to Roy. “My German isn’t up to this. Would you read it?”

“Sure,” she said. Her finger traced a path down the page and when it arrived at the bottom she stopped on the signature. “Damn,” she said.

“What is it?” Eddie asked.

“This is basically a blackmail note, and it’s signed by a man named Erich Kraft. Do you remember I told you my mother’s husband had an unpleasant son my age? That was — is — Erich Kraft. I guarantee you anything connected with either of them is no good.”

They counted six letters, written about two months apart, the last one dated November 2000. Roy had responded politely to each, saying he’d found no trace of the painting or any other treasure and was no longer actively searching. Each was more insistent than the last that he must know where to find the painting, or have already found it himself. The final letter cited a mysterious witness.

“You must deal with me honestly or bad things will happen,” the final letter said. “The painting and the gold were the property of my father, and they are mine now. I intend to have them.”

They receptionist helped them copy the contents of the binder and return the originals to the vault. Eddie put the copies into his old brown briefcase, which he'd tossed into the back seat at the last minute just in case they struck paydirt.

Following Billy Joe's instructions, they walked across the street to a fading building whose last ground-floor tenant had been an antique shop. Under a sagging tin awning they found a wooden door, repainted a bright blue much more recently than the rest of the building. Its glass window had a sign, in gold leaf, announcing that James Dean, Attorney at Law, practiced on the second floor.

The wooden stairway had seen little recent care. A single bare bulb at the top threw each step into a half shadow that made walking up them difficult. Jen tripped and would have fallen once, but caught Eddie's arm at the last second. At the top an unlighted hallway, its linoleum floor peeling at the edges, turned to the left. A man stood waiting in a pool of light at the open door of what appeared to be the building's only inhabited office. He wore the trousers from an aged blue suit, a white shirt and a black bolo tie cinched tightly under his deeply sun-lined face with a large turquoise ornament. Brown cowboy boots with blue stitching stuck out below his too-short cuffs. His white hair was swept into an enormous pompadour that reminded Eddie of the television preachers he'd seen during his college days. Jen didn't see anything unusual about it.

"Billy Joe called and told me you two would be here. Come on in and I'll tell you everything I know, which ain't much. And I am surely sorry at the death of your father, little lady. I didn't know him well, but what I saw, I liked.

"Take a seat on the couch there." He pointed to an old leather sofa. It stood under a window with a view out to Hickory Street, to the right of a roll-top desk that would have been at home in a Bogart movie. A row of filing cabinets, wooden except for a newer steel one at the end, stood against the opposite wall. Without the new-looking MacBook Pro on the desk, the room was pure 40s.

The old lawyer eased himself into an old wooden desk chair and turned to face them. He looked quizzically at Eddie. "Where do you fit in all this, young man? The banker told me you're from France, but you look American to me."

"Actually, I'm both, Mr. Dean. Roy and my father worked together during the war, and Jen brought me a letter from Roy. He didn't know my father had died."

"Where did thcy serve?"

"My father was in intelligence from 1940 on, but they served together at the end in Munich, helping recover art and treasure the Germans had stolen."

"Ah. I've heard about that operation," Jimmy said. "I was further north, in Belgium and at the Bulge, and then I got sick and wound up working in the pharmacy at a hospital in France. I was a completely green kid at the Bulge. Scared me to death."

Jen sensed that Eddie was getting impatient. She knew his next question would be a pointed effort to get the conversation back onto Sommers, and that the old man might feel rushed. She raised her hand and replied to him, "You must have some stories to tell. Could we come back in a week or two and talk more when everything is more relaxed?"

It was the right touch. Jimmy sat up straighter in his chair and apologized. "I know you're here about your father's records, so I'll tell you what I know about them.

"He came to me thirty years ago and said he needed a lawyer in Arcadia for something very specific. He wanted me to be his address of record for the safe deposit box he planned to open at Sun Bank, because he didn't want anything in the records to show his home address. It had a different name then, but Billy Joe took charge at about that time."

"That would have been in the late seventies, before I came to live with him," Jen said.

"Yes, he told me he lived by himself and had no family here. But he was worried about something, I could tell. Most people wouldn't jump through all the hoops he did to keep his address confidential."

"Billy Joe — Mr. Maxwell — said you had an emergency contact for him. Please tell us about that."

"Sure." Jimmy got up from the chair, conspicuously favoring his right knee. "Arthritis. Old age. Whatever, it makes the stairs hell."

He limped to the file cabinets and opened a wooden box standing on the top, rummaged in it and brought out an index card. "Here's the card I keep whenever a get a new client. I ask them for all their addresses and contact information, although that's blank on this one. But Roy did give me an emergency contact number just in case. 'Bout ten years ago he came to see me and said he needed to change the contact name. Said the original man died and the new man would know what to do with all the stuff in the box. And he added your name, too, in case I couldn't reach the primary."

He handed the card to Jen, who looked at it and raised her eyebrows. She turned to Eddie and pointed out the contact name, carefully written in Roy's European hand: Albert Sommers.

"Did you call Mr. Sommers?"

"Sure did. I talked to him right after I saw the notice in the newspaper a week ago Sunday, and he said he would see that Roy's bank vault was taken care of. I got a funny feeling about him, though. When I told him I was calling about some papers of Roy's, just for an instant he sounded surprised, maybe even a little bit frightened. I haven't heard anything more from him."

"The old bastard knew something was up when I talked to him yesterday. How much do you think Roy told him about the painting?" Eddie was beginning to feel like the man who finds a wasp nest but not the wasps and knows they're lying in wait for him nearby. He had a sinking feeling that Roy had been surrounded by enemies, which he'd realized early and as a result had moved his files away from his home, but hadn't spotted them when they closed in on him.

Jen said, "He never hid his interest in the painting, but he thought the search was a lost cause. I never heard him say anything different from what he told Erich in those letters eight years ago. I always thought Al Sommers was twisted in some way, but I chalked it up to his wartime injury and his nasty politics. He saw conspiracies everywhere. Do you think he could be behind Roy's death?"

"Too early to say, but it certainly is suspicious. We need to know a lot more about him. Who are his friends?"

Jen thought a minute as she made the turn toward Sarasota on Highway 70. "We used to see him now and then for dinner, but since he left the bank and his health started to fail I don't think he's been going out much. At one time he was active in Republican politics, but even they got tired of his anti-Semitic rants. He has a couple of gay friends who visit him from time to time, strange as that sounds. I think the father of one of them used to work for him in Texas — he was the guard your father met at Nuremberg. And there's a couple who look after him. They're East Germans but they've been here a long time and they keep pretty much to themselves. They live in a little caretaker's house on his property, and the story is he won't let them go into Sarasota, so they have to drive to Tampa on their days off. Otherwise I don't know if he still has any friends."

"I met Sonny yesterday. Strange guy. I'd better tell Thom some of what we found," Eddie said as he pulled the iPhone from his shirt pocket. "I hope there's a signal out here."

Jen had brought the BMW smoothly up to 70 miles an hour as they passed through a section of pine forest, broken every quarter-mile by small houses, many with old appliances and cars in the yards. They were now fully in the country.

"Good idea," she replied. "But hold on, because there's a white car a half-mile back that may be following us. I saw them move out of a parking place downtown when we left Jimmy Dean's office, and now they've followed us onto this road. It could be a coincidence, but ..."

"After what we've learned, we need to be super cautious. Do you think we should go back downtown?"

"We'll have to deal with it eventually. They probably don't know these roads as well as I do. In high school I used to come out dancing at the old roadhouses around here. Some of the gravel roads were prime stops for horny teenagers on the way back."

Thom answered his phone this time and Eddie delivered a quick summary of the day, including the indication that Al Sommers had intervened to keep the Hans Frank interview out of official Army files, and that he knew about the Arcadia bank vault but avoided telling Eddie about it. Eddie did not think that was an innocent omission.

Thom broke in. "The guy you talked to yesterday, Deus Lewis. A dog walker found his body in a park this morning, not too far from the grocery store where you told me you left him. It wasn't pretty, and you'd better figure that he spilled everything about your meeting with him."

"Arturo is in danger."

"I sent a car out there as soon as I heard. Arturo was at work, but somebody already tried to burn his house down with his wife and daughter inside. The only reason they escaped is she pushed a sofa in front of the door and slowed him down. When he forced his way in they hid in the bathroom, which has a really strong lock. She made so much noise the guy gave up but set fire to the sofa on the way out. A neighbor saw smoke and called the fire department."

"And they're OK?"

"Scared but otherwise fine. We picked up Arturo at his job and took him home."

"Any idea who the pyromaniac is?"

"No, except that the wife said he had an accent. Not one like hers, but more guttural. I think maybe it was German, or Russian, but that's a guess."

Jen called out, "Eddie, they're coming closer!"

"Oh, Thom," Eddie said, almost as an aside. "We may have somebody chasing us. We're on the way back from Arcadia, and Jen saw a white car pull out and follow us. We're going eighty-five and they're creeping up on us, so they aren't out for a leisurely drive in the country."

"Careful. There are some bad turns on that road."

"We'll be OK. Jen got to know it well during her misspent youth. She says tell you she's going to cut through the two-lane roads around Myakka City if we have to. If the driver is a foreigner, or even an out-of-towner, he won't know them."

He described Jen's BMW to Thom and asked him to alert any sheriff's deputies or highway patrolmen in the vicinity. "And tell them to be careful. If these are the guys who killed Deus and tried to murder Arturo's wife and baby, they are very dangerous and probably armed."

"Will do." Thom's tone said he didn't appreciate being told his job and Eddie made a mental note to back off.

Eddie turned up the ringer volume so he'd be sure to hear it over the wind noise. "He'll alert the highway patrol, but no guarantee they'll find us or we'll find them. Can you deal with this guy?"

"I think so. We have about a two-mile straightaway before we get to a little road called Sugar Bowl. I'll use that to see if we can clearly outrun them -- I think we can. If not, we'll head back into the farmland. I know I can duck them in there, but it'd be more dangerous because the roads are narrow."

"Ok with me. I'll watch them." Eddie tightened his seatbelt as he felt the 300-horsepower engine respond to Jen's steady push on the accelerator. As Eddie looked back, he saw the pursuers increase their speed but it was clear after only a few seconds that Jen was pulling away.

"I think we're outrunning them pretty easily, Jen," he shouted over the rushing wind.

"Good. I could maybe dig out a few more RPMs but I hate to do it on this road. You never know when you'll come up behind a truck. We're running at almost a hundred twenty now, and I'd be surprised if they can maintain a hundred for any distance without blowing up their engine. And we still have revs to spare."

The 25-mile drive to the Interstate crossroads took them less than 15 minutes, even allowing for the truck Jen had to slow down to pass. For the last five a black-and-tan cruiser of the Florida Highway Patrol pulled in front of them and Jen was able to slow to 80. She let out a sigh and looked at Eddie. "That was fun when I was 18 years old, but at 40 it's just stupid. I hope that's the last excitement I have for a while."

Two blocks past the Interstate the cruiser stopped behind a sheriff's car waiting at the side of the road. The highway patrolman, a lanky sergeant who appeared about their age, walked back to Jen's side of the car.

"We're glad you were in the neighborhood," she told him with relief.

"Me too. We're still working through what's going on, but for now the deputy in that car ahead will escort you downtown to the city Police Department. Detective Anderson is waiting for you there, and by the time you see him he should know something about what's happening."

The deputy led them through town and up the ramp of a parking garage, stopping on the third floor. As he opened the door of the unmarked white cruiser, Eddie thought he caught a murmured "Oh, shit!" from Jen as a tall blond deputy, his white shirt bearing captain's bars on the collar, reached the car.

"Been out racing the Arcadia road again, Jen?"

"One last time, Kevin. I think that was it for me."

She introduced him to Eddie as Kevin LaFarge, a high school classmate.

"Jen and I go 'way back," Kevin told Eddie. "I should have known it was her when the call came in. I was in the area and Thom Anderson said it was important so I took it myself. He's waiting for you across the street."

He waved at the entrance to a bridge that spanned a narrow street, connecting the garage to the police station.

"Old friend?" Eddie asked after Kevin had driven away.

"Part of my past. Important part. He's one of the reasons I know the country roads. It was a close call back then, but he married the homecoming queen. Now they have four kids and she runs around on him when she can."

At the end of the bridge Thom stood in a small reception area, its walls painted an institutional seafoam green. Two plastic chairs stood against a side wall, and one look at their seats told Eddie why Thom had chosen to stand. One appeared to have a dried-up puddle of ice cream residue; whatever had been dropped on the other was unidentifiable.

Thom said, "Well, we didn't find the white car. Or, I should say, we found a lot of white cars but we couldn't match any of them with your pursuers."

"When Jen put the pedal down they dropped back," Eddie told him. "At that point they were just a couple of guys out for a drive in the country."

"And that's what the Highway Patrol found — a lot of Sunday drivers. We have so many retirees here that every day is Sunday to somebody."

The door buzzed as Thom passed his card through a reader mounted on the wall. "Follow me and we can bring each other up to date on everything that's been going on today."

The desk and two small chairs left room for only one file cabinet in Thom's small office. Eddie pulled out one of the chairs so Jen could take the second one, then waited for Thom to speak. He was already concerned that the detective would be offended that he'd found the second witness, and knew policemen could be territorial about their work -- in Kuwait the civilian police called up to be MPs were among the thinnest-skinned soldiers and most likely to over-react to a slight, real or imagined. Although Thom didn't strike him as that picky, he knew ruffled feelings could jeopardize Jen's chances of learning the truth about Roy's death, so he sat quietly waiting for Thom to begin.

He did. "Your message yesterday was significant in a lot of ways. Can we go over the day again? First, how did you get Arturo to tell you about Deus?"

"Respect and patience. He had to know more than he'd told, so I just told him how important his information was to solving the case and waited for him to make the right decision. In the end, his wife encouraged him to tell me about Deus. She's the one who really got it done.

"By the way, do they have a place to stay?"

"The wife has a cousin here. That's where they went today. But there's not much room so they'll have to find somewhere else in a day or two."

Eddie turned to Jen. "They shouldn't have to suffer because they did the right thing, and they should be somewhere with some security. I'll pay the bill."

"I have a friend in the rental business. I'll see if he has something in a locked building, or at least with cameras."

Eddie turned back to Thom. "Arturo gave me a good description of Deus Lewis. I found him on the corner just where he was supposed to be, along with three of his buddies. All of them were wannabe tough guys.

"Deus saw the whole thing. It wasn't supposed to be a murder, but a kidnapping. Two men tried to hold Roy until they could push him into the car -- that's theory. Fact is that Roy recognized one of them and broke free. The car hit him as he was trying to run across the street. It can't have been moving very fast, but it weighs probably 1,500 kilograms."

He stopped to do a quick mental conversion. “More than 3,300 pounds, so it was enough. And then his head hit the curb, and that was that."

"I agree," Thom said. "That makes it murder, or something close — now two murders. But who did it?"

Jen interrupted, "In all the time I've been with Roy, I don't recall him having a fight with anyone. He told me more than once that life is too short to carry grudges."

Thom continued. “I should have been more precise. We are pretty sure who did it. That is, we found one of the men on security video at the airport. We know he arrived in Sarasota two days before Roy was killed and two other men were with him. We know they were foreign, probably Germans. What we don't know is who they are or what they intended to do with Roy. And Eddie, I'm in agreement that it was supposed to be a snatch, not a murder. But where were they going to take him for questioning? And where did they stay while they were here? If we learn that, we'll probably know who's behind it."

"How did they get here?” Eddie asked.

"Train from up north somewhere, we're still trying to find out where. We circulated the surveillance picture to cab drivers and yesterday one remembered picking them up at the Amtrak station in Tampa. It was a lucky fare for him, since he'd just dropped off a couple who were taking the train to New York. Afraid to fly.

"There were three men together, two tall and one short, and they spoke German with each other. The cabbie studied German in high school so he's sure that’s what is was. He dropped them at a motel near the Interstate, but they didn't check in. The desk clerk thinks someone picked them up in a private car, but he didn't get a make or model."

"Did you send the picture to Philippe?"

"It's not one of the two he has locked up. A witness thinks it resembles the one that got away, but on the other hand maybe it doesn’t. And we didn't get any usable prints, so there's nothing Philippe can use to compare with the car they used in Paris. And it was rented using false ID.”

Jen leaned forward, glanced at Eddie, then looked at Thom to say, "We picked up a lead this morning that may be worth something. Roy had been getting threatening letters from a German, demanding that he reveal the location of a valuable painting the Nazis stole during the war.

"They came from a man named Erich Kraft. I knew him as a very unpleasant boy my age in Frankfurt. My mother was married to his father for a couple of years.

"The letters ended just before Eddie's father was killed. He says in them that the painting and some gold belonged to his father, and he meant to have them. It's probably the gold that has him interested now, since it's gone up in value a lot recently.

"Roy wrote back once to say he'd looked for the painting for more than twenty years but never found it, and had given up the search. Kraft wouldn't take that for an answer. He said he knew for a fact Roy could find the picture, because the Nazi who stole it first had told him."

Thom stood up, a quizzical expression on his face.

"Whoa." He waved his hands. "What's all this really about? Did this start with the letter you found?"

"It did," Jen answered. "Roy asked me to deliver the letter to Eddie's father in Paris. Either he didn't know Mr. Grant had died, or he knew and just forgot to change the instruction on the envelope. It could be either, because we don't know when the letter was written."

"And it said what?"

Jen signaled for Eddie to explain.

"It was very vague. It was written in a rough code, more like jargon, but the import of it was that he was giving up the search. He gave a couple of suggestions to my father but we don't know yet what they all mean."

"But what were they looking for?"

"The most famous and valuable painting still missing. It was painted in the early 1500s by one of the Italian Old Masters, Raphael, and is usually called 'Portrait of a Young Man,' or sometimes 'Portrait of a Gentleman.' It was the pride of a family-owned museum in Poland but it spent the war hanging in the home of Hans Frank, who was the Nazi party lawyer before the war but the governor-general of Poland after the Germans invaded. That's when he wasn't fighting over it with other Nazi bigwigs.

"The painting was destined for the grand museum Hitler planned to build in Austria after he'd won the war, but of course things didn't go their way. As the Russians got closer to Cracow in 1945 Frank had the most valuable pieces of his stolen art packed up and shipped to his home near Munich. A Leonardo and a Rembrandt arrived, but the Raphael didn't, and hasn't been seen since. My father and Roy interviewed Frank just a week or two before he was hanged and they came away with a certain respect for his intelligence. They got the impression that he'd already sent the Raphael out of Poland."

Thom stopped him and asked, "Does this really trace back to something that happened seventy years ago? And a painting?"

Eddie thought a moment and answered carefully. "The painting plus, possibly, some gold. The painting would be more valuable but harder to sell. But Americans live for the here and now. We want instant gratification, short sound bites, results now, not later. Or at least that's what I keep reading in the newspapers.

"On the other hand, I have a friend, a history professor at the Sorbonne, and she and her colleagues see nothing at all strange about wanting to find out what happened to a painting lost so long ago. To Europeans, art is a big part of our patrimony, and you have to remember that some of us are still trying to decide if the French Revolution was a good idea."

"And when was the Revolution?"

"1789."

"I have to meet with the chief of detectives in a few minutes, to decide where we go with this next. But I think you two shouldn't spend the night at Jen's house until we have some of these people locked up, which may take a day or two."

Jen looked at Eddie and raised a questioning eyebrow. "No problem for me. How about that place my father and I stayed the last time we were here? The Hyatt, I think it was."

Thom said, "The Ritz is newer. The Hyatt is less formal."

"Not the Ritz," Eddie said. "I haven't seen the one here but they tend to be sort of heavy on the marble."

As they left the police station Eddie called the Hyatt and reserved two rooms on the same floor. They drove to Jen's house to pack small suitcases for what both hoped would be a short stay. They drove separately to the hotel. During the drive Eddie placed a call to Paul.

"This is turning odd and I don't really know where it's going to go. Can you come give me some backup?"

"Sure," Paul said. "There are some pretty good flights in the morning that connect into Tampa."

"Let's do it a little different. Get a flight to Dulles and meet me there day after tomorrow. I'm flying up to talk to Icky, who seems to think he knows something about this art thing."

"I haven't thought about him in a long time. Is he still CIA?"

"Yes, and now he's a division head. Let me know when you'll arrive but do it by text. I'm not going to tell anyone here that you're on the way, and I'd like you to keep it a secret on that end as well. Except for Philippe. I won't have time to call him. You may have to hang around the airport a while."

"Will do. See you then."

Eddie pulled into the hotel's parking lot and parked next to Jen's BMW just as she was closing the convertible top. They checked in and went to her room, where they pulled down the bedcovers to make it appear slept in. Then they went together to Eddie's room.

"Let's go to the bar and talk about the next step," he suggested.

The lobby bar was half-full of singles out for a good time. The adjacent restaurant had a few tables of older couples. "Earlybirds," Jen said. "But it's almost 7, and the earlier birds have been in the restaurants for almost three hours."

Eddie responded with a smile. "At home we'd just be talking about where we should go to dinner. The restaurants wouldn't be open for another hour at least, and wouldn't be crowded until 9:30. You saw how that works when we had dinner with Margaux."

"I did." The waitress brought their drinks — Johnny Walker Black on the rocks for him, a Cosmo for her.

"Here's to sorting out this whole affair in the near future," he said, and held out his glass to her. She touched it with hers and added, "and with nobody else getting hurt. I hate to say it, but it looks more and more like the people who suffer in this world are the poor unfortunates caught in the middle, like those witnesses. One of them dead, the other homeless and scared to death. And Thom Anderson knows as well as we do who did it. We just don't know how it all happened."

"And we're not going to be able to do much about it tonight," she said with a warm smile, sliding close to him on the banquette until they sat hip to hip. He put his arm around her shoulder and pulled her closer. He could feel her warm skin under the thin summer blouse she wore and it aroused him immediately.

He whispered in her ear, "What say we go back upstairs and decide what to do for dinner?"

"Outstanding idea." She slid away from the table as he took out a twenty to leave the waitress. By the time he reached the elevator she was holding the door open.

They sat on the edge of the bed as he slowly unbuttoned her blouse, stopping for a kiss between each button. He pulled the blouse out of her slacks and helped as she shrugged it off, leaving only a thin white bra with a small lace edge. He cupped each breast, then slipped the thin straps over her shoulders and pulled the bra down, kissing each of her nipples.

"They come to attention for me," he said, looking up with a mischievous grin. She was smiling happily. "I hope you'll do the same," she said, reaching for his belt.

"That's already a done deal."

An hour later they sat in bed wearing the hotel's terrycloth dressing gowns.

"You haven't lost your touch," she said with admiration.

"Nor have you. It seems like twenty years ago was just last weekend. And now about dinner. The way I see it we have two choices, go down to the dining room or call room service."

"No doubt in my mind," she said. I vote for room service. With that she rolled to him and put her hand between his legs. "You?"

He gulped, then turned toward her and pulled the robe from her shoulders. "They're open until midnight. Let's decide in a few minutes."

Room service arrived finally at 11:30, during the Late Show. With it they shared a bottle of Burgundy — "not as good as yours," was Eddie's view. At 12:30 she pushed herself away from him and said, "Into the shower for me." He started to get up and she said, "Alone. I can't do any more. I'm sore."

When he had showered he climbed into the bed next to her. She put her head on his shoulder and moved his hand gently from her breast.

He was almost asleep when she moved slightly and asked, "Eddie? Are you still awake?"

"Sort of," he mumbled.

"Tell me about Lauren. Please?"

He was silent for a moment. He knew his mother had opened the door to this question by showing Jen the family picture and that there was no civil way he could avoid it, but he had no desire to display the barely healed wounds of his past life. But he suppressed a sigh and began to to tell the story.

Almost everyone has romantic ideas about Paris, he told her, but Lauren's were stronger than most because her mother was French and had met her father there. As a young Army officer he'd learned to speak passable French, so he was able to talk to her parents. He insisted that Lauren study it as well.

"We fell in love in college, just a few months before my graduation. It was sudden, a surprise to both of us. She wanted to leave school and go with me, which I thought was a mistake but I was so anxious to have her close that I didn't fight it. She said she would finish college wherever I was stationed but for one reason or another that didn't happen. And then when I was discharged she was anxious to get to Paris. We both were."

But she learned quickly how difficult it can be to adjust to life in a foreign country. She felt trapped in a sort of expat ghetto of anglophones who were even less fluent in French than she. Most of Eddie's friends were French, and their quick dinner-table give-and-take was beyond her ability to follow. She became more and more withdrawn after Sam was born.

"When they died we were making plans for her to move back to Florida with Sam. Her parents lived in Jacksonville, so she planned to go there. I suppose we were also talking about the divorce that was almost certain to follow, although we never said the word. The marriage really was over. She was desperately unhappy and you know what that brings.

"I resisted because I didn't want Sam to grow up in Jacksonville. In Paris he was a bright and promising student with a passion for soccer, who also happened to be part American. In Jacksonville he'd still be bright and promising but at another level he'd be just another black boy. Your town appears to be a suburb of the Midwest but Jacksonville, believe me, is Dixie. I didn't want him to grow up that way."

He described the guilt he felt after their murder as a "big, stinking black dog sitting on my shoulders day after day after day. It influenced everything I did. It was all I could do to keep it from screwing up my business. It did screw up any number of relationships."

She asked him gently, "Was Aurélie one of those?"

"She was the best one. But I ran her off, too."

"That is all so sad. I'm glad you're better now. Thank you for telling me."

Neither of them moved again until the sharp chirp of Jen's phone waked them at 5 o'clock.

"Shit," she muttered as she turned to the night table to silence the offensive noise. "Hello."

She sat straight up in bed. "When?" she asked, and then, "I'll be right there."

"Eddie," she said, eyes wide. "My house is on fire."

CHAPTER TEN

My House is On Fire

Sarasota

By the time they parked behind the yellow police tape only two fire trucks remained, their bright lights illuminating a half-dozen firefighters moving in and out of the open door. Thom Anderson stood at the curb in animated conversation with a tall man whose white helmet announced he was a chief.

Jen jumped out of the car before it stopped moving. She lifted the yellow police tape and stepped under it, ignoring the single policeman across the street who shouted at her to keep out.

"Thom! What happened?" she asked the detective, grabbing his arm to pull him away from his conversation with the fireman.

"Ms. Wetzmuller," he replied. "Let Chief Benson tell you some of what he's just told me."

"Ma'am, I'm the battalion chief," he said. "I can't tell you everything that went on here, but it's clear someone tried to burn down your house. We found a plastic gasoline can in the back yard, and the back door had been forced. There's not a huge amount of fire damage, and it's mostly in the kitchen. For that you can thank your neighbor, who heard the glass break and then saw the flames a few minutes later and called us.

"You're lucky you weren't here. There was a lot of smoke. That's usually what kills people."

Thom said, "I suggested they stay at a hotel last night because of some problems with a case. You may remember — it's the death of

Roy Castor, who was run down on Osprey a couple of weeks ago. He was Ms. Wetzmuller's father, and we now know his death was no accident. She and Mr. Grant pretty much confirmed that yesterday when someone tried to chase them on the road back from Arcadia. I'm glad now they didn't stay here."

Eddie had been listening closely. He introduced himself and asked, "Chief, did the neighbor say how long it was between the broken glass and the fire?"

"Several minutes. Maybe five."

Jen interrupted to ask Chief Benson to show her the damage. They walked down the driveway toward the back yard and after they were out of earshot Eddie turned to Thom. "Do you see the same pattern I see? First they try to kidnap Roy and fail. Next they try to kidnap one of us in Paris, and as I reflect on how that went down I come more and more to the conclusion they were after Jen. They were confused because I was with two blondes that night. They failed again.

"And now they break into Jen's house, then burn it — but five minutes later. Enough time to go to her bedroom to snatch her, or both of us. I doubt if they wanted to search the house. They must have done that while she was in Paris. They were here to kidnap her, and it's probably the same people, or at least the same group."

Eddie kept to himself his thought that fire had been involved in Artie's death, and after that the deaths of Lauren and Sam. "We're dealing with something really evil here," he told himself. "It's gone way beyond a painting."

"I see the connection," Thom responded. "First thing I'm going to do is call in the state fire marshal to do a complete investigation of just the fire, if the Chief hasn't already done it. Our lab will look thoroughly at the house and interview the witnesses. The neighbor who called it in may be the only one."

"Of course that's your department," Eddie said, "but it sounds smart to me. After what we found in Arcadia I think I need to know more about Al Sommers. Can you point me toward anyone who might be able to fill me in?"

"Let's see. He sticks pretty much to himself now, since he retired from the bank, which by the way failed just a few months ago. I hear his health's been failing.

"For a starter, try Lindy Gaudet. She's editor of a weekly paper on Longboat Key that specializes in society coverage. It's mainly picture after picture of couples or groups in penguin suits holding champagne glasses and smiling into the camera. She's a bit odd — used to be a real social butterfly but got tired of it and dropped out. She likes to gossip, and she's a little mean.

"You might also talk to one of her part-time reporters. Guy by the name of Woody Matthews. He's an old-school police reporter, down to the whisky and cigars, but he knows what's going on in town."

"When I saw Colonel Sommers yesterday he mentioned a 'Woody.' He told his helper to find out what this Woody knew about Roy's death. He was surprised when I mentioned it didn't appear to be an accident."

"Same Woody. He did some investigations for Sommers at the bank. He's not a completely bad guy, but a rabid right-winger and a hard drinker. He and Sommers belong to the same church — the Church of Hate the Jews. It's not a big congregation and they keep their heads down because Longboat Key is more Jewish than Manhattan. Woody will expect you to pay him if he tells you anything. I think he makes more as a private eye than as a real reporter."

"Thanks. I'll try to see them both."

At eight o'clock the parking lot was almost empty. Eddie counted twenty spaces, but only two were filled when he arrived — a silver Buick about five years old, parked facing the offices, and an older pickup truck on the opposite side, near the back door of a restaurant. He chose a spot next to the Buick, directly in front of a sign listing the building tenants.

The Longboat Sentinel was one of eight names listed. Four spaces were blank, a foreshadowing of worse economic times to come. In addition to the Sentinel there were an accountant, a chiropractor, a fitness studio, what appeared to be a candle and gift shop, and several others with cute names giving no hint of their business.

To get there he'd driven again across the new bridge and past the restaurant where he and Jen had eaten two evenings before, then for ten minutes up Gulf of Mexico Drive, the long and narrow main highway running behind the golf courses and expensive condos lining the beach. On its other side was a line of smaller, older condos, plus all the shopping and support businesses needed by a flourishing high-priced tourist destination, from grocery stores to dentists. He'd stuck carefully to the speed limit after Thom's warning that the Longboat Key cops were particularly diligent about speeding.

He bounded up three steps to a long covered hallway leading between two rows of glass shop windows. Halfway to the end on the right he found the newspaper, its name shining on the inside of the door in bright gold leaf, incongruous next to the sheets of yellowing newspaper taped to the glass next to it.

As he opened the door he heard a chime at the end of a hallway, dingy in the semi-darkness. The newspaper-covered window seemed to be a way for the features editor to keep visitors from looking into her cubicle. Eddie didn't think the mall had enough visitors to make that a big problem.

"You must be Mr. Grant from Paris." A voice boomed at him from the depths of the hallway, and he looked up to see an enormous woman silhouetted in an office door at the end of the hall.

"I am," Eddie responded. "And you must be Ms. Gaudet. I presume Thom Anderson reached you? I hope I'm not too early."

"Lindy. I had a nice chat with Thom. Haven't seen him for a couple of years, although I know his wife. He told me some about what's going on. That was a shame about poor Mr. Castor. I really felt sorry for Jen."

"You know her very well?"

"We used to run in the same circles. We were even married to the same man. Different times, of course, and long ago. Before I looked like this." She reached down to pull at her skirt on both sides, emphasizing her bulk. Eddie figured she must weigh at least a hundred pounds more than she should.

"I didn't know that. I knew Jen had been married, but …"

"It's ancient history. He was a dashing surgeon when I met him. He swept me off my feet before I learned I was the second trophy wife. In three years he kicked me out and Jen was the next one, same story. He's still a randy old goat. He used to screw any woman who was remotely willing, including some patients. I hear he's still at it, but now he's a big wheel in town and a little more careful.

"Anyway, you didn't come all the way to Longboat to hear about my history. Come in and I'll see if I can add anything to what you know. Thom gave me some idea of what you're looking for."

Lindy lowered her bulk slowly into a large chair of webbing material. He suspected her weight gave her back problems, which she was trying to solve with the special chair.

"Lindy, I'm just here for a few days. I'm not trying to get in the way of the Sarasota police or solve Roy Castor's death, but there's an old issue that involves my father. That's what I'm trying to shed some light on, if there's any to be shed. Once I do that I can go back home to Paris. Also, I need to ask for your promise of confidence in this. I could be blackening someone's name unnecessarily and I don't want to do that."

"This is personal, not newspaper stuff. I won't print it."

He summarized his father's work with Roy during the war and the letter Jen had found and delivered to him. He told her of the Germans' effort to kidnap Jen in front of the wax museum, and of the documents hidden in the safe deposit vaults in Paris and Arcadia.

"So," she said after he'd finished. "Somewhere out there is an old painting that would be worth a hundred million dollars or so if it should turn up, maybe plus other goodies Hans Frank set aside to finance the Fourth Reich. Is that about it?"

"That's the broadest possible case. The painting may have been destroyed or taken by the Russians. There may not be any gold or jewels, or even a painting, and Hans Frank may have planned to take care of himself, not the next generation of Nazis. But someone obviously smells money and they're willing to kill to find it. That concerns me a lot."

"Thom's coming around to the view that the painting and Roy's death are related. Is that what you think?"

Eddie sat and thought for a minute, deciding how much to tell her. He wished he'd had more time to talk to Jen about her, to get a better feel for Jen's view of her trustworthiness. He decided to be open with her.

"We know from a couple of witnesses that Roy was confronted by two men. We know he was either pushed in front of the SUV driven by a third man, in which case it was clearly intentional murder, or — more likely — he accidentally ran in front of it while trying to escape. I'm inclined toward the second, but in either case the police will treat it pretty much the same.

"We know that there were two witnesses. One of them was killed within an hour or two of the time I talked to him. Someone burned the home of the other witness, after threatening his wife and child with a large knife. And did I mention, the dead witness's throat was cut with just such a knife? And now Jen's home has been burned. It's all too similar to be completely coincidental."

"Jeez. When I came here Sarasota was dead dead dead — as my favorite singer put it, dead as heaven on a Saturday night. Now we have Germans and Nazis and mysterious deaths. I don't like it at all. What can I do to help?"

The door chimed and Lindy got up to see who had come in.

"It's the feature writer and the layout man. We go to press tomorrow, so today's a busy day for him, and his office is right next door to mine. These places have chicken-coop walls, too. Let's get out of here."

"Where to?"

"Up the Key to Harry's. For my money it's the best restaurant in or around Sarasota, and they open for breakfast. This time of year we'll be able to get a table in the corner and not have people around us listening in."

One of the new arrivals had turned on the hallway lights while Eddie and Lindy were talking, revealing two dozen framed newspaper pages showing the cream of Sarasota society at one black-tie event or another. To him, they all looked the same.

"Take a look at this one," Lindy said, grabbing at his sleeve. "This was a cerebral palsy benefit in…" she squinted at the date at the top of the page "… 1992. There at the top right is Jen, with the banker she was dating at the time. He's no longer around since his bank failed ten years ago." She pointed out a slightly older version of the girl Eddie had met twenty years before. She was more mature, more obviously a woman, lovely in a green silk sheath.

"And this one is me." The woman she pointed to looked almost nothing like the Lindy of 2008, certainly no more than a distant cousin. She was slim, with dark hair, and wearing a brilliant ruby evening gown. She was on the arm of a graying man Eddie figured was in his late 40s, a man with a look of confidence.

"That was my surgeon husband. The next time we had this party it was Jen who went with him, and shortly after that she married him. It lasted three years, about as long as mine did. I went to these parties for a few more years but I was getting tired of them and of the people, but I never did get completely away from them. There's a saying here that the price of entry into Sarasota society is a tux."

Lindy struggled into the passenger seat of the rental car and directed Eddie back onto Gulf of Mexico Drive, where they turned north. After a few minutes they parked next to Harry's, a complex of converted residences with an outdoor patio facing a quiet side street.

"Nice," Eddie said. "The outdoor tables make me feel right at home, except that we have more awnings than umbrellas."

"You'll be glad to have the umbrella later in the day. Let's go inside where it's air conditioned. It will be far too hot out here before we're done."

For the next hour, as Lindy ate two orders of pancakes with bacon and Eddie had one fried egg and multiple cups of coffee, she outlined her view of the political and power currents in Sarasota.

"And now," she said at last, "we get to your man of the hour, Al Sommers."

Eddie said, "The man I saw didn't look like a killer or a major-league international conspirator. But I know he's not completely truthful because I've caught him in a couple of flagrant and important lies. And his friend Sonny gave me the creeps. Is that still an American expression?"

Lindy looked directly at Eddie. "It is, and he gives me the creeps, too. There is absolutely nothing bad you could say about Al Sommers that might not be true, emphasis on might. For most of us there are moral and behavioral red lines we won't cross. I don't think he has those. He's basically a weak man with no moral brakes. Nothing you've described to me is impossible.

"You seem like a nice young man. I know this is important to you because it's something your father wanted, but you need to be very, very careful. The threat you had in Paris and the chase out of Arcadia should tell you there's something bad going on. Thom will probably solve the murder within a few days, but for now my advice is that you get back to Paris, and don't tell anyone but Thom until after you've left."

Eddie sat back, surprised. While he'd not heard good things about Sommers from anyone, this was the first time anyone had voiced what he was beginning to believe, that Sommers, whether he was directly involved in the Paris attack or not, was probably directly behind the attempt to kidnap Roy.

"Within limits I can take care of myself. But I need to know more about him. Can you help me with that?"

Lindy paused and took another sip of coffee. She looked down at the cup and said, "Good."

"Al Sommers is a man with an extremely well developed sense of entitlement, like a lot of business executives. He has really bad taste in people and he's been responsible for a couple of his friends and fellow investors going bankrupt. One of those killed himself. I think the prosecutor looked closely at him when his bank failed but decided the evidence just wasn't strong enough to bring a Republican party stalwart to trial for fraud.

"He started a little community bank a year or two after he moved here from West Texas, where he was in the oilfield service business. He sold that business for a considerable amount of money — I was told it was around five million — and came here to make his fortune bigger yet. Keep in mind that he was already pretty old. That would have been the mid-nineties so he would have been in his late seventies, fifteen years older than I am. He wormed his way into politics and society, but on the side he collected some really strange friends."

Lindy told how Sommers had brought with him one of his employees, a skinny man named Mark Perry, whom she called "Mr.

Fixit." She indicated some of the things he fixed weren't completely legal.

"Then after a couple of years Mark died and things got even stranger. Pretty soon Mark's son, known only as Sonny — you met him — showed up with his Russian boyfriend. They bought a big house in Naples. The story was that it was halfway between Sonny's work in Sarasota and Dmitri's roots in Miami. Informed rumor says he's a collector and enforcer for the Russian mafia.

After that, she said, Sommers hired an East German couple to live in a small house on his property. They were never seen in public but the accepted story is that Sonny fills in for them when they are off duty.

"There were tales of stolen gold and silver of unknown provenance, probably Nazi. People said that would fit sommers's personality. Around ten years ago the FBI came around asking some questions about him, but nothing came of it as far as I know.

"By that time he was a big man about town in politics, and a high liver. About the time of the Internet bubble his picture was in the local daily when he presented an old German chalice to the priest of the largest Catholic church in town. He said he'd bought it on a vacation trip back to where he'd been during the war, but there were suspicions that he'd looted it when he was in Germany the first time and had been sitting on it since.

"That was about the time he and some friends were raising money to start the bank. Unfortunately they started too late and within a couple of years the real estate market here was softening, big time. Even if the casual homebuyer or newspaper reader didn't see it, the real estate insiders saw the storm brewing, or at least some of them did. They were busily reducing their own exposure at the same time they were selling thousands of new houses to unsuspecting northerners every year.

"Al got lucky. After a few years his colleagues on the board were up to here with his anti-semitism and very extreme right-wing views." She ran her hand across her eyebrows. "He wanted to close all the public schools, stop all food stamps, cut taxes even further on the rich, raise them on the middle class. And it was all done in a hostile, snarly tone. Eventually they had enough and told him he had to leave. He said OK, but only if they paid cash for his stock. He took out two or three million dollars. That was two years ago.

"Last year the FDIC showed up one fine Friday afternoon and closed down the bank. Those partners who'd borrowed money to buy his stock, or a couple of them anyway, were bankrupt, while he had cash. One of them killed himself. Al paid off the family to keep it out of court. I don't know what he has left, but I'd guess not much."

They sat for a few minutes while he sorted out what she'd told him.

"I need to go track down Woody. And I appreciate your advice but I'll be here at least another day, although tomorrow I'm flying to Washington for the day to do some background research. I am concerned about Jen, though. I think they've tried twice to kidnap her."

"My guess is she'll be perfectly safe here."

Eddie thought about Lindy's parting words as he drove back down Gulf of Mexico Drive. At 7:30 there had hardly been any cars on the road, but close to noon it was crowded and humming. He quickly counted four sidewalk cafés on St. Armand's Circle, three of them nearly full.

Lindy had arranged for him to meet Woody Matthews at Hemingway's, an upstairs restaurant and watering hole trying to trade on Papa's name. Lindy told him Woody could be found there from opening time until mid-afternoon unless he was working on a story for her or an investigation for Al Sommers or some of the other business types he knew in town.

"I have a minority partner in this newspaper," Lindy had told him. "I don't like it, but I needed the money to stay in business through the last recession, and we've performed pretty well for him. He's a money guy with almost no interest in newspapering, and he's happy to let us go on publishing our society pictures. I shut down the editorial page a few years ago when he wanted to go on a crusade to do away with the public school system and replace it entirely with private schools. He and Sommers are buddies, by the way. Woody thinks they're his friends, but they're not."

A parking place stood vacant across the street and Eddie pulled in. He took the stairs two at a time, bypassing the elevator. The bartender, a twenty-something with a mullet and two earrings in each ear, waved toward the back when he asked for Woody. "Same time, same place," he said laconically.

He could just make out a man waving at him with a beer glass from the back of the dark, wood-paneled cavern. Woody looked about sixty, or maybe fifty-five and in terrible shape. His potato nose showed the unmistakable mark of too much of the grain. His face was weathered to mahogany and his thin brown hair flew in every direction. He seemed to be about forty pounds overweight. His short-sleeved white polyester shirt was yellow at the collar and armpits. A skinny black tie hung loosely around the open collar.

Woody waved him into the seat opposite. "Lindy said you'd be here, had some things you wanted to check up on. Don't know what I can tell you but finding things out is what I do for a living." He grinned. Two teeth were missing, the rest were dingy and yellow.

"I'm here because of Roy Castor. His death is what started me off, but I'm more interested in things that went on before, all the way back to the war."

"Yeah. I heard he was there, worked on finding the Nazis' loot. Some of my friends think it was a waste of time, but you already know that since you talked to the colonel." Woody straightened visibly when he mentioned Sommers.

"He was pretty clear about what he believed, but that's not really where I'm headed. I'm interested in anything you might have heard about Roy and whether he might have had any knowledge of this treasure after he came to Sarasota."

"In other words, did he steal the painting, or whatever it is you're looking for?"

"Or did he have a good idea where it might be. Either way I'd like to know."

Woody sat back to think a minute. It was clear to Eddie he hadn't thought of Roy as a possible art thief. He held out an empty bottle as the waiter passed. "Another just like this one," he said, then turned to Eddie and asked, "What'd you like?"

"Bud," Eddie responded.

Woody went back to considering Eddie's question. "I've never heard anybody say Roy stole anything. He seemed like a straight arrow. There was always talk he might be gay, but that's pretty common in Sarasota, so nobody much cares. I did hear a few years back that he might know more than he let on about the missing painting you're chasing."

"What did that sound like?"

"Hard to say. I heard it from a friend of a friend, and his English isn't any too good. He just said he had it on good authority that Roy and somebody he'd worked with during the war were too close not to have known what happened, and that he'd like the chance to talk seriously to both of them about it. I think he said Al was going to give him that chance.

"I didn't think anything much of it, but it was the last time he talked about it. The next time I saw him I asked and he told me to shut up and forget what he'd said. Nobody's mentioned it to me until today."

Eddie asked, "Do you happen to remember about when that conversation took place?"

"Let's see… I ran into him at some kind of political celebration, I think just after Bush was inaugurated. So it would have been early in 2001, maybe February."

Eddie felt his hair stand up. Early 2001, just the time his father had died.

"Do you think this friend would talk to me? I'd make it worth his while."

"Probably not, because his boss really put a cork into him and his friend. They live together in Naples, as far as I can tell on money his friend inherited from his father, God knows where that came from. But you can try. He's a Russian — an American Russian, but still a Russian — named Dmitri. He and Sonny Perry met when both of them were in prison together, and now they work for the colonel."

He tried not to show his suspicion about Dmitri. "Are you ready for lunch? Lindy told me you'd be able to tell me what's good here."

"Hamburger and fries for me. I don't like fish much even as long as I've lived here." Eddie waved down the waiter and ordered two hamburgers and two more beers.

Woody looked at him cautiously, out of the corner of his eye. “Lindy told me you’re not just fishing, that you already know some stuff and you are looking for more about Al Sommers. That right?”

Eddie tried to phrase his reply carefully. “I don’t know much about Al Sommers personally, and it looks like he’s too old to be much of a player in anything — and I don’t really know what anything consists of. I also know you’re close to him, so I don’t want to get a turf war started because I have nothing against him. I’ll be back in Paris in a couple of days and it would be unfair for me to leave you dealing with fallout from my questions.”

Woody thought about that a minute, then said, “Al and I used to be friends. When he ran his bank I did some investigations for him and he paid me for them. But he hasn’t sent any work my way for more than six months, so I think he’s a former client. I sell a few stories to Lindy and other small papers in the area and I have a little Army pension, but I need to find other ways to make a little money. So what I’m saying is I’ll help you if I can, and it wouldn’t be good for either of us if the word got back to Sommers. So if you won’t tell, I won’t.”

“Fair enough. A couple of people say you’re good at your job and your information checks out. You know I’ll have to check it.”

“I understand that.”

“Then what can you tell me about Al sommers's relationship with Roy Castor?”

“I don’t think they was ever friends. They were in the military together, but Sommers was a hotshot pilot with medals and Roy was a grunt. Sommers tried to use Roy to raise money for his bank, but Roy wouldn’t touch that. Roy and Sommers were on opposite sides of the political divide, but that wasn’t Roy’s problem. He could just smell a rat. We have a lot of extreme right-wingers in this town, but Sommers is really rabid — and I say that as somebody who’s basically on the same side he is — and Roy was a live-and-let-live type.”

Eddie replied, “That wouldn’t have led to Roy’s death, would it?”

“Not by itself, but combined with money, who knows? I don’t know Al’s financial condition now, but last year it was pretty bad. He got on the wrong side of the stock market, and he lent some money to Sonny and Dmitri to start a restaurant in Naples, which promptly flopped."

"Did he have anything more than what he took out of the bank?"

"Well, he had to pay some of that to the family of a man who went bankrupt when the bank failed and then killed himself. But he had other resources — his own and what I'd call 'family' resources."

The hamburgers arrived and Woody stopped until the waiter had left.

"What I'm about to tell you could get me killed. It could get you killed. But I think you should know it because I think it got Roy Castor killed."

Eddie waited.

"There was always a rumor around that Al looted a bunch of stuff at the end of World War II, when he was working in Munich with Roy."

"And with my father," Eddie interjected.

"Yes. Well, that was true. He did steal a few pieces and mail them home — the post office was the looter's best friend at that time. In fact, some of them are still stored in an old fallout shelter behind his house. From the outside it looks like it hasn't been used in years, but the real entrance is in the garage. I've been in it, and I've seen it. There must be a dozen pieces of silver and gold that look like they came from old churches.

"But, and here's the important part, it's Sonny who owns most of the treasure. His father was a big-time looter and moved all of it here from Midland when Al sold the business. He stored it in the fallout shelter, too, but when his father died Sonny moved it to the big new house he and Dmitri bought in Naples. They even in a secure room just for the loot and some guns. It has six-inch reinforced concrete walls and one of those doors like you see in banks, with a combination lock.

"They've been selling it piece by piece through Dmitri's connections, some pretty shady types in Europe, maybe the Russian mafia. Dmitri's not a real full-blooded gangster but he's a dangerous man all the same, and has a reputation of being good with a knife. He was in prison for trying to burn down a federal judge's house when he met Sonny, and the two of them fell in love at first sight."

Woody paused and Eddie exhaled. “That’s a hell of a story. You ever think about writing a book?”

“I’d live maybe a week. No thanks. But I’ve had it with Sommers and I never did like his two buddies.”

“So you think this whole thing is about money?”

“Not entirely, but they’re running through theirs fast, and they got a lead from Sonny’s father that Roy learned something from one of the top Nazis just before he was hanged. Dmitri’s fence contacts got him in touch with somebody in Europe that verified some of the things they’d heard here. I think he’s one of the people they sold Sonny’s stuff to, and he’d like to buy more.”

“What do you know about him?”

“Very little. He’s German, a real tough guy, like the SS types you see in the movies. Not the effeminate ones. Dmitri thinks he’s fronting for some Arabs because he’s never interested in any of the altarpieces or angel paintings or things the Arabs’ religion doesn’t allow. He just wants valuable hard goods, like gold cups. And he never buys until the man behind him gives his OK. Nothing on spec.”

“Then why the interest in the painting?”

“Oh, he’d sell that somewhere else. And there’s some sort of family connection to it. His father was once involved with it when the Nazis had it, or something like that. He thinks there’s lots more there than the painting. A bunch of Nazi gold.”

“Did you ever hear this man’s name?”

“Sure I did. I even met him once a half-dozen years ago. He’s a mean-looking bastard. The strangest thing is his ear. He was born with only half of his right ear. It’s like somebody cut part of it off, except that his father’s was the same.”

Eddie pressed. “What was the name?”

“Erich. It was Erich.”

"You said it wasn't entirely about money. What else is there?"

"They're a threesie. Al wears the dress. I’m not sure how Sonny and Dmitri divide up the rest of the work, and I don’t want to know.”

The table had been cleared. Eddie paid the check. During Woody’s tale he had finished a cup of coffee and Woody had drunk another beer, his fifth, very quickly. Eddie decided to wrap things up before Woody changed his mind.

"Woody, you've been really helpful to me. Can I call on you again if any questions come up? And what can I pay you?"

"Sure. Call me any time, I'll give you my card. My usual fee is $50 an hour and we've been here three hours, so that's $150. Is that OK?"

"It's more than fair." Eddie reached into his pocket for his wallet, peeled off three $50 bills and laid them on the table. "And I'd like to give you a retainer for future work. Would another $200 be OK?" He showed four more fifties.

Woody looked hungrily at the money. "You bet. Sommers never paid me more than $100 for anything. You call me any time." He was relaxed and friendly.

Abruptly, Eddie leaned over the table, put his face close to Woody's and said, "If I hear so much as a rumor that you've passed this conversation on to anyone else, I'll come back and take that money out of your ass, and Sommers or Dmitri will be right behind me, if they don't get to you first. Do we understand each other very clearly?"

Woody sat back in the seat, shaken. "Yes. Yes, Sir. I understand. You don't have anything to worry about there."

As Eddie crossed the street to his car he looked carefully for followers. It seemed clear, so he started the drive back across the bridge into Sarasota proper, dialing Jen on the way.

"How are you coming with the house?" he asked her.

"Crappy. I'm here now with a contractor. Can you come?"

"Sure. I was on my way but didn't know where you were."

"Come see this mess and then we'll go and pick one of those light Burgundies you mentioned. Maybe we'll get a case. I feel like drinking a lot of it tonight."

"OK. Remember I have an early flight tomorrow. I'm going to Washington to see an old Army buddy who may be able to help. I'll be back tomorrow night."

He parked in front of a neighbor's house because Jen's was surrounded by cars. He spotted the fire chief's SUV and another that bore the seal of the State Fire Marshal on its front doors. Two pickups appeared to belong to contractors, judging from the ladders sticking out of their beds.

Smoke-stained carpet had been piled roughly on the lawn. He walked past it into the living room and found the stench of smoke overwhelming, so he hurried further, past the guest room and Roy's study, where there was no apparent fire damage, to the kitchen, which was a charred shell. A large black stain on the tile floor marked where the gasoline had been thrown. The cabinet doors had burned or were askew on their hinges, and the contents behind them were cinders. The ceiling was black. The heat must have been intense.

"Eddie!" Jen saw him from the back porch and ran into the kitchen to throw her arms around his neck. "This is horrible."

She took him to the porch to introduce him to a 35-year-old man in jeans and a blue shirt, wearing a yellow hard hat with "Jim" lettered flamboyantly on the front. He introduced himself as Jim Smith, the contractor who had done work for Jen at her gallery and whom she had now asked to repair her house.

"You're the man from Paris?" Jim asked, glancing suspiciously at Jen as he finished the question. Eddie suspected they had been more than business acquaintances at one time.

"That's me."

"Jen was really, really lucky. First, the neighbor called the fire department so quickly. Second, when her father renovated the house thirty years ago he did it right, and the ceiling of the kitchen was made of fireproof gypsum board. Without that the fire would have burned into the second floor. As is, it will be a big cleanup job and a couple of weeks' construction work. It could have been a new house. It's a good thing you weren't here."

"We were very fortunate," Eddie told him. "Detective Anderson recommended we move to a hotel after some unpleasantness that had to do with Mr. Castor's death, so we did what he suggested. It was a good thing."

"Well, we'll be ready to move ahead with the construction as soon as the fire marshal releases the house. At the moment it's still a crime scene, but we'll probably get access Monday morning. Jen's insurance company is ready to pay us, so there's no issue there. You'd be surprised how often they can be jerks."

"No, I wouldn't. I live in France, the mother church of bureaucracy."

He turned to Jen and said, "I need to go back to the hotel and make some calls, see how my business is doing. Knock on my door when you're ready to go to dinner. I need to get away very early in the morning for my flight to Dulles."

"OK," she said, then turned to the contractor. "Jim, I'll be at the gallery tomorrow. If you get the go-ahead and are willing to work the weekend just call and I'll meet you here."

They chose the hotel dining room that night because of Eddie's early flight. They each had a steak and didn't linger — by eight o'clock they were back in their room. Jen opened a bottle of the burgundy she'd rescued from her fire-damaged refrigerator but neither had drunk more than an inch before they began again to make love.

At ten she finally said, "OK. You can go to bed now."

"Not quite yet."

CHAPTER ELEVEN

History with a Surprise

Washington

Eddie looked for the fastest path through the crowd on the arrival sidewalk at Dulles Airport. He stepped between a middle-aged black woman leaning heavily on a luggage cart and a teenager who appeared to be Indian or Pakistani, both deep in cell-phone conversations. The teen's voice, in the high tenor of the subcontinent, floated above the crowd.

He had no trouble spotting his friend Icky Crane, whose six-foot-seven height would have made him stand out even if he hadn't been waiting next to his bright yellow Corvette. For as long as Eddie had known him, Icky had driven yellow Corvettes. If anyone asked, he always said he was five-foot-nineteen. The two trademarks had stuck with him all his life.

"Thanks for meeting me, Icky," Eddie said as he shook his friend's hand. Then he put his bag behind the passenger seat seat while Icky folded himself behind the wheel.

"And how is the lovely Aurélie?"

"I talked to her a couple of days ago and she asked me to pass along her regards. She's doing well. But we're not really dating now, just friends. Actually, she has married and divorced since you saw her. And how is …? Make that, how's whoever?"

"Ah. You know me, Eddie. I can't stay long in the same bed. Her name is Angela, and she's terrific. My own age, too, possibly for the first time since college. And by the way, she doesn't like Icky. It seems I'm to be Tom or Jeff, or even Thomas Jefferson Crane. Her first husband was a Virginia politician, so she's partial to Thomas Jefferson. The husband was a dreadful reactionary, by the way."

"No promises, but I'll try to remember. Where are we going?"

"Bethesda, right inside the Beltway. They moved us from Langley a year or so ago. It's never a good sign in a bureaucracy when you get moved away from headquarters, but at least all us asset chasers are under the same roof. The agency has gotten so big since 9/11 there just isn't room for us in one place, so we're spread all over the area."

Eddie recalled the day they'd first met, when they found themselves on opposite sides of a pickup basketball game their first year at West Plains University. Icky had been a high school star in Massachusetts, and Eddie, who'd come to America as the French kid more comfortable at soccer than basketball, was learning quickly enough to play a respectable game. They'd hit it off immediately and had been inseparable through college and the Army, up through the first Gulf War. When they were discharged Eddie and Lauren had chosen Paris, while Icky went dutifully back to Massachusetts to work in his family's textile business.

Both had been recruited by the CIA. Eddie didn't see much future in an organization that seemed fixed on defending against a large monolithic enemy that had already collapsed. Icky thought the agency was flexible enough to update itself, so after two unhappy years he had left the family firm and moved to Washington. Since then he'd learned five languages and been posted to a half-dozen overseas jobs. From time to time he'd called on Eddie for unofficial help, but Eddie had stopped accepting the assignments when his wife and son were murdered. He'd signaled clearly that he wanted to be left alone, so Icky had seen him only twice in seven years.

At the first, a year after Lauren's death, Eddie was a lost soul, unreceptive to friends or family. Margaux had said he was his own ghost, sliding around life and glancing off the things that once had given him joy.

The second time was a year or two later, when Icky had to be in Paris on company business. They'd had dinner at Margaux's home because she was recovering from surgery, and Icky was amazed at the difference in his friend. He was also amazed at Aurélie, whom he called "that astounding creature."

"If you get tired of her or she kicks you out, your job is to call me immediately," he'd said the next day as he tried to persuade Eddie to take on a small investigation in Switzerland.

"Wouldn't work, Icky. All your friends would think she's a raving pinko. Even the French right wing is to the left of what passes for progressive politics in the States these days. And your outfit lives in the days of John Foster Dulles. Or worse, W."

There wouldn't be any time for jokes this trip, Eddie told himself as Icky turned the Corvette smoothly onto the toll road that would take them to the Beltway and then across the Potomac into Maryland.

Icky set the cruise control. "Your call didn't leave me much time, but I've lined up some people who may be able to help. My office deals with all sorts of hidden assets, and frankly right now we're putting most of our energy into finding the sources of terrorist money. But there's a woman in the old-money section who spends a third of her time on wartime stuff -- and, believe it or not, some of the old Nazi loot has been turning up in the same places as terrorist money. She's very interested in talking to you."

A half-hour later the Corvette nosed off the Beltway and into the parking lot of a large glass-walled building. It was identical to the buildings to its left and right and reminded Eddie unfavorably of the Mitterrand library in Paris.

Icky swiped his access card at a gate separating the elevators from the entrance lobby. Outside the gate Eddie saw a Starbucks, a magazine stand, and a dry cleaner's pickup station. A uniformed guard made a copy of his American passport and buzzed him through the gate, where Icky held an elevator door. He pressed the button for the fifth floor and when the car stopped he led Eddie through a door marked only "Export-Import."

Behind the door a guard welcomed them with, "Good morning, Mr. Crane. Is this your guest?"

"It is. Eddie, we need to make another copy of your passport, if you don't mind."

Security cleared, the guard pressed a button the opened a heavy metal door leading to a stairway rising a floor to the top.

"Import-export. What do the other tenants think you do?"

"Oh, they know what we do. It just gives us a little deniability and them a little security, so everyone's happy."

"And this is your kingdom?"

"You could say that, in the sense that Napoleon's brother was king of Naples."

They paused in a windowless anteroom at the top of the stairs as Icky passed his access card through a reader. A discreet chime sounded, an LED changed from red to green, and he opened the door to lead the way down a long beige hall completely free of decoration. Halfway to the end he turned into a reception room furnished with two gray steel desks. The back wall was lined with fireproof file cabinets, each of which had a combination dial in the center of its top drawer.

"Eddie, this is Stella Marcos, my right hand." Stella stood to greet them. She was a tiny Filipina, who without her tall heels would hardly have been five feet tall. She wore her jet-black hair in an elegant French twist echoing Margaux's style.

"Stella. Delighted," he said.

"It's really Estrella, but no one could handle that."

Icky's office was larger but no more elegant. His desk was T-shaped, with its own conference table, and was larger than Eddie had expected.

"Where we came from you had to be a bird colonel to get this kind of setup."

"That's still the way it is. But don't confuse Washington with the outside world. Out there the colonel or the one-star really have serious responsibilities. Here we're a dime a dozen. At least I'm not some general's aide."

He turned serious. "Eddie, I know you have a real problem going, and I intend to help solve it. My initial information is that it may be more serious than you know -- although I'm not sure how anything could be more serious than what you've been through."

"Do you think this is connected with the murder of my family?"

"Too early to say. They may be totally separate crimes, but let's just say we've found some evidence in looking at the missing painting that might lead back to someone who might have been a part of the murders. But it's too early yet. We have miles to go.

"When you called, I asked Carole Westin to start looking around. Her official job is dealing with the old lost assets, most of which are the property of Jews deported and murdered during the war. But like all of us, she's been working mainly on finding terrorist money. Yesterday I asked her to put that on hold for a day or two and work on the painting and anything that might be related to it. Needless to say, she was very familiar with Hans Frank.

"I'm pretty sure now that what I thought was going to be a freelance project for an old friend has turned into something that just might move one of our old cases forward. Let's hope we can work together again on it."

Two minutes more of small talk, then Icky held up his hand and said, "Here she is now."

"Eddie, please meet Dr. Carole Westin, director of our recovered assets branch. Carole, this is Eddie Grant of Paris, my old company commander and the guy with the intriguing problem I told you about yesterday."

Carole Westin appeared to be about 35, although Eddie thought he might be off by five years either way. She had hair nearly as black as Estrella's and an olive complexion that would have marked her as Mediterranean, perhaps Italian, except that the name didn't match. Maybe it was a husband's name, but there was no wedding ring. She wore a beige shirtwaist dress that looked expensive, and gold earrings that matched a simple chain necklace. She reminded him of a picture of Margaux at the same age that had sat on his father's desk.

"I'm sorry to have dropped this on you on such short notice, but Icky may have told you this whole affair came up rather suddenly."

"I was sorry to hear of your friend's death …"

"It was very hard on his daughter, but that is what led to my call. Maybe something useful will come out of it."

"Let's go across the hall to a conference room and get out of Icky's hair," Carole said. "Excuse me, out of Thomas Jefferson's powdered wig." She looked at Icky with an impish half-smile.

She sat down at the head of a steel conference table and signaled to Eddie to sit at her left. "Is there anything specific I can tell you now?" he asked.

"May I just summarize what I know, then ask you to fill in any obvious blanks? Then I'll tell you what we have found so far and see if that sparks any new ideas." Eddie had no objection.

"First, your recently deceased friend worked with your late father in the Allied Central Collection Point in Munich. As part of their work they interviewed Hans Frank just before he was hanged but he didn't give them any useful information about the missing Raphael, other than to indicate it might have been shipped earlier than the other paintings.

"Mr. Castor stayed in the Army a few months longer than your father, still in Munich, then was mustered out and returned to St. Louis. But soon he went back to Germany, where he settled in Frankfurt and opened an antiques business. He spent thirty years building it, plus or minus, then sold it to a German company and retired to Florida, where he lived for another thirty years until his recent untimely death. One of his acquaintances in Sarasota was his commanding officer in Munich, Lieutenant Colonel Albert Sommers.

"Your father returned to the family business in New York State, married but it didn't last, and after three years or so moved back to Paris, where he was very successful in selling much of the steel that went into rebuilding Europe. There he married your mother, whom he knew from his cloak-and-dagger days with Army intelligence. The family business was ultimately sold to another American steel firm that had no need for a second European CEO and he retired, but he had the good judgment to recognize that the domestic steel industry was on the skids and sold his stock in the acquiring company as soon as he legally could, a good decision since it went bankrupt a dozen years later. As a result you and your mother are among the wealthiest Americans in France or anywhere else. You have done a successful job of preserving your assets and hers during the current economic unpleasantness. I take it from your investment activities over the last eighteen months that you expect things to get worse."

"Much worse," he replied.

She paused to push a hank of shoulder-length hair behind her right ear.

"Is that a fair summary of our starting point?"

Eddie nodded and told her she seemed to have a good grasp of everything he'd known before Roy Castor's death.

"There are a couple of things we know that you may not yet have heard, and I'd like to get them onto the table early." He nodded at her to continue.

"First, Colonel Sommers is a more complicated character than he might appear on the surface."

"I suspected that," Eddie said. "I interviewed him day before yesterday and he certainly wasn't anxious to volunteer information. In fact, he lied."

Carole continued, "I'm not at all sure how pertinent any of this is to the case at hand, but Colonel Sommers is well known to my office as having been a mid-level thief during his time in Munich. Like too many GIs, he just couldn't keep his hands off the material he was supposed to be preserving. He seemed to favor old religious silver. As far as we can tell he's never overtly sold any of it, and we never were certain exactly what he took, so the Justice Department took a pass on him. The FBI did give him a once-over about ten years ago, but couldn't find enough evidence to move forward and he was a pretty small fish."

Eddie interrupted her. "Roy's daughter Jen and I found some of Roy's files in a bank box yesterday and I'd say his behavior in Munich was consistent with what you just told me. For example, my father did a long report to Sommers about his interview with Hans Frank, and later sent the pink copy to Roy with a notation that the original wasn't in the files where it should be. The clear implication was that Sommers had plucked it out for his own purposes. In it there's a mention that Frank may have sent one painting separate from the others, which could have attracted his attention."

"That's consistent with what we know. Many of the looters were enlisted men who just accidentally-on-purpose forgot to turn in everything they found and mailed a few pieces home, but he picked through everything and chose the pieces he wanted. It doesn't appear he was particularly good at it, but he really abused his position. But as I said, nothing's going to happen to him on the criminal front. It's just been too long and he's too old."

"I understand that, but he went out of his way to try to convince me he wasn't interested in art and didn't know much about it, but his dining room walls are hung with a half-dozen nice oil paintings. Not museum-quality by any means, but if he chose them he knows something about painting. On the surface it would make sense that the gold is the big target here, but the painting might also be important. Also, he knew about the safe deposit box where I found the Frank interview report but he didn't mention it to me. Then the next day when we left the bank Jen and I were chased at very high speed by someone the police could never identify."

Carole asked him to go through the story of what had happened since Jen had turned up at his door. She questioned him especially closely about the attack at the Hôtel Chopin, and asked him to repeat his description of the attackers, then she laid two photos on the desk before him. One was black and white, poorly focused, and showed a tall man dressed in 40s style standing between two French policemen, each of them holding an arm. It had been cropped so that only half of each policeman was in the frame, but it was clear they had their man firmly under control. The other appeared to be a frame from the same surveillance video Thom had shown him.

"We're really interested in this guy," Carole said, tapping her index finger on the surveillance clip. "We're pretty sure he was in the group that tried to kidnap Mr. Castor, and we think he may have been the man who cut up the French hotel clerk so badly. "Our embassy asked the Paris police for the mug shots, but they only got two of the three Germans so we had to make do with our own — this is from the camera in the long-term parking lot at Sarasota airport, and it shows this man stealing the car that hit Mr. Castor.

“Here’s one of a man with almost the same name taken sixty years ago, from our own files. Obviously they aren’t the same person, but you can see more than a superficial resemblance.”

Superficial? Eddie thought the resemblance was uncanny.

“Who is this? They could be brothers.”

“We think they’re father and son, the Krafts,” Carole said. Both are named Eric, the son with an h.

“What’s most interesting is that the photo of the father was taken in 1947 when he was released from Santé Prison after he’d served two years for collaborating with the Germans. At the time he told a wild story about how he’d brought a truckload of gold and a valuable old painting to Paris on behalf of Hans Frank, who was a relative -- his mother’s side, I believe, but that’s murky. But there was no evidence of either the gold or the painting, so the police put him down as a windbag. As soon as he got out of jail he hightailed it for Germany, where he went to work for the Stasi. Later he surfaced in Frankfurt, where he died in the eighties.”

Eddie caught his breath. “What then?”

“We aren’t sure. He was in the shipping business and probably was involved in some undercover work on behalf of Stasi. Frankfurt was on its way to becoming a huge financial center, so there would have been a lot of opportunities for industrial espionage. But the agency just didn’t have the resources to chase every East German spook, so he fell off the radar.”

“Let me fill in some of the blanks,” Eddie said. “One of the things he did was marry Jen Wetzmuller’s mother, Gutrud, who was Roy Castor’s office manager and maybe his sometime lover. She died in 1980, but Jen remembers that he had an unpleasant son who looked just like him.”

“Ugh. The two of them must have been a pair.”

“No doubt about that. It means that there may have been something to the father’s tale about the painting and the gold, or at least the son is convinced of it. But why now? Why is this coming to life this year, and not next year or fifteen years ago? And what has the son been doing all this time? And could Al Sommers have heard the father’s story?”

Carole said, "The price of gold could have something to do with it. It's more than tripled in the last four years, which would make it very attractive to someone with a cash-flow problem. And young Erich may have found a lead, or met somebody who thinks he can find the treasure. Or he might have found someone who could sell the gold. It would have swastika markings cast into it, so all banks and legitimate gold dealers would recognize it as wartime loot, unless of course he can find someone to melt it down for him, which wouldn't be easy, or sell it to someone who didn't care. He was pretty young when the wall fell, so he wasn't ever an official Stasi agent, but since then it appears he's been hanging out with some of the more disreputable Stasi alumni, including some with terrorist connections. That, by the way, is the intersection of your case and my usual work."

Eddie thought for a minute before responding. "And it may have something to do with Sommers's health. Jen told me he was in really good shape until a year ago, but now he's in a wheelchair and on oxygen part of the time. He might have decided it's now or never."

"There's something else that's bothering us." Carole pointed again to the second photo on the table.

"We've enhanced the parking-lot shot, which was pretty good to begin with. Here's a blowup of the man you see at the door."

The photo was clear. It showed a man in his 40s, with short brown hair, wearing a brown jacket that looked like leather.

"We know the men Philippe's people arrested were German, so we started looking for this one among the pictures TSA takes at immigration checkpoints."

"Did you find him?"

"No, which bothered us. The Sarasota police found out that three men arrived in Tampa via Amtrak a couple of days before Mr. Castor was killed, then took a cab to Sarasota, where they slipped away.

"Imagine our surprise when we found out this German had arrived in Atlanta from Frankfurt and gone through immigration as a U.S. citizen, with a valid U.S. passport."

"How could that be?"

"You have to keep in mind that TSA's facial recognition software is very good, but it's not yet perfect. It picked out this face from among a group of passports issued to naturalized citizens almost ten years ago, so there's still a little bit of doubt about the identification, but I doubt he'll want to try renewing it."

"That's a surprise. I'd think the pre-naturalization checks would have turned up his background."

"That should have happened, except that he had a legend that seems to have been years in the making. You're looking at citizen Erich Wetzmuller, who was vouched for by his loving sister, Jennifer Gutrud Wetzmuller."

Eddie stood up to get a closer look at the pictures. "Merde!" he said softly. Then, "that would explain some things."

"Such as?"

"Just a feeling I've had that Jen wasn't playing this completely straight. She was just a little evasive, like her mind was elsewhere. And she reacted very strangely when Philippe Cabillaud mentioned the clipped ear. She didn't seem really surprised. And I could never figure out why the people who killed her father would wait 10 days to go after her, when they could have done the same thing in Sarasota. Maybe they were spooked when Roy died and got out of town as quickly as they could."

Carole asked, "Do you think she set her father up for the kidnapping?"

"I doubt it. I don't believe Roy had ever indicated to her that he knew where to find the painting, but they had the idea — and I'm told this was from Dmitri — that my father knew where to find it. So they may have figured Roy had the same information. But why would they wait seven years?

"In any case, it's pretty clear to me now that they wanted to kidnap him and sweat the hiding place out of him, because they thought he knew where it all was hidden. But he didn't know where it was, or is, but they were pretty sure he did. And then when he tried to escape from them and instead ran in front of the car, accessory to kidnapping turned into accessory to murder.

He paused a moment, then added, "She must be tough, to deal with all of that and string me along as well."

Carole said, “Hard to say. Her business is in serious financial trouble, and the police suspect she may not have passed on all the money she took in from selling paintings that she took on consignment. Her inheritance from her father will take care of that, because as this sort of scam goes it was pretty small beer. There’s a competitor who’s about to go to prison for stealing millions.”

“How do you know all that?”

“We have friends who have friends. Unfortunately, Florida is home turf for an astounding number of very inventive scams. Most of them have absolutely nothing to do with us, but now and then somebody like citizen Sommers will come along, and then we get involved, just for the information — CIA isn’t, officially, a law enforcement agency on American soil. One contact like that generally leads in a lot of other directions. For example, the Sommers lead came from a disgruntled employee while he was still in Texas. It led us to Sonny Perry and the hoard he inherited from his father.”

Eddie paused for a second. “I heard about Sonny’s record just yesterday, but not from the police. I wonder why Thom Anderson never mentioned any of this to me?”

“For all he knows you’re part of the deal — you’re sort of European, your father was present at the start and stayed in touch with Roy over the years. And, you’re sleeping with her. Down there I’m not certain which is worse, all that or speaking French.”

“Well, I’m most definitely not part of any art or gold scam. But do you think I may have trouble with the local police before this is over?”

“I don’t think so. Icky talked to the local chief about it. You certainly don’t need the money, Raphael isn’t your taste in art, and you’re a Special Forces officer with a bronze star and a V, so I don’t think they’ll bother you. No, I think they believe they’re dealing with a local bad apple, or several of them, and if they can solve it on that basis they’ll be happy.”

“That’s good to hear. There’s one more thing that will help you, I think. The witnesses to Roy Castor’s death said Roy shouted at one of the kidnappers, ‘You’re no better than your father,’ or words to that effect. That picture of Eric the older when he got out of Santé prison sort of looks like the right ear might be a funny shape, but the surveillance photo in the parking lot just shows the left ear. If you can find a picture of that other ear it might square the circle."

"Thanks," Carole said. "We'll look for another view. I'll get your phone number from Icky and call you if I find anything else."

Eddie crossed the hall to Icky's office and waited in the anteroom for a few minutes until the door opened. A three-star Air Force general wearing a glum expression emerged and Icky walked him to the security door at the end of the hall. He returned and signaled with a nod that Eddie should come in and take a seat at the long conference table.

"Was Carole helpful?"

"I'll say. It seems the woman who brought me into this, and with whom I've been pleasantly sharing a bed, may be part of the other side. At least she has some friends who aren't on the same side Roy was or I am." He smiled ruefully at Icky. "It's funny, but I thought of her as the soft 20-year-old I knew. I wonder if she's changed or was like this when I first met her."

"Doesn't matter, take it from a serial philanderer. What are you planning to do about it?"

"Basically nothing. I'll wrap up in Sarasota tomorrow and go back to Paris the next day and forget the whole thing. If my father could put it out of his mind I should be able to do the same."

"But what if this was all tied in some way to his death? Or Lauren and Sam's?"

"Then of course I'll reconsider," Eddie replied. "But right now it looks like we have a group of local gangsters with financial problems — my bedmate among them, unfortunately — and they'll have to answer to the police for Roy's death. From what Carole told me I wouldn't be surprised if the FBI paid a call on one of the helpers, a scumbag named Sonny Perry who inherited a bunch of his father's Nazi loot. Another source told me he's been selling it through the Russian mafia."

Icky said, "Perry. I've heard the name. In that case I suggest you get back to Paris and avoid the shitstorm that's bound to hit real soon. Please tell your mother hello for me, and if you see Aurélie tell her I'm still interested."

"I'll probably talk to her today. She and some of her academic friends have helped me figure out what's going on here. They identified the missing painting."

"Friends like that help a lot."

"Oh, and one other thing. When this started to get sticky I called in Paul Fitzhugh. He should be waiting for me at Dulles now, and he'll shadow me quietly from here on. I've given him your cell number."

"Paul. A good man. I'm glad he's still with you. Tell him to call me any time."

"Tonight and tomorrow are the most likely," Eddie said.

"Unfortunately, I can't take you back to the airport. OK if Stella calls a cab for you? You can have a coffee downstairs until it arrives. It will be a Diamond Cab."

Icky walked Eddie to the security door then down the stairs to the elevator and shook his hand. "You'll be OK alone from here. It's a lot easier to get out of this place than it is to get in."

He stopped for a minute, then looked Eddie in the eye. "Can I call on you for help again?"

"Not quite yet. Maybe soon, but not quite. Let me get all this out of the way first. But I sure as hell owe you now."

In the lobby Eddie walked into the tiny coffee shop and ordered a latte. "What size?" the barista asked.

"Venti," he responded."Whatever happened to small, medium and large?"

"Then it wouldn't be Starbucks," said the barista with a grin.

Eddie bought The Washington Post and sat on a bench to await the taxi. He called Paul, who had been fighting boredom for four hours in the United Airlines passenger lounge, to say they would be returning as scheduled. He laid out the plan for Paul to follow him from the airport in a rental car.

Then he summarized Carole Westin's bombshell and said, "the security level obviously has to be higher than I thought. Let's try to get through the next 48 hours and go home." And he gave him cell phone numbers for both Thom Anderson and Icky Crane.

Paul was silent a few seconds then said, “Feels like we’re back chasing some really bad guys. I have your back.”

CHAPTER TWELVE

Trapped

Sarasota

Eddie watched Paul pull his bag from the overhead bin as soon as the 737 stopped at the gate. He waited and left a few minutes later, and as he walked past the Hertz lot he saw Paul putting his key in the door of a Chevrolet. He knew from the brief description Paul had texted him that it was red, but the car stood in the umbra between two overhead lights, which made it look an indefinite muddy color, but definitely not red. The German proverb "Bei Nacht sind alle Katzen grau" forced its way unbidden into his mind.

He made certain Paul saw him, then drove the rental Ford through the parking lot toll gates and turned down the Tamiami Trail toward the Hyatt, less than fifteen minutes away.

As Eddie turned off the Trail onto Boulevard of the Arts his iPhone chirped. Paul said, "I got stopped at a light. There's a white Buick that's been behind you for a while. It's just making the same turn you did. Careful. I'll be there in a minute."

Eddie passed through the archway leading to the Hyatt's outdoor parking lot. He drove to the end, looking for the best-lit space available, and on his way back up toward the hotel building found one and turned in. He immediately got out of the car, then opened the back door to reach for his briefcase. At that moment a large white sedan came to a screeching stop and Dmitri the Russian jumped from passenger seat. Eddie saw he had a black automatic pistol in his hand.

"Leave that," Dmitri said roughly. He opened the back door. "Get in here and lie on the floor."

Eddie knew looking around for Paul would tip off Dmitri, so he dropped the bag and did as he was told. Dmitri sat down and put his foot on Eddie's leg, pressing him to the floor. With his free hand the Russian frisked him efficiently but took only the iPhone from his shirt pocket. He flipped it into the front seat and said, "You won't need that." It would be impossible to get up before Dmitri could fire the big pistol.

The driver — Eddie was confident it was Sonny — started immediately. Eddie felt a short right and then a left as they went back out through the same archway he'd driven under less than two minutes before. They turned right and then right again, so he knew they were headed south on the Trail. From there on, they appeared to make random turns at random intervals and he quickly lost track of their location.

Paul had arrived too late to stop the abduction but he saw Eddie's bag on the ground and sped out of the parking lot less than 30 seconds behind. He had put both Thom's and Icky's phone numbers into his speed dialer, and first he tried Thom. Voice mail answered and he left an urgent message. He ended with, "I'm not going to call 911 now because these men are killers. If they're stopped they might be desperate enough to kill Eddie before anything else can be done."

He dialed Icky, who was at dinner with Angela and did not sound pleased to be interrupted. His tone changed when Paul introduced himself and explained what had happened, and that he hadn't been able to reach Thom.

Icky took charge. He told Paul to keep trailing the white car while he started alerting people who could help. "I think I can find the cavalry," was the way he left it.

Paul did not know Sarasota at all, but the GPS map told him his quarry was working steadily east but backtracking often to keep Eddie confused. Finally they passed under the Interstate on a road the GPS identified as Bee Ridge. A mile to the east, after they'd passed a fire station and the road had narrowed, they turned right onto a narrow lane. To follow them would have been obvious, so Paul passed the turn and parked in the lot of a strip mall. The GPS map told him the kidnappers had turned into a dead-end road, so somewhere on that long block Eddie would be found.

Thom picked up on the second call and confirmed that Sommers lived on the road where the car had turned. “It’s the second driveway on the right,” he said. “The house is a long way from the road, and there’s a barn behind it. Eddie told me the only way in is the front gate, which is opened electrically from inside the house.”

Icky had called and together they were assembling a team of officers from the county sheriff and the FBI. Thom would participate even though it was in the county, where the sheriff’s authority held sway, rather than in the city. “This is going to take a few minutes. Can you keep watch while we put the team together?”

“Sure,” Paul told him. “I’ll walk down and hide in the bushes across the street. I’ll silence my phone but I’ll feel the vibration.”

“OK, but be careful in case they left a lookout on the road. We’ll have to figure out how to get in. Maybe we can come in through the back some way. Let me know what you see.”

In minutes Paul found a stump nestled into the bushes across the narrow road from sommers's house. He sat on it and hoped most of the mosquitoes had gone in for the night but soon realized enough of them would still be around to torment him. He could see the house clearly, plus about two-thirds of the barn behind it. Lights were on in the house, on the left side. From Eddie’s description Paul thought he was seeing the living room.

The barn appeared to be dark, but after a few minutes one side of the garage door opened and he could see the white sedan inside. A tall thin man came out of the door and closed it quickly, then disappeared behind the house.

He tried to sit very still, which was becoming more and more difficult as insects chewed on his arms and climbed up his ankles. “At least these are our own bugs,” he thought ruefully. “In Kuwait they were real nasty desert bugs. I can live with these.”

He carefully called Thom, keeping the screen of his iPhone covered with his hand so its light wouldn’t be visible, and whispering. “The car is in the barn and I saw one man come out, so there’s probably still a man in there with Eddie. I don’t see any guard on the front, but it would take a while to get to the house and barn even if you can force the gate open. There seems to be a fence behind the barn. Can you come in that way?"

"We're looking at that. Stay in touch," Thom responded. "We're only about 15 minutes away."

Inside the barn, Eddie would have been happy to have only bugs on his mind.

Dmitri had fastened his wrists together behind him with plastic flexcuffs while he was pinned to the floor of the car. The only thing of interest he'd seen on the drive from the airport was a dark stain on the inside of the door, which he suspected was Deus's blood. He'd been at Sommers's home when Deus was killed, and Sonny was there at the same time, so he must be riding in the back seat with the killer — no surprise. It did not make him confident, although he was certain he could take Dmitri in a fight. That is, if his hands weren't cuffed behind him and the other guy didn't have the gun.

The car slowed and made a right turn, then followed a winding route until it stopped and the driver got out. He heard the sound of a gate or a garage door being opened. He'd heard the driver make a call on his cell phone and say only "gate," which he'd figured was meant to have the roadside gate open when he turned through it. So now they must be on the Sommers property and were probably entering the barn.

The driver returned and drove another two or three car lengths, then got out again. Eddie heard a wooden door slam, and then saw bright lights come on outside the car. Dmitri took his foot off Eddie's leg and walked around the car to open the door at his head. He grabbed Eddie's arm and said, "Get up," and yanked him to his feet. For sure, Eddie thought, this guy is strong enough to be very dangerous, even without that gun.

He blinked in the bright light. Sonny had been on his best behavior when Eddie met him the first time, but now his blank face signalled that he was a killer, and might kill even here on his home turf, even though it would be harder to escape the consequences. Be careful. Go slow, Eddie told himself.

He shifted his weight from side to side to relieve a cramp in his left leg. He stood before Sonny and Dmitri, who reminded him of the two Germans he'd seen in Paris, Mutt and Jeff.

Sonny spoke first. "You stuck your nose in where you shouldn't have and now you're deep in the shit. It's up to the boss, but if it was my call I'd shoot you and drop your body in the Gulf."

He turned to Dmitri and told him gruffly, "the pit." Then he opened one side of the garage door and walked out, closing it softly behind him. Eddie hoped Paul was watching the door at that moment.

Dmitri took his arm tightly and moved him toward the front of the car, where he opened a door into a darkened room. When he flipped the light switch Eddie could see a steel trap door set into the concrete floor and secured with a padlock. Dmitri pushed Eddie backwards onto a bench against the wall, then took a key from a nail above the steel door and opened the padlock. He pulled the heavy door up, then motioned for Eddie to walk down a narrow concrete staircase.

"Once you're down there you can make all the noise you want and nobody will hear you," he said with a sneer. "Have a nice day."

The steel door slammed too close for comfort as he worked his way down the steep and narrow stairs, hampered by the tight flexcuffs. He counted the steps to the bottom — 14, which meant the wet and dirty floor he finally reached was about 12 feet below ground. The only light was the little that leaked through the cracks around the trap door, and Eddie knew that would disappear as soon as Dmitri turned off the room light. He willed his eyes to adjust quickly.

He had maybe 30 seconds, enough to tell he was in a room the size of a Parisian bedroom, with a dome at the top of the far end, the old entrance to the fallout shelter. The wall to his left appeared to hold several narrow shelves containing cups and other small objects, probably the loot Woody had mentioned. If the shelves had originally been full, then Sommers's stolen fortune was indeed dwindling dangerously toward nothing.

He took a step toward the shelves and tripped, falling hard over a long object lying on the dirt-caked concrete floor. The object moaned and moved, and Eddie realized he had fallen over a second prisoner — he looked into the battered and bruised face of Woody Matthews.

"Jesus, Woody, how did you get here? I thought these guys were friends of yours," he asked. At that moment Dmitri turned out the light and the old shelter went dark.

Woody was silent a moment, then moaned again. "Is that you, Mr. Grant?"

"It's me. What are you doing here?"

"They found out I talked to you. I didn't tell anyone. They came to Hemingway's today and told me Mr. Sommers had some work for me, would I come with them. I couldn't refuse those guys. They didn't even take me to Sommers. They drove straight into that garage, opened the trap door and threw me down the steps. That was after they beat me up pretty good. I think they used a piece of garden hose."

"Woody, you said you'd been down here before. Do you remember if there's electricity? Are there lights?"

"Yeah, the light was on when I landed here, I think. I got knocked out when I hit bottom. But I remember they turned on some lights when they brought me some filthy chicken soup to eat. What time is it now?"

"About 10."

"Must have been three hours ago or so. When they left they made a big deal of unscrewing the light bulb and taking it with them."

"Do you remember if they had any tools or supplies down here? Maybe there are some candles or another bulb or something. We have to get moving on this, Woody. Wake up."

Woody shook his head groggily. "I don't remember, but a fallout shelter would have some kind of backup. Feel around under the shelves and see if there's anything there."

"I can't do that very well. They cuffed my hands behind me. You'll have to get up and do it. Are you tied up?"

"No, I can do it. Point me in the right direction."

Woody crawled to the wall under the shelves and began to feel his way from the stairway toward the far end where Eddie waited.

Almost immediately he said, "Here's something." But after another minute he moaned, "It's just a niche, like where you'd put a lantern. There's an old plate in it that feels like tin, and some candle wax on the bottom, but nothing we can use for the cuffs."

"Remember where it is, though. We might think of some use for the plate," Eddie told him.

After 10 minutes of feeling the wall carefully and checking the ground under it Woody had found nothing. But then he said, not so optimistically this time, "Here's something. It's a little metal box, and it's pretty heavy."

"Look — sorry, feel — in it for anything that might cut them, a razor blade, wire cutters, a pair of pliers. We need to get these cuffs off."

Woody grunted. "Feels like a spool of some kind of wire. Here's a couple of screwdrivers. Something waxy, feels like a candle. Aha! Pliers!"

"You're a good man, Woody. Is it the kind with wire cutters near the hinge?"

"Feels like it. It's old and loose. Feels rusty. This place is probably wet all the time."

"We'll have to make do. I'm going to turn my back to you and you feel the flexcuffs and find a way to put the pliers on them. These cuffs are tough plastic. It will take some work."

He slid back until he could reach and feel Woody's jacket, then he felt Woody's fingers probing the cuffs, looking for the best place to cut. His breath smelled strongly of stale beer. Then the fingers went away.

"I dunno if I ought to do this. If I help you get out Sommers is going to be really pissed."

Eddie paused, reaching for the right words. "Woody, if you don't get me loose we're both going to be killed. Sonny made that clear to me. Somehow they found out you talked to me, and they're afraid I talked to other people, and they're right, I did. So you'll be a hell of a lot better off taking a chance on my side than with Sommers. I guarantee you he'll feed your body to the fish 'way out in the Gulf."

The fingers returned. "I guess you're right. We're better off sticking together. I never did trust the bastard anyway."

Eddie felt the pliers slip between his wrists. Woody grunted as he strained to make the old tool slice through the tough 21st-century plastic, but at last he exhaled and said, "That's it." The cuffs fell off and Eddie quickly rubbed his hands together to restore the circulation. A thousand pinpricks rushed to his fingertips.

He reached out to find Woody and touched his shoulder. "Woody," he said, trying to sound as serious as possible, "We are in real trouble here. I think we can get out, but we'll have to work together, and we'll have to be ready when they come back for us. Are you ready to work on it?"

"Ready as I'll ever be, I guess. I never trusted Al but I didn't think he was this bad. Or do you think it's those two fairies pulling the strings?"

"Don't kid yourself. Sommers is the key to this whole thing. Sonny and Dmitri will do what he says as long as it makes sense. In a way they're like well-trained dogs. They know what their job is and they rebel if they're asked to do something else. So don't kid yourself that all three of them aren't working together."

"Do you think we can take one of them if he comes back for us?"

"That has to be the play," Eddie said. "But we have to figure out the means. We're pretty sure there's electricity down here, because they took the light bulb when they left you. We know we have a screwdriver or two in the tool kit."

"Two," Woody said. "They felt as rusty as the pliers, though."

"OK. They could be makeshift daggers if it gets to that, but I'd rather trust to the electricity. You're not an electrician, are you?"

"Me," Woody answered with a short laugh. "One of the reasons my wife kicked me out was I never could do anything around the house. Electricity scares the shit out of me."

"Well, let's see what's in the toolbox. Push it over here to me."

Eddie felt carefully through the old metal box and found just what Woody had found. The spool of wire seemed more of a cable, a single solid wire inside insulation. He pulled some of it off the spool and figured there must be more than twenty feet.

"What kind of light bulb was in here?" he asked Woody.

"Just a wire hanging from the ceiling. I'm surprised you didn't hit it when you stood up. It's pretty low."

Eddie stood again and waved his arms around until he found the hanging cable. It was an old cotton-covered wire attached to a socket that would hold a single bare bulb. A short string served as a switch. Very gingerly he passed his finger over the edge of the empty socket and bent it slowly toward the central contact.

"Shit," he said, pulling back quickly. "That circuit is definitely hot."

His next urgent need was for light, so he set Woody to feeling every inch of the shelves carefully, looking for matches to go with the candle stub he'd found in the toolbox. "It makes sense they'd have some way to light the candle if they were concerned about backup," he said, and Woody agreed. "Think of where you'd put matches if you didn't want anyone to knock them off, and start there. Maybe the top shelf."

Woody began to run his hands along the top shelf, which was only a few inches above his head. "Watch out!" he shouted as one of the stolen cups clattered to the floor and rolled away. "Sorry." In less than five minutes he found a large box of matches. He passed it to Eddie, who hefted it and felt along the edge and decided they were wooden strike-anywhere matches. "Every kitchen in America used to have those," Woody said.

The box held a dozen. He struck one on the sandpaper striker, but it fizzled. The second caught and burned, and Eddie held it over his head. He looked first at Woody, who had been beaten badly. His lip was cut and had bled down his chin onto his shirt, and one eye was black and almost closed. One sleeve was half ripped from his shirt, which appeared to be the same one he'd worn when Eddie interviewed him at Hemingway's.

Then he looked at the hanging light fixture and saw that the socket was attached to the cord with a single screw. Everything in the shelter seemed to date from the fifties or sixties, before Sommers's time, except the staircase he'd built from the barn. That might have been there all along, too, Eddie thought. Maybe Sommers is just taking advantage of a previous owner's paranoia.

Woody handed him the candle and Eddie touched the dying match to its wick. It gave a dimmer but steadier light that he figured would last long enough to get the electrical work done. Then they'd have to snuff it out and wait for Dmitri or Sonny to come for them. The wait would be tense.

"Woody, go get that tin plate and let's put the candle on it. Then you hold it while I work on this cord and try not to electrocute myself."

"What are you going to do?"

"I'm going to make an electric chair for whichever one comes down those stairs. We should be able to at least stun him and take the gun, and then maybe we can work our way out and over the back fence."

"That fits," Woody said. "In Florida they call the electric chair Old Sparky."

Eddie pulled his shirttail out and tore off two long strips. "We'll need some insulation up there to keep the wires from crossing. If they do that it will trip the circuit breaker and kill our power, and it might tip off our friends as well."

The first screwdriver he tried was too large, the second fit the setscrew holding the light socket together. He took off its cap and unscrewed one of the wires, which he turned back to keep its uninsulated tip out of the way. Then he unscrewed the second wire. Both were now bare.

"Put the candle on the shelf and let's see how much wire is on that spool. I want to use half of it for each side of our little trap."

They estimated that they could use two twelve-foot lengths. Woody used the pliers to cut it at about the center, and then to strip an inch of insulation of each end. When he had one wire stripped at both ends he handed it to Eddie, who tested the cut ends. "Good and sharp. That's what we need."

Eddie took the pliers and twisted the new cable firmly to the end of the existing drop. Then he wrapped the joint in one of the cloth strips he'd torn from his shirt and tied it tightly. "Merde," he muttered as he brushed the other hot wire. A minute later he said it again.

"Rinse and repeat," he said as he twisted the second wire onto its power source. "Be sure we keep the far ends of those wires away from each other, and off the floor. It might be wet enough to short them."

"The candle is just about gone," Woody said with alarm just as Eddie stood back to admire his handiwork. "OK. You can put it out now. We may need it later. Sit down on the floor and act confused when they come in."

Paul's phone vibrated in his shirt pocket, interrupting his fruitless effort to keep the bugs away from his sweating face.

Thom said softly, "We're around the corner next to your car. Can you come brief us on what you've seen?"

"Sure." With a great sense of relief stood up and walked as silently as he could down the edge of the road.

At the parking lot he found a half-dozen cars parked around his rental. Three of them were marked deputies' cars from the Sarasota County Sheriff, another was Thom's black Crown Victoria, plus two nondescript sedans. He walked up to the closest deputy, a five-foot-six black woman carrying a lethal-looking pump shotgun in her right hand and a bulletproof vest in the left. The nametag on her shirt said Ginepri. The stripes on her sleeve said sergeant.

"I'm Paul Fitzhugh and I'm looking for Thom Anderson. Can you point him out to me?"

She looked at him sourly. "He's city. This is a county and federal operation. But that's him over there with the FBI guys."

He walked over and introduced himself. Thom said, "We need to wait just another minute or two while the judge signs the warrant. These two men are FBI agents, and we have six uniformed sheriff's deputies, which should be enough. What did you see?"

Paul explained that he'd seen the door open and a man come out of the barn, leaving the light on inside. "From that, I think there's one more man in there, and Eddie."

One of the agents said, "We knew about this Eddie fellow, but who are you?"

"I work for him. I was his company sergeant in Desert Storm. He helped get me through a bad wound and we've been working together since."

Ginepri appeared to be the senior deputy. She walked over and told them the judge had signed the warrant. Her plan was to go in over the back fence separating sommers's property from a vacant lot, and that a truck was already in place there with ladders and other tools they might need.

Thom asked Paul to ride with him. When they were in the Crown Vic he said, "We're pretty much guests here. My authority doesn't extend beyond the city limits, and we're out in the county now. The FBI is involved because of the federal angle — the stolen stuff they think Sommers has. But they sure wouldn't come out in the middle of the night like that if somebody in Washington weren't really interested in this case."

"Eddie was in Washington yesterday talking to an Army buddy of ours who's in charge of recovering old treasure. That's probably where the pressure comes from."

"I know. A CIA bigwig named Icky Crane. He told my chief his real name is Thomas Jefferson Crane but people call him Icky after Ichabod, and if we saw him we'd understand."

The little convoy drove through a subdivision with more vacant lots than houses until it pulled up near a pickup with the sheriff's logo on the doors.

Deputy Ginepri told Thom, "We're going to put three ladders on this side, then pull up three more and put them on the other side to give us a stairway down. We'll have to be really quiet, but if you and Thom want to come over after we and the FBI agents are in, feel free. Just be careful."

Paul grinned. She was a stocky 35-year-old with hair in a businesslike bun and the no-nonsense demeanor that spoke of deep experience. He was a grizzled veteran who'd survived being shot in the head. They'd both been around and knew he would be careful. Very careful.

Each of the deputies carried a ladder to the fence but held it a foot off the wood in case Sommers had installed an alarm system. To the left of each stood another deputy carrying an identical ladder, ready to pass it to his partner as soon as he reached the top. The FBI agents stood behind the deputies, waiting.

All eyes were on Ginepri as she surveyed the little line to make sure everyone was ready, holding her hand in the air. When she was satisfied, she dropped her hand and three ladders landed almost inaudibly atop the fence. Three men scampered up them until the fence was waist high, then turned to receive a second ladder from his partner below. They placed them gently on the ground inside the compound, then stepped over the fence and climbed quickly down to ground level. They drew their guns and turned toward the barn twenty feet away, watching until everyone was in place.

Ginepri had divided her group into two squads, one for the barn and the other for the house. She waved the house group on its way and led the remaining deputies around the barn. Paul followed her closely. His goal was Eddie and he figured four big men should be able to handle Sommers in his wheelchair and his one scrawny assistant.

The three deputies, Paul, and Thom walked carefully on the grass around the barn. They stopped under a window and Ginepri looked carefully inside, then ducked quickly. She turned to the men following her and held up one finger of her left hand, then stuck up her thumb and held her hand out to simulate a handgun.

She called Thom to her side and asked him to stay, and when the others had reached the front of the barn to make a noise at the side in an effort to bring out the man inside. "It'll be easier to get him if he opens the door himself," she said. He nodded.

They took up their positions on each side of the door. Across the yard, they could see the other team looking carefully in the windows of the main house. She reconsidered and signaled to Thom he should wait. The sound of the break-in at the house might flush out their man.

Paul stationed himself under the window so he could look inside and learn the layout after the action started. He still had no idea how the barn was laid out and until he knew that it would be too dangerous to enter.

The deputies and FBI agents at the back door of the house could see through the kitchen into the living room, where Sonny sat watching television. They could not see Sommers and hoped he had gone to bed. The largest of them first tested the door but found it locked, then without ceremony kicked it in and charged through.

Sonny jumped up from the sofa in front of the television and reached quickly for a drawer in the table at its end. One of the FBI agents put a hand on his wrist. Don't make a sound, he whispered. Sonny didn't.

"What's going on out there?" Sommers called from his bedroom. The other FBI agent and a deputy followed the sound and quickly arrested him.

The deputy who kicked down the back door was six-foot-four and weighed 230 pounds. The door split at its lock like a ripe melon and separated easily from its frame, and the glass in two of its four panes splintered and fell inside the room. Dmitri heard the noise and knew immediately what it was. He had no thought of leaving the barn.

As soon as he heard the attack on the house, Paul stuck his head above the window frame to see Dmitri stand up directly in front of him, fortunately looking the other way. Dmitri glanced at the barn door, then ran around the white car to look out the window on the other side, where he could see that every light in Sommers's house was on. He ran quickly toward the door at the front of the car, heading for the entrance to the fallout shelter. Paul knew now where Eddie was held, and that he'd reached the moment of greatest risk to his friend.

He tested the window and found he could raise it. He turned to Thom and made a stirrup sign, then pointed up at the window to indicate he would go through. Thom hesitated, then laced his fingers together. Paul rolled over the windowsill, dropped to the floor and crept to the door Dmitri had used. Then he stopped and listened.

The padlock clattered as Dmitri dropped it on the steel door, then Paul heard him grunt as he lifted the heavy door. Then a shout and a single gunshot. Dreading what he'd find, Paul dashed to the open cellar door.

CHAPTER THIRTEEN

Old Sparky

Sarasota

Woody sat on the floor in the center of the shelter, where he'd been when Eddie found him. "My head hurts," he complained.

"It'll be better soon. One of them will come down here to check on us, or the police will arrive. It's the same to us. We just have to be ready."

He took a position standing against the wall opposite the silver cups, holding his hands behind him as they'd been when he was flexcuffed. He held one of the electrical wires in each hand, being careful to keep the ends separated.

They waited. The silence was almost absolute. They hadn't heard anything since Dmitri had slammed the trap door but in the silence Eddie could just make out the vague sigh of air moving, almost a low whistle. He focused on it and decided it was the wind passing over the old steel door he'd seen in the original domed entrance to the shelter. It wouldn't help us to go out that door, he told himself. It's in full view of the house, and the noise would alert whoever's in the barn.

He'd kept his watch. The dial had long since given up the last of its illumination, but he estimated he'd been locked in for about two hours. If Paul had called the police at the right time, they should have something organized pretty soon. Or at least he hoped so.

Another wait. It was probably only 15 minutes but it felt like eternity. Eddie moved around, rising to the balls of his feet to keep his legs from cramping. He stretched his arms up to the ceiling and put his hands on the rough concrete, one at a time to keep the bare wires away from each other.

Suddenly there was the sound of something scraping on the floor above, then a thud from the steel door at the top of their stairs. "Woody. Ready? Somebody's about to open the door. Lie down. Play dead," Eddie said in a hoarse whisper.

There was the sound of metal falling on metal, the padlock dropping on the door after Dmitri unlocked it. Then the stairway flooded with light and Dmitri shouted to them, "Stand away from the door. You guys are my ticket out of here but I'll shoot the first one of you to move."

He walked slowly down the steps. Eddie first saw his feet, then the gun.

"Woody's badly hurt and I'm still tied up," Eddie told him, hands behind his back. The gun sagged slightly.

Dmitri stepped into the room. He looked first at Eddie, then over at Woody's supine form on the floor. "Is he dead?" he asked. He could have been asking about a stray dog found lying in the street.

The brief distraction was all the time Eddie had. He jumped on Dmitri, grasping his gun hand by the wrist and bending it down, at the same time forcing the sharp end of the wire deeply under his skin. A howl of pain and surprise filled the little room, then stopped suddenly as Dmitri realized he was in a fight for his life.

Meanwhile, Eddie reached across him with his other hand and drove the sharp end of the other wire as hard as he could into Dmitri's stomach. The sound stopped and his body went rigid as the electricity coursed through him. In a final involuntary reaction, his finger tightened on the trigger. The blast was deafening in the tiny concrete space. Dmitri fell like a stone as Eddie pulled the wire from his stomach then reached for the gun, a Glock 9mm. It hadn't been used by the Army during his time because it had no external safety lever, so he handled it very carefully. He considered putting it in his waistband but changed his mind and laid it on the top shelf near where Woody had found the matches. Dmitri lay motionless on his back, knees in the air, his face a rictus of pain, eyes staring.

He kicked Woody's foot and told him to stand, then shouted up the stairs. "This is Eddie Grant with Woody Matthews. We have Dmitri. Identify yourself before you come down those stairs or be shot."

"You wouldn't want to do that, Eddie. The area is secure."

"Jeez, Paul, I'm glad to hear from you. Do you have the cavalry with you?"

"Right behind me. Another group stormed the house and got Sonny and Sommers. At least I think they did. I didn't hear any shots. How's Woody?" he asked as Paul came carefully down the stairs.

"Woody's been beat up pretty bad but he'll survive. You used to be a pretty good medic. Take a look at Dmitri, would you? I think he shot himself in the thigh. It's bleeding like he hit that big artery."

Paul felt his neck for a pulse and said, "We should get him an ambulance just in case, but I think he's past help."

"The cops!" Paul said. He dashed up the stairs and unbolted the barn door. "Eddie and Woody Matthews are safe. Dmitri's been shot and looks pretty bad. You'd better get an ambulance out here," he told Ginepri. Her expression said she wasn't happy to be kept waiting outside the door, but she said nothing. The drama had taken only 30 seconds.

"We put one at the nearest fire station just in case. I'll get him," Ginepri said, raising her radio to her lips.

Eddie came slowly out of the back room, supporting Woody's half-conscious weight on his shoulder. "You'd better get one with two beds. They beat Woody up pretty badly."

"I never did like the bastard," Woody mumbled.

"Sommers clammed up and called his lawyer," Thom told Eddie as they sat in the detective's small office. It was 8 a.m. Neither had been to bed, and Eddie had been waiting patiently in the office while Thom and another detective questioned Sonny. He'd occupied the time hunched over his MacBook Air, composing his own statement of what had happened from the time he arrived at the airport. It had reached ten double-spaced pages.

Paul was doing his own statement, in longhand, in a neighboring office. He'd resisted learning to type and didn't own a computer.

Thom came back into the office and told Eddie, "Sonny finally quit talking. He did tell us Dmitri killed Deus and set the fire at Arturo's house, but that's no surprise because Dmitri's dead, and we know Sonny was somewhere else at those times. I'm pretty sure Sonny was more than an onlooker, but when we pressed him on his role in the fire at Ms. Wetzmuller's house he shut us down completely, which means he was there. I expect he'll get a lawyer from the same firm Sommers uses, and that Sommers will pay for it, so I have a lot of hard detective work ahead of me before we can bring them to trial."

He said the FBI agents had brought the silver cups and other loot into the interrogation room and tried to get Sommers to explain how he got them, but he'd refused and said Dmitri or Sonny must have planted them there. "If the rumors are right there's a lot more stuff like this in their house in Naples. We've started the process of getting a warrant and I hope to go down this afternoon to take part in the search.

"Just so you know, the FBI is planning to interview Ms. Wetzmuller later today. I heard one of the agents say she has a brother who might be involved."

Eddie nodded. "I don't think he's a real brother, but the son of the man her mother was married to for a couple of years when Jen was a teenager. I learned in Washington yesterday that she sponsored him for citizenship ten years ago and claimed he was her brother, but it was a false name. He's the one in that picture you have of a man standing outside the Navigator on the airport parking lot. I'm pretty sure he was the kidnapper Roy shouted at — he knew him from when he was a teenager and, according to Jen, he was a really bad character even then. God knows what he's like now.

"I have a hard time believing she was a willing partner in all this, but yesterday I heard some things that make me wonder…" He shook his head sadly and added, "I think if you'll call Dr. Carole Westin in Icky Crane's office she'll give you more information."

"I talked to Mr. Crane day before yesterday. He said you're one of the good guys. Were you two in the Army together?"

"He was my number two in Desert Storm, and Paul was our company sergeant. The three of us go 'way back — I've known Icky since were college freshmen together."

"Ah, now I understand a little better," Thom said. "I'll call Dr. Westin as soon as I can, because I sure don't want the Feds hijacking my murder investigation. If they catch him they'll hide him somewhere I'll never find. There's going to be a lot of press if they arrest a big looter, and they love publicity. Me, I just want Roy Castor's killer in prison. I'm also going to whisper to Sonny that Sommers is trying to hang it on him. That might help us get something."

Eddie told him the story of Eric Kraft the father, Erich the son, and his new identity as Erich Wetzmuller. "Carole should be able to tell you if he was spotted leaving the country, but I'm sure he's back in Europe right now. Problem is, we don't know where. It would be a lot easier to get him if Philippe could find him in France."

"Wouldn't he have to coordinate it with other police departments if Erich is not in Paris?"

"There's only one real police department in France, and that's the national police. There are municipal police and local branches and different divisions, but it's the Interior Minister who's in charge, and Philippe has his ear."

The iPhone in Eddie's shirt pocket chimed. Caller ID told him it was Philippe.

"Philippe? I'm with Detective Thom Anderson in Sarasota right now."

"He will be interested in this too." Eddie turned on the speaker and laid the iPhone on Thom's desk. "I just came from talking to the Germans and they're willing to give us a little bit of information right now. Not much yet, but I think they will talk more after they understand they're going to be in jail for a very long time if they don't.

"They tell me their boss was contacted by someone named Sonny and asked to pick up Jen for questioning because the effort to talk to Roy had been a failure. They did not confess to killing Roy, however. They also didn't admit to ever being in Sarasota, but we'll be able to determine that from Customs records.

"Can you see if there is a Sonny in this case anywhere in Sarasota?"

Thom said, "I can tell you right now. We arrested him last night at Al Sommers's house. His partner in both life and crime, a Russian mobster named Dmitri, is dead. Sonny spent time in federal prison for securities fraud, which is where he met Dmitri."

Eddie asked, "Philippe, can you ask them another question? Do they know anything about Artie? Or Lauren and Sam?"

The policeman responded, "I'll pass that question on to the team that's actually doing the questioning, but don't get your hopes up. These guys are tough, and they won't want to admit to knowing anything about another crime, especially murder. They've obviously learned how our system works, and they know they're looking at going to trial and starting their sentence within a month or two."

Thom interrupted. "You can do it that fast?"

"Our system is a little different from yours," he answered. "Our code goes back to Napoleon, not England. The only part of the United States that uses it is Louisiana.

"An investigating judge will look at the evidence on both sides before the trial starts. There's no endless cycle of motions. They won't be released on bail, and even if they were they'd have to go back into prison for the trial. When it's over they will start their sentences. They have the right of appeal and that works in a few cases, but for a violent crime like this there's a very small chance of winning on appeal, especially since half of Paris saw them chasing Eddie that night."

As Eddie closed the call from Philippe, a uniformed policewoman knocked on the frame of Thom's open door and said, "The lawyer for Sonny Perry has arrived, Detective. He'd like to see you along with his client."

"Is it a white-shoe guy from Sommers's law firm?" Thom asked her.

"No. That's what I expected, too. It's a young guy we've seen around the courts a lot for a couple of years, Ted Sorenson, the public defender."

Thom made a face. "He beat the shit out of me on cross a year ago. We got a conviction but it might have gone the other way. Ted knew his guy was guilty as sin but he's what you'd call a forceful advocate."

Eddie responded, "You have a lot of evidence, though. If this guy is smart and can keep his client from a murder charge here, he may let him talk. Meanwhile I'm going back to the hotel now and you can call me if you need me. I'd appreciate your seeing if there is any possible connection between these guys and my father's death in 2001. It's a remote chance. My wife and son were killed the same year by somebody who also burned the apartment, but it would be a lightning bolt if these guys were connected in any way with that. Still, if there's anything there I'd like to know and so would Philippe. Otherwise I'm planning to go home in a couple of days and try to forget that I ever heard of Raphael and his damned painting."

Eddie let himself into his room at the Hyatt and found that the maid had already been there. A note on the bedside table said, "Call me when you're back. I have a meeting with the contractor and then I'll be at the gallery. J."

He sat exhausted on the edge of the bed and puzzled through what he knew so far. Jen was in legal trouble, and might already be answering the FBI's questions. She did sponsor Erich Kraft for citizenship under her own name, falsely claiming he was her brother, but he couldn't recall that she'd ever said a positive word about him. She'd thought he was nothing but trouble when he was a teen.

So what had happened six or seven years before to make her commit immigration fraud for someone so unpleasant? It was after her marriage to the surgeon had ended. He supposed her gallery was well established, but there could have been financial problems at the time. No small business is very far from bankruptcy, and a recession could sweep in at any time, like a summer thunderstorm. A recession had begun in 1997. Was that it? He would just have to ask her, but not now. Sleep was what he needed. He took off his clothes and crawled under the cover.

And then he sat straight up, wide awake. Of course! In 2000 Erich Kraft was writing threatening letters to Roy about the painting. That had to be the connection. If he was as rough as he seemed — and the knife attack on the hotel clerk left little doubt about that — he would have threatened Roy or Jen. Perhaps she bought him off with citizenship. It wouldn't be easy to assemble all the documents he would have needed, but it could be done, with help.

Sleep. He had to get some sleep. He remembered nothing from the instant his head hit the pillow until the chime of his phone waked him four hours later.

"Eddie, it's Thom. Are you awake?"

Momentarily confused, Eddie mumbled, "wait just a minute," then went to the bathroom to splash his face with cold water. He sat naked on the edge of the bed and pulled the bedspread over him for warmth against the blast of the air conditioning.

"OK, now I'm conscious. What's up?"

Thom said, "First, we got the warrant for Sonny's house in Naples. I'm on the way there now so if the call drops out I'll call you back in a couple minutes. AT&T has some dead spots. Actually a lot of dead spots.

"Second, we got some movement from Sonny. I talked to the prosecutor and he'd appreciate it if you'd pass it on to your friend in the French police so they'll have it quicker, and he'll follow up in writing soon. He also gave me carte blanche to keep you updated on the case, both ours and the Feds', but don't tell them that."

"I appreciate that a lot."

"Sonny was really pissed that Sommers wouldn't pay for his lawyer. He thinks he's being thrown overboard, which of course he is. My own view is that Sommers is running out of money and that's the reason, but I kept that to myself. I think your instinct that this is a case entirely about money is probably right."

Sonny had heard Sommers tell Dmitri to follow Eddie, so Dmitri had waited near Towles Court in his Buick and watched Eddie meet Thom, then followed him to Arturo's house and on to his meeting with Deus.

"I saw a big white car pass behind me right after I let Deus out at the grocery store. That could have been him."

"Good chance," Thom said. "Because at the time you were interviewing Sommers at his house, Dmitri was working Deus over really hard in a park not far from the grocery store. He got all the details Deus gave you, plus I'd guess some more, because when it was finished Dmitri cut his throat and left him there dead — he knew too much. We found his blood in the Buick."

Eddie said, "He probably didn't go after Arturo because you already had him as a witness. I guess Sommers sent him back the next day to finish the job. What else?"

Thom was silent for a minute. "I don't know where this goes, but something has been in the air for a while. Two days before Mr. Castor's death, Sonny was delegated to pick up a group of Germans at a hotel on the Interstate and take them to the caretakers' bungalow next to Sommers's house. One of them looks a lot like the picture from the surveillance camera at the airport. We did a photo lineup and he picked him out. He took all three to an airport hotel in Miami the day after Mr. Castor's death. And then a week later he flew to Paris himself. He tried to lie about it, but we have his passport with the entrance date and the date he returned to Tampa airport. We think he was there to question Ms. Wetzmuller after the Germans kidnapped her."

Eddie said, "That's not really a surprise, except that it ties Sommers tightly to Roy's death."

"Yes, but what he told us next is. He remembers seeing the same guy before, he thinks in 2001. He's sure because the guy has a big notch out of his right ear."

"Then it's Erich Kraft. He was writing threatening letters to Roy the year before. I bet he came here to put on more pressure, and somehow persuaded Jen to help him get citizenship, which would make it much easier to get in and out of the country."

"That would make sense. He says Ms. Wetzmuller brought Kraft to see Sommers during that first visit, on a Saturday, when Sommers wasn't at his office. Sonny was there for part of the meeting and got the impression Kraft was an art buyer from Germany. Anyway, she left and Kraft and Sommers talked for a couple of hours, although Sonny didn't hear all the conversation."

"Wait. He said Jen introduced them? Personally?"

"That's what he says."

"Most likely he was looking to buy some of the loot. Sonny would have been a better seller," Eddie said.

"Yes," Thom said, "But remember Kraft was already chasing Mr. Castor for the Raphael and whatever's with it. Sommers's and Sonny's own loot would have been peanuts next to that. No, I think he wanted Sommers to help him find the big trove. He was just doing the same sort of detective work I do every day.

"And if that's not enough, I went through the recent calls on Sommers's cellphone. It seems that just a few minutes before Mr. Castor was killed he placed a call to a French cell phone registered to Erich Kraft — but the phone was roaming in Sarasota. He must have been tipping off Kraft that Roy was on the way. That call by itself will earn him a life sentence."

"Wow," Eddie said. "Good thinking on your part. Did you hear anything about Woody? He was pretty beat up. Will he be OK?"

"He was tougher than you'd think. The hospital released him a couple of hours ago. He's to come in tomorrow and give us a statement."

"How did they know I'd talked to him?"

"I haven't figured that out yet. He said he didn't tell anyone, and Sonny said no one was following you that day. I don't know if I believe either of them."

"Did they threaten Lindy as well?"

"I don't think so," Thom replied. "I called her and she said not. At least they didn't kidnap her, but I wouldn't be surprised if she'd talked to them. Does it matter?"

"I don't think so, no. You haven't asked me if I told Jen."

"No, I haven't, and I don't plan to."

"I didn't. I can't say why, but something kept me from it."

"That may be the best thing you've done for her."

When the call ended, Eddie looked at the iPhone clock — one o'clock. "Merde," he muttered. "If I hurry maybe I can find Woody."

In 20 minutes he had showered and shaved and 10 minutes after that he parked across the street from Hemingway's, just as Woody walked out next to a short man who looked like an F. Scott Fitzgerald impersonator, down to the center part in his blond hair. The man waved his arms around in agitation, and it appeared to Eddie that he was trying to convince Woody of something.

Woody's left eye was black, with a thick bandage above it. Another bandage on his right cheek came precariously close to his mouth. His right arm was in a sling but there was no cast on it. Eddie remembered he'd landed on that shoulder when he was thrown down the stairs. He looked profoundly unhappy, and he was having none of what the slim man was trying to sell him. Twice he shook his head defiantly and when the blond left him at the next corner, after he'd tried one last time to make his case, Woody refused to shake his hand.

Eddie followed on foot as Woody turned south. Lindy had said he lived alone in a one-bedroom apartment he'd bought after his divorce 20 years before, but hadn't said it was on Lido Key, the barrier island adjacent to St. Armand's, although that explained his fondness for Hemingway's — he could drink all day and then walk home. The property must have appreciated enormously, Eddie thought. Maybe he won't be so bad off when this all blows up, as it seems to be doing.

As Woody turned onto the sidewalk of a three-story green apartment building Eddie caught up with him. "I'm glad to see you're not in the hospital, Woody. I was afraid you were hurt bad when they took you off in that ambulance last night."

Woody turned his head to look at Eddie and took his hand out of his pocket to wave Eddie away. "Stay the fuck away from me, man," he said, obviously frightened. "I'm already in enough trouble for talking to you."

"Woody, like I told you last night, I didn't tell anybody I'd seen you. Why would I do that? I'm not here to cause problems like that."

He paused. Then he asked, "Who was that you came out of Hemingway's with? He looked like he was trying to sell you a used car from the 20s."

"You may as well know. That was Perry Andrews. He's the money partner in Lindy's newspaper. He's the son of a bitch who told Sommers I talked to you. He tried to tell me Al didn't have me roughed up, that it was all Dmitri and that snake Sonny, but I know better and I told him so. He also said I shouldn't testify against any of them, if I knew what was good for me. I told him what he could do with that."

"He's the one who's Sommers's friend? Lindy told me about him."

"Yeah. She told him. The bitch."

"Really? That must be how they knew I'd be at the airport. But she struck me as pretty nice when I met her."

"Don't kid yourself. She's made more people unhappy here than hurricanes. And the one she hates most of all is your girl Jen, who she's convinced stole her husband. I think she's right about that. Jen was flittin' about in public with that hifalutin' doctor while Lindy was still married to him and living with him, and everybody in their circuit knew it. And I guarantee you that the minute you left she called that partner to tell him all about your meeting. She probably told him about your trip to Washington, too."

Eddie knew Jen was self-centered and not discriminating about her sexual partners but was surprised to hear Woody's take on Lindy because it was so different from the image she'd displayed during his long conversation with her.

"That's sure not the woman I saw," he said.

"Don't kid yourself. Right after Lindy's fancy doctor left her there was a big poison-pen campaign against Jen around town. I was never completely sure Lindy started it, but Jen was, and she fought back. She told the story to all the society advertisers and Lindy's advertising dried up. She was about to lose the paper when she found that investor asshole you just saw, and he bailed her out. That's also when she started getting fat."

"That's something to keep in mind," Eddie replied. "Here's another question. You mentioned last time that Dmitri told you Sommers knew someone like Roy who knew about the missing painting. Did he tell you more about who that was?"

"Nah. He said it was an old geezer, older than Roy even. He lived in France."

"Paris?"

"Maybe. But I think it was somewhere else. I got the feeling Dmitri wasn't too strong on the geography of France. He wasn't an intellectual, you know."

"Could it have been Rennes?"

"Cudda been. It sounded something like that, but most of those French words sound the same to me anyway. Anyway, I'm going in. My head hurts and I need to take a pill and get rested up for when that young detective gives me the third degree tomorrow."

CHAPTER FOURTEEN

The Decision

Sarasota

Eddie walked the two blocks to Lido Beach, took off his shoes and socks and rolled up his trousers, and began pacing the sand, trying to sort out what he knew and what it meant. Sommers was clearly a key player in the conspiracy that resulted in the death of Roy Castor, and it looked like he was behind the death of Artie, too. Was this Sommers's plot or Erich Kraft's? Or was there a dark presence in the background? He had a disturbing feeling that there was a kingpin lurking in the wings.

"I'm surrounded by evil," he heard himself say aloud. "I've been in bed with it. Where do I go from here?"

He realized he couldn't abandon the chase until he'd found the painting, that this was the time to re-engage. True, there were hundreds of stolen artworks still missing, but this was one that had captured the imagination of a small group of determined and amoral men with no qualms about killing to find it. And it just might lead to his family's killers.

He looked out over the Gulf of Mexico and gave himself a pep talk. You're in this now, Grant. Nothing to do but follow it to the end, wherever it leads.

Feeling better, he walked back to his car and drove slowly to the hotel, dreading the confrontation he knew was coming. On the way, he called Thom's phone and got his voice mail. He left a message saying he had information that would help him question Woody and Sonny. And he asked Paul to meet him.

He called Philippe as he waited in the hotel room for Jen to arrive. It was ten p.m. in Paris and Eddie found him at dinner at a restaurant on Rue de Sèvres, just a few blocks from Aurélie's apartment. Philippe took his portable into the street.

"We're just finishing, and I don't mind a bit skipping the coffee. It's lousy here. It's just an informal dinner with Aurélie and the Sorbonne friend she's been seeing." Eddie felt a momentary twinge. "Also, I had dinner with Margaux last night and she'd like to hear from you."

"Philippe, I know I should call her but I don't know what to tell her at this point. I'll try to think of something.

"Also, the local prosecutor has delegated me to give you some information that may help on your end. And, he'd like help finding the man who was driving that night outside the Chopin. It already seems like a hundred years ago, but it was just last week. We — they — think he was the man who grabbed Roy Castor."

He went on to explain his own suspicion that Erich Kraft was responsible for Artie's death, aided by Dmitri. He went through Erich's immigration story and Jen's help in getting him American citizenship.

"And I don't know if she was directly involved in setting up Roy's kidnapping, but she certainly introduced Kraft and Sommers shortly before Artie was killed. If I had to guess I'd say she did stupid things with consequences she never imagined, but the police may find it's more than that. Bottom line, I don't think we can count on her for help because it's going to be a full-time job for her just to stay out of jail. And I have serious doubts about her loyalties."

Philippe heard Eddie out then asked, "What are you going to do? You'd certainly be justified in coming home and dropping the matter."

"Until I re-interviewed Woody Matthews this afternoon that's exactly what I intended. No, I'll be back in a couple of days to work on it there. I'll call you so we can talk about the next step. I'm beginning to take this personally. And it's time I re-engaged with my own life.

"Do you think Aurélie would like to be involved? I haven't responded very well to the stuff she's sent me. I hoped I wouldn't have to pursue it."

"You should ask her yourself."

"I will. Please tell her I'm reading her information right now."

He placed the phone carefully back on the table and plugged in its charger. Then he opened the MacBook Air and waited for his inbox to synchronize with French Gmail. There, among messages from his accountant and the manager of his language school, he found two long messages from Aurélie — one he'd already read, and a new one dated today, which he opened.

From: Aurélie Cabillaud

Subject: History of the lost painting

Cher Édouard,

This is what we know so far, including the material I sent you earlier. I've put it into English in case you need to give it to someone else there.

The missing painting is almost certainly "Portrait of a Young Man," a self-portrait by one of the great masters of the High Renaissance, Raphael (or more completely Raffaello Sanzio da Urbino), who did his best-known work in Rome 1509-1520, mainly working for two popes, Julius II and Leo X (one of the Medicis).

I've talked to several art historians and a couple of gallery people and they tell me it's the most valuable painting still missing from the war. When "The Rape of Europa" came out in 1995 the general estimate was it would be worth $100 million. I don't know who would buy it, unless they wanted to hang it in a cave somewhere and admire it privately, but there are people like that. Maybe a rich investor in Russia, China or one of the Gulf countries.

Raphael lived in a time when patronage of the nobles was the source of all money, and he went right to the top. He trained in

Urbino and then in Florence, but moved to Rome where he was introduced to Pope Julius, who put him to work immediately. Michelangelo, on the other hand, had to wait around for months before he could start his work.

The highlight of Raphael's relatively brief career is the first room he did for Julius, known as the Stanza della Segnatura. It contains a sequence of paintings, one of which is called "The School of Athens." I mention this much detail only because "Athens" contains his only undisputed self-portrait, and it is the similarity of the missing painting that convinces most experts it is Raphael's own portrait of himself. This is the art world, of course, so there are other opinions, but the majority vote seems to be that it's the real thing.

Michelangelo painted the Sistine Chapel ceiling at the same time. One story holds that Raphael had the Vatican guards let him go into the chapel after hours so he could admire the painting. It seems to have had some impact on his work. Michelangelo called him a plagiarist.

He was also an architect, and at one time had a contract for the design of St. Peters, but after his death Michelangelo's work was kept instead.

Raphael was born in Urbino, a town with a long artistic tradition, where his father was court painter to the local duke. He died young in Rome, at age 37. One popular rumor is that he died of a fever brought on by too much sex with his long-time mistress, but the truth is probably something absolutely pedestrian and in any case it doesn't matter now and that story isn't very likely, as we know.

The Portrait was painted in 1513-14, when he was 30 years old. It's not very large, about 22 inches wide and 28 inches high, and it's painted in oil (which was a relatively new medium at the time) on a wood panel, which means it couldn't just be rolled up and stuffed in the corner of a suitcase. It would require some protection and would take up some space.

There doesn't seem to be much if any record of who his client was or what happened to the painting after its death. But almost three hundred years later a young Polish prince, Adam Jerzy Czartoryski, traveled to Italy and bought it, along with Leonardo's "Lady with an Ermine" and some Roman antiquities.

He took his purchases back to Cracow, where they became the center of the Czartoryski family museum, except for a period during some political unpleasantness when they were in Paris. Just before the Germans attacked in 1939 they were sealed up in the basement of a country house in the vicinity, but the Germans found out about them anyway. Hans Frank, the governor general of Poland, confiscated the Raphael, the Leonardo, and a Rembrandt. There was an internal squabble with Göring over all three, but they wound up hanging on the wall of Frank's home in Wawel Castle in Krakow.

Here's where it gets interesting. As the Russians were closing in on Krakow early in 1945, Frank wrapped up his looted treasures and sent them off to his home in southern Germany, not too far from Munich. All three of the famous paintings were on the travel manifests — you know how the Germans had to document everything — but when the shipment arrived there was no Raphael. For a long time the prevailing theory was that Frank's personal curator had stolen it, but he denied it. Frank's own son wrote a bitter book well after the end of the war and speculated that his mother traded it for butter, and that it still hangs on some farmer's wall. We can't ask Frank, of course, because he was hanged by the Nuremberg tribunal in 1946.

One of my colleagues has made a special study of the Nazis' thefts and says he's never seen evidence that the painting was in Frank's house in the year or so before he moved — or that it wasn't. That doesn't prove anything, but it holds out the possibility that the painting could have been moved long before Frank took the others to Munich, in which case it could be just about anywhere.

Always,
Aurélie

The door hummed, then opened slowly. Jen entered with a bright smile that looked forced.

"I just came from the house," she said. "Jim was able to start this afternoon so we went over details for a couple of hours."

"You'll be glad when the work is done and you can move back in."

"I suppose we could go there now if it weren't for the fire. I heard on the radio that the police have arrested Al Sommers and poor Sonny Perry, and that Dmitri is dead. Is that why I didn't hear from you last night?"

"More or less. I was pulling into the hotel lot last night when Sonny and Dmitri kidnapped me at gunpoint. It was a close call. Let's go down to dinner and I'll tell you more." She did not look surprised.

Paul waited for them at a table for four in a remote corner of the dining room, Eddie pointed the way there.

"Jen, this is Paul Fitzhugh, who works with me in Paris. We served in the Army together and he's been part of our group since. And he's the main reason I'm still alive to talk to you tonight."

She sat without a word, her face rigid. "What's going on here?"

Eddie spoke plainly. He didn't want to leave room for misunderstanding. "Paul and I are returning to Paris to do some serious rat hunting. I thought this whole affair started when your father was killed, but the things I've learned in the last couple of days make me think it may have started with the death of my own father in 2001, or before."

"How could that be?"

Paul put his hand on Eddie's arm and picked up the story. "Ma'am, the dead Russian — Dmitri — was a known member of the Russian Mafia, an enforcer who worked mainly in Miami. We know he went to Rennes in June 2001 and was there the day Eddie's father died. We now know — and Eddie, you haven't heard this before — that Sonny was there, too. Artie Grant was kidnapped, interrogated and murdered, just as it's clear your father was murdered. The difference is that he died before they could question him. They would have done the same thing to Eddie if he hadn't outsmarted Dmitri and killed him."

Jen looked at Eddie with surprise. "You killed Dmitri?"

"I electrocuted him. He shot himself at the same time and probably would have died from that, but I did kill him."

Paul continued, "Artie was almost 90 years old at the time, and his heart just couldn't take the beating. Finally, they put a plastic bag over his head to frighten him, make him believe he would suffocate, and he had a heart attack. They put his body in his car to fake an accident, then doused it with gasoline."

Eddie asked, "You're sure?"

"Yes," Paul said, "The police and prosecutors have opened up to me, I think completely. They have a full confession from Sonny. I am sorry.

"Sonny also explained the long delay between 2001 and Mr. Castor's death. Sommers thought things would go smoothly when your father was kidnapped, because Erich Kraft was experienced in such things, according to a reference he gave Sommers. Kraft would question Mr. Grant, using intimidation if necessary, he would tell them where to find the painting and everyone would leave as friends. It was a major miscalculation on his part, just like it was a major error to trust a thug like Kraft.

"He was so bummed by Mr. Grant's death that he called off the entire project. Then he ran short of cash and the price of gold started to shoot up, so he reactivated it. He thought he could control the Germans but he was wrong there, too. He should never have tried to snatch Mr. Castor off the street."

Jen started to push back her chair but Eddie told her sharply to stop.

"I don't need to know much from you, but I do need a few things, and we're not leaving until I have them. First, tell me about your fake brother, Erich Wetzmuller. And I do know he's fake, that he's Erich Kraft, and he was involved in Artie's death and Roy's. And I know you sponsored him for citizenship. I just don't know why."

"Why? Why?" Jen's demeanor shifted in an instant from resignation to rage. "You saw those blackmail letters. When Roy didn't come up with what the bastard wanted he came to see me. He told me he'd kill both me and Roy if I didn't. And he raped me. Not once, but repeatedly. Every time he came to town. He made me introduce him to Al Sommers. But I didn't know he killed Roy. I would never have done that. God knows I'm no saint, but I wouldn't kill my own father."

Her shoulders slumped. She reached for her purse, but Paul snatched it quickly from the table and looked inside. Then he handed it across the table and she took out a tissue and dabbed at her eyes.

"Did you think I'd have a gun? That's not me, but I wish I'd killed that bastard and his father when I was a kid, or when he came back into my life.

"I was happily working in the shop when he came through the front door one day. He's a big man and I like big men…" A wan smile for Eddie. "Then a second later I saw his ear. It was missing a notch. I'd seen it before on my mother's East German husband and I knew instantly I was in trouble.

"He was nothing but sweetness and light at first, entirely different from the vicious teenager I remembered. We went to dinner and he told me his father had died. I knew it already, from Roy, but I didn't tell him. He came home with me and I gave him my second bedroom, but in the middle of the night he came into my room and raped me. And it wasn't just sorta rape, I didn't want him at all but he forced me.

"The next day was a Saturday, potentially a busy day at the gallery. But he told me he wanted to meet Al Sommers. I thought if I gave him what he wanted he would leave town, so I took him out there and left him. Sonny brought him back later. Roy was in France consulting on a film, so Erich stayed three more days and then he disappeared as silently as he'd arrived."

"The Loire dinner party," Eddie muttered.

Jen continued, "The next time he appeared he wanted something more specific. He'd been officially living in the States for six or seven years and had a green card, and he wanted me to vouch for him to become a citizen. It wasn't until I signed the form that I realized he'd also stolen my name. The son of a bitch had renamed himself Erich Wetzmuller.

"I didn't see him again until last year. I finally got up the courage to tell him if he touched me again I'd cut his dick off and feed it to the garbage disposal, and after that he stayed with Al. He seemed to have lost interest in me."

She put her face in her hands and wept, her back heaving as she sobbed.

"I've done such stupid things. All I wanted was to live my own life my own way." She looked at Eddie, tears streaming down her cheeks, and put her hand on his. "And I so hoped that we …."

He did not move, could not move. “Jen, there can’t be a we, not now.”

Paul asked her, more gently, “Do you know what he was here for last year?”

She wiped her eyes and blew her nose. “He was working with Al and somebody in France on finding the missing Raphael. Al was having money troubles and he wanted to restart the search for some treasure he thought might be hidden near the Saint-Lazare railroad station in Paris. There was supposed to be some gold with the painting and the price was going through the roof. It was a fatal combination of need and greed. Erich was representing someone over there. I never found out who. But it was money Al needed. His bank had failed and the legal problems from that almost wiped him out. He had some church silver he brought home at the end of the war but there wasn’t much of it left and he was having a hard time selling it since the FBI came and questioned him about it. It made him afraid to try.”

“Do you know the identity of his partner in Paris?” Paul asked.

“No, I never heard the name, but I could tell Al was afraid of him, and so was Erich. Roy and I went to dinner at Al’s house a few years ago, while he was still riding high as the hotshit banker. Sonny was there and they all talked quite openly about the painting. Roy told them how he’d tried to trace it but failed. He’d picked up one good lead at a dinner party but it turned out to be a dead end. He said he’d quit working on it several years ago when his friend died. That was Mr. Grant, I guess.”

CHAPTER FIFTEEN

It's Good To Be Home

Paris

Eddie stepped out of the bathroom in a well-worn terry robe Aurélie had given him during their too-short time together five years before. He walked across his bedroom to the open window, where coffee and a pot of hot milk waited, still rubbing his wet hair with a large towel that matched the robe. He'd made the coffee before his shower, but the steamed milk was in a heavy porcelain pitcher and it held the heat. Hot enough, he thought as he took the first sip, then turned his attention to the half baguette, butter and jam on the plate next to it.

He tore off a piece of the crispy bread, buttered it, then added a small dot of strawberry jam. Then he sat back with a satisfied sigh to watch the play of sunlight turn the stone towers of Notre Dame a golden honey color.

"Damn," he muttered, "It's good to be home."

It was his first full day back from Sarasota. Last night had run late, a dinner with his mother at her home. Normally Martine made dinner and left it, but for her son's return Margaux had made dinner herself and brought a fine Bordeaux up from her cellar. She wanted all the details about his week in Sarasota, and he'd given them to her for hours, unvarnished. The news he'd brought of how Artie had died had been difficult for her to absorb. She had wept quietly as he told her the story and Eddie — who normally kept his emotions tightly in check — had shed a few tears as well. When he left at midnight both were exhausted but agreed to meet for dinner the next night at Pierre-Victor, and to include Philippe.

"Ask him to bring Aurélie, too," Eddie said as he left. "She gathered a lot of interesting information for me and if she'll help it will make everything much easier."

"Why don't you ask her yourself?" his mother responded.

"That's what Philippe said. But I don't want her to think it's personal."

"It's not?"

He raised one eyebrow and walked through the repaired front door into the waiting elevator.

Today he had to plan the next step. He'd given up any idea of dropping the search for either the Raphael or Erich Kraft, although the painting had faded into near insignificance after he learned that Erich was his father's killer — for that, he would pay dearly. He didn't want to just turn it over to the police. He thought Philippe would eventually find Erich but he wasn't so sure he would search for the treasure with the same diligence, and it was the treasure that would lead to the mastermind behind Erich.

"The art is detective work," he said to himself. "Paul and I can do that, and if we track down Erich so much the better. We need to find out what's behind Erich. He was an apparatchik, not an art critic. He wouldn't know what to do with a Raphael if it arrived in the mail."

A half-hour later he left for his mid-morning appointment with Philippe, who in semi-retirement had borrowed an office in the Préfecture de Police on the Île de la Cité. From long habit he walked, starting with the stairs down to the lobby and continuing on a path that took him down Rue de Rivoli under the looming dark stone wall of the Louvre, across the north arm of the Seine on the Pont Neuf, along the charmingly named but in fact utilitarian Quai de l'Horloge, then across the center of the Île to a side entrance of the prefecture, where a suspicious policeman demanded his identity card but softened considerably when he heard Eddie was there to visit Philippe.

With a halfhearted salute he waved Eddie through to a wide staircase. On the third floor, Philippe waited at the head of the stairs.

They walked to the end of the hall and into a large office full of heavy wooden furniture, ornately carved, the chairs tightly upholstered in red. A flag stood in the corner behind the oversized desk.

"Bigger than I had when I was a commissioner," he said with a broad grin. "It's temporary and I don't know how long I'll get to keep it. The next one may be a cleaning closet, so let's get this all wrapped up. Tell me about your adventures in Sarasota."

Eddie told the story of his kidnapping and narrow escape, then of the arrest of Al Sommers and Sonny Perry, and the death of Dmitri.

"With just an electric outlet and a pair of pliers? Very creative," Philippe said.

"Not a lot of choice," Eddie replied. "We had a couple of screwdrivers, but he had a Glock. The Americans say you should never take a knife to a gunfight, and screwdrivers wouldn't even have been as good as knives."

"What is your next step?"

"I want to go down to the Loire and talk to an old art dealer. He gave a dinner party in 2001 that Roy Castor attended. Roy's memo to Artie said this dealer intimated he knew where some World War II art and maybe some other valuables were hidden. He claimed later it was just the wine talking, but Roy thought it was significant enough to ask Artie to follow up, which he did, but the old guy wouldn't talk. Things might have changed by now, if he's even still alive."

Philippe thought a moment then responded, "I may be able to help with that. I used to do some work among the art dealers, maybe twenty years ago, and I know a few of them. I'll make some calls and try to have something ready for dinner. What was this guy's name?"

Eddie opened his old brown briefcase and found Roy's message to his father and Artie's unmailed response.

"Artie went to see this man on his next-to-last monthly inspection trip to our property in Rennes. He wrote a report to Roy but never mailed it, and Margaux found it in his office. Here's the name. Jacques Ranville d'Estres. He used to have a gallery near the Champs Élysées."

"Jacques! That old thief. I got pretty close to arresting him in the late eighties, but couldn't quite get enough evidence together to satisfy the magistrate. He was guilty as hell of diverting funds from his customers. He paid a big tax penalty, as I recall, then he sold the gallery." Philippe beamed at the prospect of another shot at his old adversary.

"It's too bad you can't talk to his wife. Former wife, actually. She died about five years ago but she was really the crooked one.

"They were like two scorpions in a bottle. They married right after the war and together built a tiny gallery into a pretty good business, after time had washed away most of the stench of collaboration. But she'd fuck anything. He finally divorced her in the sixties but they couldn't come to an agreement on the gallery, so she continued to work there. It drove him crazy."

Eddie asked, "Could she have anything to do with the missing painting?"

"Impossible to say. She handled a lot of Jacques' business with the Nazis before they married. She could easily have been the round-heeled source Roy asked about. I heard she made a pass at Artie once, but I don't think anything came of it.

"I'll call him and soften him up. He'll probably think I have something new on him, but of course I can't say that. But I'll talk to him today if he's there."

"That would be great," Eddie said. "I'd like to go down and interview him as soon as possible. We can make more detailed plans at dinner."

Dinners with Margaux were normally sparkling affairs, but this one dragged. Philippe had Eddie go over the story of Sonny's questioning three times, and would have asked for a fourth if Aurélie hadn't put her hand on his arm and told him, "Enough. If Édouard thinks of anything else he'll tell you. Let's go on."

"If you say so," Philippe responded sourly. "But the prosecutor in Sarasota is playing games with me and I suspect he's going to resist giving me everything he has until they've tried Sommers and Sonny Perry. Of course I want both of them tried here as well, but I know we won't get that. But I do want Erich, and I was hoping Eddie might think of some little fact he'd overlooked."

Eddie said, "I agree with you, by the way. Prosecutors are prosecutors, and the one in Sarasota is going to protect his case by telling us as little as he can get away with. So we'll have to dig Erich out of his dunghill ourselves. Jacques Ranville may be a help. Supposedly Roy Castor and an unknown other person went to him after the dinner and asked about his broad hint that he knew something about a painting. He said, as I recall, it would someday rise like Lazarus."

"I talked to him today," Philippe said. "Old Jacques hasn't changed much. He's always been crooked, but that's hardly even illegal in his world. He did think I had something new on him, and he understands he needs to respond fully to your questions. He'll see you at 10 day after tomorrow. Is that a good time?"

Eddie responded, "The only better time would be tomorrow, but that will do." He turned to Aurélie, who'd been quiet since the dinner began, other than her effort to keep her father from hectoring Eddie. "Would you be willing to go with me? It would improve our chances of getting worthwhile information. Your stuff has been really helpful so far."

She pulled an iPhone from her purse and made a show of checking her calendar. "Day after tomorrow. Thursday. I'm clear that day, but I do have to teach the next. Can we do it in one day?"

"I think so. It's less than an hour and a half on the TGV, then a drive of less than an hour. It may be a long day but we can do it. Are you game?"

"What's my role?"

"We can talk more about it on the train down, but you're our expert on the art itself, and I hope you'll be able to tell when he's lying, as he surely will. Can you talk to one of your specialist colleagues about questions we might put to Jacques, and what lies he might tell us?"

Philippe added, "I don't know how long he'll be able to talk to you. He's 92 years old and sounded weak."

The TGV pulled into Gare de St. Pierre des Corps near downtown Tours at nine o'clock. Fifteen minutes later they drove away from the Hertz parking lot in a blue Renault Megane, the largest and fastest car available. A minute later Paul followed in a white model. In less than a mile they crossed the River Cher on the A10, with a brief view down at the east tip of an island park named for Balzac. Eddie immediately looked for the exit to highway D976, which would take them the twenty miles up the river, past the famous Château de Chenonceau with its often-photographed arcade spanning the river.

"There's the main entrance," Aurélie said a half-hour later, pointing to a stone archway marking the only visible opening in a high brick wall that extended for several hundred yards ahead of them. On the wall next to the entrance an elegant new sign advertised "Château Tours." Under the name and telephone number, "Corporate Retreat" was repeated in French, English and Japanese.

"We drive to a service entrance two hundred meters further, then turn in and follow the dirt road for 100 meters. His house is on the left. Used to be a groundskeeper's cottage."

As they turned, Eddie saw Paul's car pass behind him. They had agreed he would wait in the parking lot of a country hotel five hundred yards away.

"Does he always follow you like this?" Aurélie asked after they passed through the gate.

"Only when there's somebody out there trying to kill me," Eddie replied with a rueful smile. "This is the first time that's happened, but I don't want us to take any more chances than necessary and he's very good at his work."

The cottage was larger than they expected. Like the three-story chateau just visible in the forest behind it, it was constructed of cut stone several shades darker than the 19th-century buildings of Paris, most of which were built using limestone quarried deep beneath the city. Four stone steps, two of them with chips broken out of the tread edge, led to the ornately carved entrance door. A brass plaque that said simply, PRIVATE, was screwed to its center. The right end was a quarter-inch lower than the left, which made the entire door seem off balance.

"Well, here we go," Eddie said, as his hand reached for the lion's-head door-knocker just above the plaque. "Wish us both luck."

"We'll find out whatever he knows," Aurélie said. "If we do it right, that will be more than he wants to tell us."

The sound echoed back at them. After a minute Eddie lifted it to knock again, but stopped when he heard a loud voice inside shout sourly, "Attendez! J'arrive!"

"That doesn't sound like a weak old man," Aurélie said as she tried unsuccessfully to suppress a smile.

The door opened to reveal an improbably tiny figure, fully a foot shorter than Aurélie in her low-heeled shoes. "I didn't know there would be two of you," he said with no sign of friendliness. He looked at Aurélie and smiled, making Eddie glad she had agreed to accompany him. "Monsieur Flic didn't tell me there would be an attractive mademoiselle. Please come in."

"You make the introductions," Eddie whispered quickly as Aurélie walked past him through the door.

Jacques was dressed like a city Frenchman's idea of an English country gentleman out for a walk in the woods. He wore heavy forest-green trousers with a brown flannel shirt under a worn houndstooth jacket sporting leather patches at the elbows. Wellington boots with many miles on them stood just inside the entrance next to an empty brass umbrella stand. He wore corduroy slippers.

Inside, the house looked smaller. The entrance door opened directly into a generous living room, which contained enough overstuffed furniture for two rooms, all upholstered in dark colors. Dark, heavy wainscoting topped with a chair rail surrounded the room. Above was an expensive and once-elegant wallpaper depicting country hunting scenes, mainly of baying hounds chasing terrified foxes, probably left over from decorating the main house.

An open door to the right, beyond a carved oak dining table with six chairs, led to a small kitchen. To the left was a closed door that probably led to the bedroom. It was essentially a one-bedroom apartment. Jacques led them across the room to a fireplace with one large leather chair to the right and two smaller visitors' chairs on the left. He eased himself into the large one.

"You know that I am Jacques Ranville d'Estry, Jacques to all my friends. My old friend Philippe didn't say there would be two of you, but of course you are both welcome."

Aurélie hurried to introduce them. "Jacques, I am Aurélie Cabillaud, and Philippe is my father. I am here today to help my friend Édouard Grant. I believe you have met his father Artie Grant, who visited you in March of 2001 to ask about a certain dinner party you gave."

"Mr. Grant. I remember him. At first I thought he was just a rich American businessman but we had a long talk and I realized he was deeply knowledgeable about rural France. I believe he said his wife was French."

Eddie said, "Yes, my mother is Margaux d'Amboise. My father was part of American intelligence and met her father at the little town of Bompas, near Perpignan, when he came in by submarine to help the Resistance coordinate D-Day attacks with the Allies. Artie — my father — grew up in Paris, as I did.

"Unfortunately, Artie died a month after you met him and we believe the dinner party you gave may have a connection to his death. May we ask you some questions about it?"

"I regret that he is dead. He was not a young man, though. About my age, I believe."

"That is true,"Eddie said, "and if he had died a natural death it would be easier for my mother to accept. But he was murdered in Rennes. I just learned last week that the people who kidnapped and killed him did so because they thought he knew the location of the famous but missing Raphael painting called 'Portrait of a Young Man'."

"Murdered!"

Aurélie spoke up. "Édouard was able to confirm this only last week in Florida. He had a very narrow escape from the same people, so it's very important that we learn as much as you can tell us about the dinner party."

Jacques stood up abruptly and asked, "Would you like a cup of tea? I always make one for myself about now."

He returned with three cups and a steaming teapot on a wooden tray and set it on the small table between them. He carefully poured two cups and offered them to Eddie and Aurélie, pointing to the sugar, then poured one for himself. He did not speak until he had sat back in the chair and taken two sips of the tea.

"May I call you Édouard and Aurélie?" he asked, then without waiting for an answer continued.

"Édouard, I have to confess that I did not tell your father much when I met him. Times were much different then. I was still the master of the chateau…" he waved his hand in the general direction of the large house "… but it is no longer mine. I had some reverses in the stock market and some tax problems, so I was forced to sell it three years ago. As part of the sale, the new owners gave me a lifetime lease in this small house and an income although not a grand one. I have absolutely nothing to lose now, and I doubt that Commissaire Cabillaud is going to chase someone 92 years old, even if there were something I should suffer for, which I doubt. In any case, I no longer care much one way or the other."

"Neither of us can speak for the police, but we have no desire to bring you trouble," Eddie said. "The only reason we're here is to follow up on the meeting you had with Artie. It has come up now because Roy Castor was killed about three weeks ago in Sarasota, Florida, by the same people who kidnapped and killed Artie and who kidnapped me in Sarasota. They would certainly have killed me if I hadn't managed to escape."

"Roy is dead? That's terrible. Well, I'll tell you anything I can but I'm not at all sure it will help you."

"I remember that party. It was a big one I threw to celebrate the end of filming a TV show. I'd invested in yet another program about the art the Germans had stolen. As I recall, it was a joint venture between one of the French channels and one of the German ones. That was when I had money." A brief, wry smile.

Jacques sat back. He set the teacup aside and picked up a much-used pipe, carefully loaded it, then continued without lighting it.

"That was a pretty good group. Roy was there. Of course I knew him from earlier, though not well. He brought a friend from the Marais with him, which was pretty bold for him. The times I'd seen him before he was fully in the closet. The director sat on my right. One of those hostile German dykes. Then there was the producer, the narrator, a couple of others. All told I think we had a dozen people. I didn't often get the chance to throw a dinner party that big.

Eddie prodded him. "There was another man there, I think. When my father visited you the year after the party, you told him this other man had been much more insistent than Roy."

Jacques thought for a minute. "Yes, I remember him. He was a businessman and art collector who'd also put some money into the movie, so the producer invited him. I think he was more of an agent than a collector, because most of the art he bought was never seen again. I presume he sold it to people who put it on their living room walls and left it there. Not much of it in France, I'd guess."

"Why do you say that?" Eddie asked.

"Because it was all non-representational stuff, almost no people in it. He was a secular Arab, so if I had to venture a guess I'd say most of what he bought went to the oil billionaires."

Eddie pursued him. "What did you say that got Roy and this Arab so interested, anyway? And what was his name?"

"He called himself Alain Alawite, but it was a made-up name, a joke. I never knew his real name, but it should be easy enough to find out. He's an investor in businesses that go after the Muslim immigrant market. One of them was a chain of low-priced halal burger restaurants with stores all over France. I don't think he's an Alawite, even if he did adopt the name. He's a desert Arab, from Saudi Arabia or another one of the Gulf countries. He speaks French like a native, too. Must have learned it young.

"Like I told both Roy and Artie, I didn't really tell them anything they couldn't figure out with some common sense. I had a lot of wine so I may have overstated it a little, but was getting fed up with the director. She was talking on and on about how all the remaining paintings were gone forever, most of them to the Soviet Union and the rest lost to American military looters. She might be right, but I still didn't like it, so I said I was pretty sure there was unfound treasure in Paris, and that one day it would rise like Lazarus. That was a mistake. I don't think anyone picked it up, but I never should have mentioned Saint-Lazare."

They sat for a moment. In the corner a large clock ticked as its pendulum swung slowly. Jacques lighted his pipe and exhaled blue smoke.

"Jacques," Aurélie interjected. "Édouard's father was killed within weeks of his trip to see you. We know some of the story behind his death, but not all of it, and you're one of the few remaining people who can tie all this history together, if for no other reason than to give Édouard and his mother a sense of closure."

Eddie and Aurélie knew from their talk with Philippe that Jacques was a proud man who had once been prominent in Paris society. He'd bought the old chateau in the seventies, then in the eighties he had sold his highly regarded art gallery near the Champs-Elysées to a multinational conglomerate that was also buying auction houses.

He thought he would have enough money to support himself in luxury for the rest of his life, and 2001 was his final high point. But then had come 9/11 and the tense estrangement between France and the United States that resulted from the Iraq invasion. The stock market slumped and tourism went flat. The business tycoons he depended on to fill the vacation apartments in his chateau quit calling. Taxes went unpaid.

As a result, he'd been forced to sell the chateau to an American hedge-fund manager and his wife, who had redecorated it and started a marketing campaign to bring groups of culture-starved executives and their acquisitive wives to the green Loire, where they could play the châtelaine of the manse but not be too far from Paris for the shopping. He was not poor but he was bitter, especially when the guests mistook him for the groundskeeper.

"All right. I'll tell you the story. I don't have much to lose any more, but I'm not anxious to get in trouble with either the police or the Nazis. God knows I've seen enough of both.

"It was one day in 1944, just before the Liberation. The boche were jumpy as hell because they knew the Americans were headed toward Paris. Of course, their newspapers didn't say that — they were always in the process of turning them back, except that every day they were turning them back from closer to Paris. The Resistance papers had more information, but we still didn't know much.

"Anyway, I'd made friends with a young man a couple of years before. His father had been a French Army officer who was killed on the Maginot line. His mother was German, so of course his loyalty was suspect to both sides. She moved back to schoënes Deutschland right after her husband was killed. The boy gravitated toward the Germans. God, was he an overcompensating super-Nazi. When the Vichy government was set up, he went there and became a member of the Milice, the French cops who were basically a front for the Gestapo, even though he was just a kid. Then for some reason of his own he moved back to Paris and applied for a job in my warehouse. And then one day he disappeared without a word. Just didn't show up for work. No message, nothing.

"A week later, a customer came in to see me. He's not a name you'd know any more, but he was a real Count, one of those whose titles go back six or seven hundred years. A lot of the make-believe nobles today trace their titles to Napoleon, but this guy went back further than that. Much further. His estate in the south was wiped out in the Revolution, but he still had his city mansion and a lot of other real estate in Paris. He was very comfortable.

"Weird man. Very Catholic as only the old French landowners can be, but most of them stayed away from the Nazis if they could. Not my Count, though. He was fully in bed with them. A complete, loyal Nazi. And he was a very good customer of my gallery. For that matter, I was a good Nazi too, or at least I talked the talk. You had to be those days. I even sold a few paintings to people like Haverstock who were collecting for the grand museum Hitler wanted to build in Linz after the war. It was to be the new Louvre. But I was never part of that group, although my wife was close to them. I was hardly more than a kid when the Germans invaded in 1940. The gallery was small, and they let me stay as the Aryan front man. The owner had already left for Belgium, where he survived the war and moved to New York. I made payments to him for five years and then the gallery was mine, and it was all on the up-and-up."

Jacques paused for a minute to think, then continued.

"The battle for Paris started on August 19. It was the last week in July that the count came to see me. He told me my warehouseman would visit me at some time during the next two weeks. He would be driving an Army truck and would have valid papers. I was to get in the truck with him and show him how to get to the count's home in the 17th arrondissement. There we would leave the truck in his garage and return by métro. I would receive a suitable reward when the task was finished.

"I knew immediately of course that it was something the Nazis had stolen to finance their renaissance, the Fourth Reich. I thought the true believers were foolish, but I didn't tell the Count that. And I did exactly as he said."

The clock ticked loudly in the corner.

"Jacques, what was the name of your warehouseman?" Eddie asked.

"Eric Kraft."

CHAPTER SIXTEEN

The Painting, 1944

Paris, July 1944

The old métro car had been new well before Verdun, but now it was long past a decent retirement age. It bucked and groaned in complaint as the driver stopped none too gently at Denfert-Rochereau. Line 4 at 6 o'clock was a workingmen's train, filled with old men in blue cotton tunics and trousers who had watched their prime fade first slowly then, after the occupation began, at lightning speed. Most had come to view the Germans as just another burden to bear. The occupation would end or they would die, it didn't matter. They were too old or sick or broken to fear conscription for weapons work in the Fatherland.

The train finally shuddered to a complete stop. A young man lifted the silver latch of the last door of the last car then, out of habit, stuck his head out to peer suspiciously up the platform. There was no longer any particular risk but there used to be, and he had formed the habit of always riding in the last car and always looking first. If they're looking for me they'll catch me, he thought, but I'll make it as hard as possible. From the last car I can always duck down the tracks.

The crowd at Denfert-Rochereau was lighter than usual. He stepped across the six-inch gap between the car and the platform, putting his weight carefully on his good right leg before stepping out with his gimpy left. An underfed woman wearing a homemade brown dress allowed herself a vague smile, just a slight upturn at the corners of her thin lips, when she saw his limp. She came immediately to the conclusion that he was a mutilé de guerre deserving of her pity, not the scorn she had first felt. She wondered for an instant if the large notch in his right ear was also from honorable military service and decided it was.

She was wrong on both. The limp was a gift from a fellow milicien in Toulouse who'd refused to arrest an old Jew — his former teacher — during one of the weekly deportation roundups then backed up his point with an extremely sharp knife. The stabbing resulted in the limp as well as his separation from the Milice and a quick decision to move back to Paris, but he would neither forgive nor forget. Three months later he had slipped back into Toulouse under his own name and begun a search of the whorehouses favored by the miliciens. It was a short search — in the second one he found his nemesis puffing atop a tired-looking whore and very quickly, without ceremony, cut his throat. When the whore screamed for help he cut hers as well, then escaped out a back door and hid in a warehouse he'd picked out months before. Two days later he used the new papers arranged by a friend of his mother's to hitch a ride back to Paris. The friend was a Frenchman with an inner Nazi struggling to get out, and the newly minted Eric Kraft hoped he never learned the first use of the new identity he'd so carefully constructed.

Up the stairs, slowly, and out of the métro station. He followed the exposed tracks of the suburban commuter line for a half-mile, then turned left into a small lane whose name sign had long been lost, more an alley than a street. Three doors down, he pulled open the cracked once-blue entrance of the Hôtel Saint-Paul, a crumbling six-floor building that had been a cheap residential hotel for as long as anyone in the neighborhood could remember. It had once sheltered French tourists from the provinces but now was home to impoverished workers who could, if they were careful, afford its rent and one meal a day at the cheap cafés in the neighborhood. He'd lived there two years, most of it in a tiny room directly under the roof that baked him in summer and froze him in winter, and had bad ventilation all the time. Only six months ago, thanks to his new job at the art gallery near the Champs-Élysées, he had been able to move to the relatively luxurious third, where the ceiling was higher and he had two windows. The job wasn't bad and the owner was a decent guy despite his transparent pretense of being from a noble family. Jacques de whatever, that's what his name should be. Jacques de Chose Truc.

Eric crossed the minuscule lobby in three steps, only once catching his dragging foot on a roll in the threadbare carpet, which long ago had been the color of the door. The owner sat glumly behind the splintering counter, frowning ostentatiously as he read one of the approved occupation newspapers. He handed over the key to Room 305, looked up briefly and grunted, something he normally did only if the rent were a day late.

The key turned wrong in the lock. He was certain he'd locked it that morning but it wasn't locked now. If they were coming for him they would have been watching the lobby as well as the room, so he pushed open the door, unsure, and stepped inside.

A tall SS officer stood up from his only chair, folding a newspaper. He had stubbed out a Gauloise in the souvenir ashtray from Toulouse that had sat untouched on the table for six months.

"May I see your ausweis, please?" The officer, a major from the insignia he wore, was not unfriendly. His French struggled under the dead weight of a heavy German accent.

"Not a bad fake, but a fake nonetheless," he said, shifting to German and returning the papers. "You were hard to find. It was only when I went to see your mother that I learned the name you are using now. How did you become Eric Kraft?"

"Long story, but there are people in the South — on both sides — who would like to do me harm. Eric Kraft was the name of a cousin on my mother's side. He was killed in 1940 but his body was never recovered and officially he is still alive, as you can see."

"Creative. You are going to need all that creativity and more.

"I am Major Steinhauer and I serve in your uncle's headquarters in Cracow. You are to return there with me. He needs you for a special mission and I don't believe he trusts anyone outside his family." A thin smile.

"I took the liberty of packing everything I found. It fit easily into your small suitcase."

“I don’t have much. No one does,” Eric responded.

“Then let’s go. My car is around the corner. We will go to the Hôtel Wilhelm, where you will receive new papers and a uniform. We will be together every minute until we reach Cracow.”

“Do you mind telling me what is going on?”

The major smiled a second time and said, “You’ll become Lieutenant Eric Kraft of the SS, on assignment. We will return together to Poland, and there your uncle will explain your duties further.”

“And if I refuse?”

“Either way you go into a German uniform, which you should have done the instant you left the Milice. If being a lieutenant isn’t your taste, you can be a private. You will still go to Poland, except that as a private you’ll go in a troop train and fight the Russians. It would not appeal to you. I know. I have been there.”

“Do you have orders for me?”

“I have better than just orders. Here is your authorization to travel anywhere you wish within the Reich and to call on all units of the German military for any help you need.” He held up a sheet of heavy paper covered in dense Fraktur script at the top, French at the bottom, and headed Laissez-Passer. It was signed,

Heil Hitler!
Hans Frank
Obergruppenführer SS
Governor General of Poland

The next day they sat sweltering in a Wehrmacht train rattling east toward Germany. The trip passed in a blur of wounded soldiers evacuating in panic ahead of the Allied invasion forces, plus a few officers and sergeants on administrative missions. They changed trains first in the heavily fortified border zone near Stuttgart, then again in Dresden, where they mounted an ancient six-car train pulled by a wheezing steam engine from the Great War.

The first part of the trip was uneventful because all the cars bore large red crosses on their roofs, but the train from Stuttgart was unmarked. Within the last month, Major Steinhauer said, American and British Mustang fighters had begun strafing trains as they returned from bombing missions deep inside Germany.

"But where is the Luftwaffe?" Eric asked.

"It's not very effective any more," the major answered. In fact, the newly aggressive tactics of the fighters had nearly eliminated the Luftwaffe as an effective defense, with the exception of some of the new and very fast Messerschmidt jets, which had the speed to strike and run before the Mustangs could respond. Even so, some of them were shot down.

Two hours out of Stuttgart the train came to a sudden stop in the middle of an open field and the engine whistle sounded an evacuation alarm. Eric and the major jumped hastily from the first car and ran for a ditch 100 yards away. From there, they saw two silver Mustangs with bright red tails blow up their engine with machine-gun fire, sending shrapnel flying far over their heads, then fly off toward their airbases in western France.

"There is a rumor that all the Mustangs with red tails are flown by noirs," the major said as they waited for a second attack. "That can't be true. The Jew Roosevelt might want it, but the officers of the American Army would never allow it."

They waited twelve hours for a repair crane and replacement engine, then resumed their trip.

Finally, after four days of interrupted sleep and meals of cold sausages, the old train came to a halt in Cracow's main station, shabby after five years of war, with damaged engines and freight cars scattered about the yards like a child's building blocks. But the tracks were clear.

The town swarmed with replacement soldiers on their way to fight the Russian army, threatening from the east.

"We'll walk," the major told Eric. Each picked up his single bag and they set out toward the looming brick hulk of Wawel Castle, a mile away toward the river.

A guard saluted as they approached its imposing main door. Eric offered his laissez-passer, which the guard looked at carefully. The major said, "Please tell the Governor-General I have returned with his nephew, who awaits his instructions."

"Sir, I have orders to take you to him as soon as you arrive. Please follow me." He turned and led them up the stairs. At the top Eric heard him tell another guard "… the Governor-General's nephew…" and the door opened immediately.

The second guard beckoned for them to follow and led up a broad staircase to a double door, where a lieutenant sat behind a table. Soldiers stood at attention on both sides of the door. The lieutenant took the laissez-passer, then picked up a red telephone, waited several seconds, and said, "Sir, your nephew has arrived." He then stood up and signaled to one of the guards, who opened the door and with a nod indicated they should enter. Several men waiting on benches — Eric spotted at least one general — glowered as they went in.

The major came to attention before the desk and saluted. "Herr Governor-General, I am pleased to have found your nephew."

"Thank you, major. Please wait outside."

Eric had not seen his uncle Hans since he was a schoolboy ten years before, and thought he looked worn. He had less hair, much less than Eric's own father, who had a full head of lush brown hair at the same age. He could not easily identify the changes in his uncle, who still had the close-set eyes and pinched mouth of a small-town accountant but somehow looked meaner and at the same time soft and round-faced. He did not look like a man with life-or-death power over ten million people.

"So," he said. "You are Eric Kraft. Did you have a problem with the Frank name?"

"Uncle, the Frank name would have got me killed. I was attacked by a colleague who wanted to excuse his old teacher from deportation and my leg still suffers from the stab wound he gave me. My mother sent me to a friend who created the new identity for me. Major Steinhauer says it's a good fake. Of course I would prefer to use my mother's name, and yours. I was pleased when she took it back after my father died."

Hans Frank signaled to Eric to sit down. "And the old Jew. Was he deported?"

"I saw to that, uncle."

"Good."

Frank had a reputation throughout the Reich for his zeal in purging Jews from the rump Poland that was now called the General Governate, the four districts that had not been absorbed directly into the Reich. Legend held that the governor of Czechoslovakia had once posted a sign announcing the execution of seven Jews, and Frank had responded with scorn that if he put up posters for every seven Jews he killed there would be no trees left in Poland.

Hans Frank sat still behind his large oak desk. As he waited, Eric looked around the room, his eyes stopping first at a painting hanging on the wall behind his uncle.

"Do you like that, Eric? I believe I shall call you Eric, so we can avoid confusion."

"It's very pretty."

"It's much more than pretty. It is one of the great treasures of western civilization, and it was wasted on the Polish peasants. It is called 'Lady with an Ermine' and was painted almost 500 years ago by Leonado da Vinci. One day, after this war is won, it will hang in the Führer's grand new museum in Linz, to honor his birthplace and one day his memory. In the meantime, he has entrusted it to me, along with several others like it."

Frank had swiveled around to look at the painting. He stretched his hand to his right as he turned back to face Eric. "The one over there is a Rembrandt."

He turned the other direction and pointed to a smaller painting. "Do you recognize that one?"

Eric stared a minute at the exquisitely framed painting that hung to the right of the door. "It looks familiar."

"And so it should. It hung on the wall in that gallery where you worked for a month after you started."

Eric did not understand Frank's fascination with the paintings. Within the family he had the reputation of a single-mindedly political Nazi, perhaps slightly more refined than the criminals and street brawlers who had filled the party's ranks before 1933, but only because he was educated — a lawyer who had Hitler's ear and, in fact, had been Hitler's personal lawyer. Rumors said he fought bitterly with the other old lions of the party leadership, especially Göring, the obese Luftwaffe chief.

"Nephew, I am telling you all this not because I want to educate you about art. It's too late for that. It was too late long ago, since my poor sister failed to develop an appreciation for beautiful things. She even married a Frenchman, although on the one time I met him he did appear to be cultivated. I'm glad you have grown up in the warrior tradition of our German ancestors.

"What I am about to tell you is top secret. More, it's Führergeheim."

Eric nodded. He remembered that his mother thought her brother Hans was pompous and vain, and so far he'd seen nothing to convince him she was wrong. She said you could tell by his language — as he'd risen in the party and then the government it had become more and more bureaucratic. Eric understood now what she had meant.

Frank continued, "I have been charged by the Führer with putting aside resources for the future in case they are needed. You must never repeat that, because you would be charged with defeatism and certainly shot if it got to the wrong ears, but our Führer recognizes that we must have a fallback plan and he has entrusted part of that to me. I assume he has also asked other senior commanders to do the same, maybe all of us. They will no doubt send assets different places, some of them inside Germany. But I consider that too risky."

Eric's task, he said, would be to take a truck of art and gold back to Paris, where it would be hidden by a trusted collaborator until the end of the war. If Germany won in the end, the treasure would be there for the taking. If not, the Allies would quickly make friends with a new Germany and the treasure would still be there to finance the next incarnation of the Reich.

"You might call it the Treasure of the Fourth Reich, but I wouldn't say that outside this room."

As Frank droned on, a glimmer of understanding turned slowly into a frightening realization that this was not the rescue of the Reich but the rescue of Hans Frank, who after the war would have a fortune waiting for him in Paris. He nodded dumbly, struggling to keep his face blank as he began thinking of ways his uncle's plan could benefit himself as well.

Frank pressed a button on his desk and the lieutenant appeared at the door. “Sir?”

“Please ask Major Steinhauer to come in.”

Frank told Eric that Major Steinhauer was in charge of preparations for his journey and would see that he had new identity papers and uniforms. He should be prepared to leave in two days.

Eric spent most of those days with a mousy captain whose name he never learned. The captain was, or had been until he lost his left arm in Africa, a navigator for a tank battalion, and he took very seriously his duty to find the safest and fastest route across Germany and France for Lieutenant Frank. He had been a mathematics teacher before he was drafted in 1941 and had the teacher’s interest in keeping records, which also made his Wehrmacht masters happy. He vacillated between licking Eric’s boots and pulling rank, but the knowledge that he was instructing Hans Frank’s nephew tipped the balance toward obsequiousness.

“You’ll have to drive north, around Czechoslovakia,” the gray captain said. The Russians were already threatening and had told the Czech government that any lands they liberate would be turned over to the civilian government. “It’s too dangerous. If you were in a larger group it would be OK, but as a single truck you might be attacked by the partisans. Better to drive a little farther and risk the American airplanes. After a day or two, depending on how far you can go, you’ll have to drive at night and find shelter from the fighters during the day. I suggest the forests rather than army posts, which will be targets.”

They marked out a route from Cracow northwest to Dresden, then southwest through Nuremberg, bypassing Munich, to Memmingen, the small city where Eric had grown up and where his mother still lived. The 400 miles from there to Paris would be the most dangerous part of the trip, and would have to be driven at night because the Allied air forces had almost unchallenged control of the air throughout France. By the time Eric arrived they might be almost at the gates of Paris.

“What will I be driving?” Eric asked.

"A small truck of some sort, probably a two- or three-ton, and probably made in France. A Citroën or Opel won't attract attention on either side of the Rhine, since we took a lot of French civilian vehicles for our own military."

"You can see the results in Paris. The streets are empty," Eric said.

The captain leaned over the map table and rubbed his stump. "It still feels like I have my arm, and sometimes it hurts. The surgeons say that will go away eventually, but …" He grimaced in pain.

"I suggest you avoid the cities and look for food and fuel in the smaller towns. Most of them will have a Wehrmacht post commanded by a lieutenant or sergeant, and your papers will get you anything you need. You'll leave here with quite a good supply."

He paused and straightened up, then put his hand on Eric's arm. "I know I don't have to say this, and I hope you won't take offense, but you haven't been in Germany in a while. All of us in active service must remember times are very bad for our families. Your papers will see that you get everything you need, but remember never to take everything a farmer has. If we do that, his family doesn't eat."

"I'll remember," Eric responded. "I've seen some pretty bad behavior in Paris and I don't want our own people remembering me that way."

"Good. Now, if you go directly toward Dresden then pass it to the south you should be safe enough. There are several municipal forests along the back roads, although I don't know how many of the trees have been cut for firewood."

They discussed the merits of trying the autobahns versus the country roads, with the captain advising against the autobahns, especially in the western part of the country.

"The Allies are now bombing Berlin and the Ruhr from our old bases in France as well as from England, and they have a new long-range fighter escort called the P-51 Mustang. There is no way to defend yourself completely, but if you stay away from industrial areas and big cities you'll have less chance of being hit."

"The P-51. Major Steinhauer and I had to wait 12 hours for a new engine after a pair of Mustangs shot up our train not far from Stuttgart. They are dangerous, although from a distance they look like fireflies," Eric said. "Is it true that the Mustangs with red tails are flown by black pilots?"

"It is true, and they are very skillful and dangerous pilots. I suggest you keep far away from them," the captain said. He rolled the map carefully using his one hand and handed the roll to Eric. "Go with care, lieutenant. The Governor General himself came to give me my instructions, so I know your mission is important to him and to the Reich."

He looked at his watch. "You have just enough time for lunch, then you are to meet Major Steinhauer and go to the garage to make the acquaintance of your new truck. Heil Hitler!"

Lunch was a meager affair of one sausage and a small pile of potato salad. The wurst tasted mostly of filler, and Eric avoided thinking about what kind of meat might be in it. He thought the filler might be oatmeal or bread, but more likely turnips. Before he left Vichy he'd heard of the red barrels of dried turnips marked "for prisoners only" that had gone on the deportation trains with the haggard crowds of deportees he and his milicien colleagues had rounded up. Earlier, the food had been better, because the thousands of young Frenchmen drafted for munitions work in Germany were in theory volunteers donating their labor for the good of the Reich and Marshal Pétain. They deserved better treatment, at least until they arrived in the Fatherland, from which many of them would never emerge.

Thin as it was, lunch was a better meal than he was able to scavenge most nights in the bedraggled cafés around the Hôtel Saint-Pierre. He was grateful at least for that.

The junior officers' canteen occupied a high-ceilinged room in the southwest corner of the castle. He asked the old Pole who picked up his dishes how to find the garage, but got only a blank stare in return. He was tempted to lash out but decided it would be too much trouble, and there was a good chance the old man didn't know in any case. The other lieutenant sharing his table hadn't known.

Oh, well, he thought. I'll just start looking. Someone will know how to get there.

But as he pushed his chair back, he heard his name.

"Kraft!" It was Major Steinhauer calling to him from the front door. "Come quickly." He signaled with an impatient wave.

Eric caught up with him in the hallway. "I'm glad you're here. I couldn't find anyone who could tell me how to find the garage."

"It's not far." The major led the way down a hall for fifty paces then turned into a staircase that led down to the ground floor. At their right stood a door, which he opened to find himself in the garage, an immense room full of staff cars. The nearest was a six-wheel Mercedes bearing fender flags — his uncle's official car.

The major beckoned to a sergeant, whom he introduced to Eric as the senior guard. "Lieutenant, please show the sergeant your laissez-passer."

The sergeant stiffened when he read it, saluted, and said, "I will tell all the guards you're here, licutenant."

The major led him to a repair bay at the back of the garage behind Hans Frank's grand Mercedes. There, surrounded by canvas panels, stood a prewar Citroën two-ton truck. Two Wehrmacht carpenters were painting the wooden bed.

"Eric, this is your duty. This truck must get to Paris safely and intact," he said.

Eric leaned close to hear him over the sound of the large ventilation fans. "You will leave today. The cooks have prepared enough food for several days and will store it in a trunk. There are also blankets and other bedding. We will put up the canvas top, giving you a place to sleep if you need to avoid the American fighter planes by parking in a forest during the day. As an officer you will have a Luger as a sidearm. The armorer will be here soon to issue the pistol as well as a carbine with 200 rounds."

"But," Eric interjected hesitantly. "But what about the cargo?"

The major smiled. "The cargo is safe." He patted the wooden sides of the truck's bed. "The entire cargo is under the new bed they are painting now. There will be one more box, under the seat in the cab."

He led Eric out of the carpenters' hearing.

"Eric, you have been chosen for one of the most important missions in Germany. We soldiers work hard to do our duty, but seldom does our work result in the salvation of the nation. Yours, on the other hand, just might.

"The Governor-General gave me this duty because he knows I believe strongly in it. I have tried to give you the best information possible, but there is one more thing I need to tell you."

"And what is that?"

"You will not be alone on this trip. You will have another lieutenant to assist you. He is older than you and also a native of Memmingen. I had intended that he would make the trip with an enlisted driver but your uncle wanted someone more trustworthy. We discussed it and he suggested your name, then sent me to find you. I think he was right, although it certainly wasn't easy." He smiled slightly.

"Who is the other man," Eric asked.

"I know this will sound unusual, but he is a priest. The Governor-General brought him here and they are very close. Your uncle is becoming more and more religious. He and Father Otto pray together several times a week."

"A priest? In the SS? I knew there were a few in the Wehrmacht, but not the SS."

"Father Otto is here now so your uncle can protect him. But he has been away from his flock for four years, so he will return with you. It will be your decision, but your uncle and I will approve if he remains in Memmingen and you go on alone."

"Jesus! My uncle, a senior Nazi, with his own private priest. I thought only the old French Nazis were still interested in God."

The carpenters had left and removed the canvas privacy walls, giving Eric his first chance to look closely at the truck. It was at least six years old and battered. Only the bed had been painted. The rest of it looked like it was just back from the front.

As he ran his hand over the hood he heard a footstep behind him and turned to find a Wehrmacht mechanic in grease-stained overalls. He appeared to be in his mid-thirties, wearing regulation eyeglasses with thick lenses that caused his blue eyes to appear out of focus behind them. His blond hair was cut short.

"I'm Schmidt, sir. This is a good truck. She's a Citroën 23R, the best we could do right now. She was built in France in 1939 but hasn't had a lot of hard duty, not as far as we can tell. She'll give you an honest 45 miles an hour on a good road, less if you have to move cross-country. We put on a new set of tires and gave you two new spares as well, and you'll have enough fuel to fill up twice, although I'm sure you can get gas from any army post if you need it.

"You should blend in wherever you go. There are thousands of these still in service. One of the officers told me 14,000 were built and we only took 6,000 for army use."

Schmidt walked him around the truck, pointing out the twin gas tanks behind the cab, the windshield that swung out from the bottom to let air flow through the cab, and the blackout headlights. In the bed he showed Eric the tool kit he had assembled personally, the two spare tires bolted to the left side, and the spare battery in a wooden box with the jack, next to the tires.

"It's a lot of stuff," Eric told him. "Still, there will be room for us to sleep."

"Yes, there should be. You and Father Otto should find it cozy back there." For an instant Eric thought he was going to add something but the moment passed.

"Let's go over the controls. Do you know the truck?"

"Not this one, but I drove another Citroën when I was in the Milice, in Toulouse."

Schmidt showed him the gearshift pattern and cautioned him against using reverse any more than necessary. "I think the gear is wearing, and we don't have a replacement for it here."

Eric felt a tap on his shoulder and turned to find Major Steinhauer and a dumpy man wearing a baggy uniform. Looks like he slept in it, Eric thought.

"May I present Father Otto? Father, this is Lieutenant Eric Kraft, with whom you'll spend the next few days."

Eric put out his hand. The priest moved a small brown canvas bag to his left hand and shook Eric's limply.

"I am so pleased to meet you. Of course I know your mother well and she told me about your life in Paris."

Eric shot a quizzical look at the major. "Of course I had to tell him your real name so he would make the family connection," the major said. "No one else knows."

Eric calculated quickly. His mother had moved back to Memmingen only after his father's death in 1940, so he could have known her only briefly.

"I can see you're curious. I met Frau Frank during her visits to her family but I've not seen her since your father's unfortunate death. She was a strong member of the parish."

Eric spread the map on the hood of the truck.

"Father, we have 600 miles to cover, probably at an average speed of 20 miles an hour, and that's if we're lucky. On the way here from Paris the major and I watched our train being blown up by American planes well inside Germany, so there's no telling what this trip will be like. I hope they'll ignore a single small truck on its own, but they might not.

"In any case, we have 30 hours or so of driving ahead of us. It's summer, nights are short, so we may be able to drive for only five or six hours when we get closer to the French border."

He turned to the major and said, "We are ready to depart. May we leave now?"

"Of course. You'll have an escort out of town, but when you get to the highway you'll be on your own. Drive carefully. Much depends on you."

Eric climbed into the driver's seat. The priest heaved himself into the right side of the bench seat and crossed himself as a guard on a motorcycle signaled to follow him out of the garage, then led the way along the river to a military highway that led to the northwest, toward Dresden, almost three hundred miles away. For all but fifty miles they would be in rural Poland and thus reasonably safe from air attack, so they would drive through the night and find an Army post near Dresden to verify the one-armed navigator's route suggestion.

They stopped once, at the little town of Görlitz. Father Otto had driven the last hour and had found a sheltered spot by the bank of the river. They took blankets from the small trunk the carpenters had fastened to the bed.

"You sleep first, then we'll change places," Eric told the priest.

Two hours later he shook Otto's shoulder and told him, "it's eight o'clock. Let me sleep for a couple of hours and we can get back on the road."

Eric awakened to a breakfast of sausage and dried eggs, which the priest had heated on a small alcohol stove, along with water for ersatz coffee.

Better than the stuff I get in Paris, Eric mused, and he was glad to have it. If the good father can cook some, this may seem like a short drive.

During the long night's journey they had begun to exchange personal information. Eric learned that the priest had lived in Memmingen for twenty years and that St. Anselm's was the first parish he had ever served. For five years he was the designated cook for the four priests, and to fill their larder he had made friends with many of the parishioners, who then contributed food for the priests' table.

"One of my favorites was a farmer. He was very generous. Every year he slaughtered a hog for us, and one year he gave us half a cow. She was an old dairy cow, tough, but we'd never had so much beef.

"He was a widower with one son and four daughters. I will always remember the son, a beautiful boy who was twelve when I knew him, and a faithful altar boy. It was sad when he was killed at Stalingrad."

Eric told of how his mother had been sent by her stepfather to school in Paris early in the twenties, primarily to clear the way for his own younger children in his new family. There she had met a dashing young captain of the French cavalry and married him over the objection of her stepfather but with the surreptitious support of her mother, who had always dreamed of living in Paris. The captain was so persuasive, Eric said, that he was born nine months after their first meeting at an Army dance.

As a boy Eric had lived two years in Berlin, where his father was a military attaché at the embassy.

"That's what got me interested in Germany," he told Father Otto after breakfast. "The Germans seemed so organized, so full of purpose. This was before the Führer and the economy was in shambles, but they seemed to know what they wanted. The French seemed weaker, less determined. Anyway, I suppose that's why we're all here today."

Outside Dresden they found an army post where they learned there had been no bombing along their planned route for two weeks. "Before that the Americans bombed by daylight, and they had escorts. From Nuremberg south you will have to travel by night and hide during the day," the intelligence officer told them.

He pointed at Schweinfurt on Eric's map. "Here's where the danger is greatest. The industrial plants around here and Regensburg have been bombed without end since last year. There is no way to predict when they will be back, but you'd better plan to stay completely off the roads during the daylight hours from there to Memmingen."

Eric looked at Father Otto, then back at the intelligence officer. He said, "That's only 180 miles. If the roads are good, we can get to Nuremberg today."

The two-lane highway was clear of civilian traffic and most of the military traffic they saw was driving east to reinforce the troops fighting the Soviet army.

Military police patrols stopped them twice but both times Eric's laissez-passer worked its magic. The policemen saluted and waved them on.

As sundown approached, Eric drove deep into a forest north of Nuremberg. Once they had to stop to move a tree blown over by a bomb that had missed its target by miles, then just as the forest plunged into darkness they found a sheltered place in a grove next to a brawling stream.

"That's all for today," he said as he turned off the engine. "We stay here tonight and tomorrow. If the roads aren't too cratered or the traffic too bad we should be at my mother's for breakfast the next morning. Otherwise we'll have to find another campsite."

Eric was confident they would reach Memmingen without having to stop again for fuel or food. Once there, his mother would do her best to feed him better on the final run to Paris. It was less than five hundred miles and he planned to do it alone, leaving Father Otto behind.

The priest put together another meal of sausage and potatoes with a few reconstituted eggs on the side, and he brought out a loaf of rough, dark bread.

"Otto, does the Governor-General eat like this?" Father Otto had asked him earlier in the day to drop the priestly title, both for their safety and because he recognized Eric was never likely to be one of his parishioners. For the same reason, he'd suggested they use the familiar "du" in conversation. One military policeman had given them a suspicious look when he'd overheard the formal address, which was not expected among soldiers of equal rank.

"It sounds strange to them and no policeman likes to hear strange things. It makes them nervous," Otto had told him, and Eric had to concede he was probably correct.

Otto thought the food in Hans Frank's mess at Wawel Castle was better, and lamented that living conditions would be worse yet when he was fully back in the civilian world.

Eric had a different view. "Say what you like about this, but it's no worse than what I had in Paris. Before the war, eating in Paris was heaven, but since the invasion the Wehrmacht has stripped France of almost everything of value. However this comes out, it will be a long time before Germany and France are friends again. If they ever have been."

"Is there any doubt in your mind how this will end?"

Eric changed the subject. Even a theoretical discussion of the war ending in Allied victory was enough to bring accusations of defeatism, which for a soldier would lead either to a quick posting in the east or summary execution. Even priests weren't to be trusted. Some of those who'd remained in Paris were ostentatious Nazis who loved to preach that the occupation was God's punishment for the high living and loose morals since the Great War. The ones he'd met in Vichy were worse, since their leaders came from the old Catholic establishment of rural France.

"Did you say my mother was a strong member of your parish?"

"I may have overstated it a bit. I was transferred from St. Anselm's to St. Boniface in early 1940 and that's where I met her. She took part but I don't think her heart was in it. But I'll always be grateful to her for suggesting me to her brother."

Eric sat up straight. "She recommended you?"

"It was kind of her. I'd had some problems at St. Anselm's and the pastor sent me away. She thought I would be happier in an army post. She wrote, and a few weeks later I had a uniform and orders to travel to Poland."

"Why are you leaving?"

"It's been long enough, and there's an opening at Saint Anne, a small parish made up mostly of old people. I will be a good pastor to them."

Eric had not intended to ask, but curiosity got the better of him. "Your problems at St. Anselm's. Were they …?"

"I sinned miserably," Otto said. In the dim light Eric saw him put his head in his hands. "I was weak. There was a lovely boy, son of the farmer who had been so good to us…"

"The one killed at Stalingrad?"

"Yes. And he was not the only one." Otto wept quietly. "I'm certain God has forgiven me, but I can't forgive myself."

"This departure from Cracow. Is there anything like that behind it?" Otto crossed himself and murmured, "so many beautiful young men."

Eric broke the uncomfortable silence. "All that is between you and your conscience, if you have one. We'll only be together another day and then we can forget that this conversation ever happened."

"Please," Otto said, sniffling.

Eric got up and started to take a walk but realized he could get irretrievably lost in the dark woods if he wandered too far from the truck. He and Otto had listened carefully for almost an hour before their dinner and had heard nothing, not even a large animal.

"The bombing has probably run off all the wildlife," Otto had said

"We don't want to meet a wild boar or a German unit, and we definitely don't want to surprise anyone. Anyone camping here is likely to be trigger happy." He adjusted the luger so it rode more comfortably on his belt.

They agreed to keep watch in two-hour shifts. Eric slept first because he had done most of the driving. Otto's driving experience was long behind him and he had caused the truck's old gearbox to grind menacingly one too many times for Eric's comfort. He'd agreed without objection that Eric would do all the driving except where the road was straight and level, and Otto would handle the cooking and cleanup.

Midway through Eric's second sleep shift the truck moved. He thought Otto had climbed into the cab to be more comfortable, turned over, and forgot about it. But soon it rocked and awakened him again, and he heard the harsh sound of wood breaking. As quietly as he could, he took the luger in hand and crept out of the truck bed, trying to stay on its centerline so it wouldn't move under his shifting weight.

Shoeless, he crept to the passenger door. A dim light shone through the window, so he moved away, out of its range.

He needn't have worried about being seen. Otto had removed the bench seat and pushed it out onto the hood through the open windshield and was completely absorbed in attacking the crate of gold bars. The breaking sounds Eric had heard were the nailed wooden crate being pried open. Otto held the gray top in both hands as he looked closely at the black lettering. "Deutsche Reichsbank" identified it as the property of the German central bank.

Just as he reached the door, intending to pull it open and confront Otto, he saw the priest knock on the back window of the cab.

"Eric! Eric! Get up quickly. Come see what we have!"

Pistol in hand, Eric opened the door and said roughly, "just what the fuck do you think you're doing?"

"Don't you know about this? Your uncle told me I could take two bars back to Memmingen with me, and you can do the same. See, they packed this crate with four extra bars. That's two kilos of gold for each of us. It's worth more than a major earns in an entire year."

"That's not our gold to take. It belongs to the Reich."

"But the Governor-General said we could have two bars for all our work and danger. Didn't he tell you?"

Eric paused. "He did say there would be a gift for me, but I think he meant I would get it in Paris. How much did you say it is worth?"

"He told me each bar is a kilo. At the official rate each of them would be worth more than 1,100 U.S. dollars. He suggested I take it to Switzerland and exchange it for Swiss francs."

Eric holstered his pistol, still suspicious, but Otto had so many details that the story could be true. Just maybe.

"I have to believe you because I was told to expect some sort of gift. Let's nail the crate back together and get the truck ready in case we have to leave on short notice." Eric watched Otto put the two bars in the side pockets of his uniform jacket, then pound the nails he'd removed back into the walls of the crate.

"I'm going back to bed."

When he woke the sun was up. Otto hummed softly as he worked at the alcohol stove.

"You should have waked me for my shift," Eric said sharply to him.

"I thought I'd upset you so much already that you'd prefer to sleep. Anyway, I wasn't a bit sleepy."

They shared an ordinary breakfast of eggs and potatoes, washed down by the dreadful ersatz coffee. When they'd finished Otto took the dishes to the brook and scrubbed them in the cold water.

"Dishes are clean but I'm not. I think I'll wash up and take a nap. We'll be here all day?"

"Yes, we can't leave until dark. I haven't heard any bombers but they could come any time. Don't go all the way into the stream. It's running too fast."

"I'll just wash up on the bank," Otto replied.

He carefully hung the heavy uniform coat on the lowest branch of a tree at the water's edge. Then he removed his undershirt and laid it on the coat.

Eric asked himself how anyone could allow himself to gain so much weight, and how he found the food it would take to provide so many calories, although he suspected he knew the answer. At least three rolls of fat danced above his belt. A good match for his three chins, Eric thought.

He watched Otto drop to his knees, then reach down with both hands, splashing the cold water under each arm and then all over his face and head. He moved at the moment Otto leaned further out over the stream.

As he splashed his face a second time, Eric grabbed the back of his neck in a vise grip and forced his head under the water. He put his right knee on Otto's back and forced his chest to the ground. Otto thrashed and kicked for more than a minute. When he was still, Eric counted another two minutes second by second, then released his grip and stood up. Otto's head hung loosely under the surface of the water. His dead hands floated back and forth in the current.

Eric rinsed his hands. "A pederast I could accept," he said gently to the body. "A thief, perhaps. But not both."

He took the gold bars from Otto's pockets and returned them quickly to the crate under the seat, nailing it tight. Then he pulled Otto's heavy body from the water and dressed him. The undershirt was hardest to manage, but when he was done he had the fully dressed corpse of a lieutenant, with no visible sign of how he had died. With difficulty, he carried the body to a clump of bushes a dozen yards away and laid it face down where it could not easily be seen from the dirt track they'd used to enter from the highway.

I should bury him, Eric said to himself. But the animals won't get him for a day and I'll be miles away. He moved the truck a few hundred yards closer to the highway so he wouldn't be near the priest's body if someone stumbled on it. As night fell he drove back onto the highway and pointed south toward Memmingen, but as he neared Augsburg a military police car stopped him to warn that there were air raids further south.

"Memmingen," he asked?

"They're raiding the airfield," said the MP sergeant, a dour north German who'd been very suspicious of Hans Frank's laissez-passer. "Go there if you want, but it will be dangerous."

Eric looked closely at the map and found a route that would take him directly across France to Paris. He took inventory of his food and spare fuel and decided getting the treasure to Paris before it fell to the Allies was more important than a visit to his mother, and without Otto there was no other reason to visit Memmingen. He would see his mother after the war ended.

He stopped for the first day in the Schwarzwald and the second in a municipal forest near the small town of Chatêau-Thierry, an hour's drive outside Paris. Two hours before sunset he began the final leg, anxious to arrive before the curfew because he wasn't certain how much weight the laissez-passer would carry in Paris. Hans Frank had many enemies in the Wehrmacht, and he was far away.

Coming from the south, he avoided the busy Porte d'Orleans, instead taking the Rue de la Tombe Issoire, turning into Rue Hallé a block south of the tiny street where he'd lived in the poor Hôtel Saint-Pierre. "I'd better be certain the old bastard has a room for me tomorrow," he muttered.

A hundred meters and he turned under the carved-stone archway of a rundown apartment building that hid a second equally squalid building behind it, and behind that a defunct auto repair shop. Its owner had gone out of business soon after the Germans requisitioned all private cars in 1940 and he'd quickly found there was no living to be made repairing bicycles. He drove into one of the unused repair bays and closed the door behind him, then changed from his lieutenant's uniform to the worker's clothing he'd worn for his job at the gallery. Only when he was no longer recognizable as a German soldier did he remove the truck seat and carefully take out the crate of gold bars, which he wrapped in a blanket.

He muscled the 55-pound crate up the winding stairs to the narrow landing on the third floor, then deposited it as quietly as he could in front of the right-hand door. A tired-looking woman apologized as she shepherded a small boy by him on her way to the floor above. He knocked — two sharp raps, a pause, two more — and waited for his sometimes girlfriend Édith to open the door.

"Where have you been? I haven't seen you in two weeks." She smiled but her tone was sharp. He normally visited her at least twice a week and wanted more but her husband sometimes came home on the weekend from his job as a traveling salesman. Eric was suspicious that the agricultural equipment was a cover story but didn't push the issue with Édith.

"Can I stay tonight? I'm just back from Poland and I have to deliver a truck tomorrow."

"A truck?"

"My boss bought one and sent me to pick it up. The Wehrmacht let him have an old Citroën for deliveries, but I had to drive it back all the way from Poland."

"What's in the blanket?" she asked.

"My pay for the trip. It's heavy, so don't try to pick it up or you'll hurt yourself." He pushed the crate to the back of a closet in her unkempt living room and closed the door firmly. She pulled a battered wooden chair out from the decrepit table that separated the corner kitchen from the tiny living room and sat down. "I'll show it to you tomorrow after I get back from delivering the truck. Right now I'm exhausted. Is there anything to eat?"

"Nothing. I was going to go out to one of the neighborhood places."

"Don't. There's some food in the truck. It's German army chow but we shouldn't let it go to waste and besides we can spend the time better if we stay here." He leered at her. She smiled back.

He ran quickly down the stairs and returned with all the remaining food — Uncle Hans had been generous. There was enough to last them for several days, so long as they could eat sausages, potatoes and dried eggs. He wrapped it in the remaining blankets, which he planned to share with her.

When he got back to the third floor the door stood ajar the way he'd left it. He found her sitting in the same chair and laid the package before her. "All this came with the truck. They gave me a lot because nobody was sure how long the drive would take. Let's enjoy it while we can."

Édith slowly fried the dry sausages until they gave up a little fat, then threw in potatoes. When they were done she added the dried eggs and water, stirring until she had made a recognizable omelet. She added a slice each of the dark bread, then put the dinner on the table with a half-bottle of red wine that had been open too long. They ate in silence until she pushed back from the table and said sardonically, "Vive le Wehrmacht."

Then she took his hand and led him into the bedroom.

CHAPTER SEVENTEEN

The Count

Château Tours

"And after he brought the truck you never saw him again?"

The old man looked away at a corner of the room before he turned to answer Eddie's question.

"He was supposed to come back to work the next day, but he didn't show up. Then two years later he appeared at the gallery and said I owed him wages from 1944. I did owe him for a few days, but I felt sorry for him and gave him two weeks, sort of severance, even though times were tight for me then and my wife gave me hell for it. He really looked rough, but two years in Santé would do that to anybody. The Count spent six months there and died only a month or two after they let him out."

"He was in Santé?"

"His girlfriend wasn't what she seemed. She and her husband were both in the Resistance, and when Eric left to deliver the truck that morning she ran to tell her friends about him. When he came back she was gone, the gold was gone, and two men were waiting for him. They spirited him down into the old quarries near the catacombs with some other collaborators they'd captured and kept him there until after the Liberation. He was one of the first to be tried, and there was serious thought of just shooting him, but in the end he got a sentence of two years at Santé. He came to see me as soon as he got out."

"Did the Count ever say anything more about the painting?" Eddie looked at Aurélie, hope in his eyes. She shook her head slowly to say he shouldn't expect luck that good.

"He acted like he didn't know what Eric had brought from Poland. When he got out of prison in 1945 he sent me a note saying I could have the truck if I wanted it, and I went over to see him and look at it. His daughter told me his health was very bad, and I shouldn't bring up thc past.

"But I did ask him. He told me he had called his contact with the SS and an officer had come with a driver to get the truck the next day. A couple of days later they brought it back and put it back in his garage. The bed had been repaired, and it was a foot lower than it was when I first saw it."

Aurélie asked him, "Do you think he was telling you the truth?"

"In his position I'd have told the same story. Anyone would have.

"I hired a mechanic to get it running again and brought it back to the gallery, where I used it for a couple of years and finally sold it."

Aurélie said, "A daughter? Tell us more about her."

"Yes. A lovely girl, pretty notorious. She went around with a Saudi prince who was supposed to be the unofficial ambassador to Vichy, even though the Saudis had broken off relations with Germany before Poland and were sort of passive allies of the Americans, in return for protection. He preferred Paris to Vichy — who would blame him? — although he went home right after the war. Somebody told me he was one of 2,000 princes and had a family back there. They had a child, a son.

"It turned out that she was a Communist and a member of the Resistance, and had funneled back a lot of pillow talk he'd picked up from the Germans. She wound up getting the Order of Liberation from DeGaulle himself. That would have killed her poor father if he hadn't already died. He was an unrepentant Nazi until his last breath. She became a Gaullist — hell, everybody did, even me — and she was a big deal in Paris society for a while. But when her son came of age he moved back among the Arabs and her health began to fail, and she finally died in the seventies. Nobody wanted a house that grand right next to the railroad tracks, so they tore it down to build new apartments, and that was the end of the story."

Eddie asked him, "Did they look through the house for the painting?"

"I imagine so. When the daughter died everything was sold and the house stood vacant for a couple of years before it was torn down. It's probably in a bank vault somewhere, waiting for the right owner to show up."

"You wouldn't have any idea where that vault might be?"

"Me? Hardly. I was never on anything but commercial terms with the Nazis. If I knew where it was I'd have figured out a way to get it earlier, when it would have done me more good."

"And Eric. Did you ever hear from him again?"

"Not directly. When DeGaulle came back to power in 1958 the government was in chaos, a mess. It was all he could do to handle the rebellion in the colonies, so he did his best to close the books on some of the old postwar issues. That winter a couple of men from one of the new intelligence services came to see me at the gallery and asked about him. I told them about the truck, which they seemed to know about already. They didn't know where we had taken it and I let them think Eric had driven it away alone. They did tell me that five crates of gold were nailed into a fake bed. That would be worth a lot of money today.

"The standard Reichsbank crate held twenty-five one-kilo bars. That would have been worth almost thirty thousand dollars to Eric, if he'd been able to get away with it. God knows what it would be worth today."

Aurélie did the math quickly and said, "Almost nine hundred ounces. Each of them is now worth nine hundred dollars, so a crate would now be worth almost a million dollars. The price has tripled since 2001. So that's why this whole thing came back to life now?"

"It confirms what Sonny told the police," Eddie replied. Then he said to Jacques, "I believe we're beginning to understand what's happened, but please go on about Eric Kraft."

Jacques continued, "Anyway, these intelligence men told me something of Eric's life after the war, including the prison term. After I saw him he went looking for his old girlfriend and found her, along with her husband, in Lyon. He killed both of them but didn't find the gold he'd left with her. They told him the Resistance had traded it for several of their colleagues the Nazis had arrested and were threatening to kill. He cut their throats and set fire to their apartment. Burned down the whole building.

"And then he headed east. First he stopped at Memmingen to see his mother, but she'd been killed in an American air raid at about the same time he would have been there. Then he went on to Berlin and landed in the Russian sector, where he joined the secret police, who were glad to have him — he had their kind of skills. I never heard anything more about him."

The old man turned to knock the ashes out of his pipe into an ashtray with a cork knob in the center.

"He's dead by now."

The sound of the heavy briar pipe against the cork knob reverberated against the walls, like the sound of a drum far away.

Eddie said, "He died in Frankfurt during the eighties but he left behind a son who's very much a chip off the old block. He's the one we're trying to find now."

Jacques leaned forward almost imperceptibly and turned his head away from them to study the ceiling. His mouth moved slightly, then closed.

Eddie moved to ask another question but Aurélie held up her hand.

The grandfather clock ticked slowly, until Jacques broke the silence.

"I think I can help you," he said. "God knows I shouldn't, but enough people have died."

He looked directly into Aurélie's eyes, then at Eddie.

"Eric's son came to see me not two weeks ago. He was pleasant enough, but I could see the mean streak under the surface. The deformed ear wasn't the only thing he had in common with his father."

He made them wait while he went to refill the teapot, then carefully poured each of them a fresh cup.

"Erich came here unannounced a week ago last Thursday." Eddie and Aurélie looked at each other — that was the day they'd been accosted by the two Germans outside the Hôtel Chopin.

"He introduced himself and told me his father had been grateful I gave him more money than I owed him. He said he and his friends thought they were very close to finding the Raphael and a lot of gold that his father had brought to Paris at the same time. He just wanted to know if I could add anything, because his boss had found a buyer for the painting in China, or maybe Russia. In any case, to one of the new billionaires.

"He was only interested in the day his father and I took the truck to the Count, and I told him just what I told you.

"But…" He pushed himself upright and walked to an ornate marble-topped chest near the front door. "I was feeling lightheaded that day, not very sharp. You try being 92 years old and you'll soon see it's no bed of roses. It's just better than the alternative.

"I told him I would probably feel stronger the next day and I'd try to think of more about the Count. He gave me his phone number and asked me to call him. He said I'd have to leave a message but he would call me back."

He pulled a slip of paper from a drawer and handed it to Eddie. "This may help you. Please don't tell him I gave it to you. I may be old but I'd prefer to grow older yet."

Aurélie asked, "Did he threaten you?"

"No. He was on his good behavior. He knew my situation here and told me there would be a reward if I helped them find the treasure. I wouldn't have any objection to that, but I just don't know anything more."

"Did you call him?"

"The next day. He called me back in a couple of hours and I told him I couldn't think of anything else I hadn't told him, but I would call again."

"Who answered the phone?"

"It may have been a restaurant or a shop. Anyway, it sounded like there were some people there, but they weren't loud. I'm pretty sure I heard some Arabic in the background, although the man who answered the phone spoke good French."

Eddie and Aurélie spent the train ride back to Paris rehashing their conversation with Jacques. Paul, as usual, sat in the car behind.

"Do you think Jacques told us everything he knows?" Eddie asked.

"No, but I think he gave us enough to let us figure out the rest. And I think what he told us was the truth. He seems really sad to be at the center of something that's caused so much unhappiness.

"That expression 'rise like Lazarus' interested me. You don't hear it a lot these days. The Count's townhouse was not that far from Gare Saint-Lazare. Maybe that's the connection."

"It certainly could be," Eddie said. "And Saint-Lazare — St. Lazarus — was supposed to have been the first bishop of Marseille after he was raised from the grave, so there's a French connection, or maybe it was just hot air. What we really need now is the chance to squeeze Erich."

She laid her hand on Eddie's arm and smiled. "It shouldn't take much detective work to find him, if that's what you want."

"You know damned well I want him in hell," he responded sharply. She pulled her hand away quickly. "Sorry. It's just something I have to do. Erich must have a string-puller somewhere, and it sounds like neither of them will rest until they find what they want. I need to find Erich first, then his puppetmaster."

"I know Philippe will be glad to hear what happened today. It will make his job easier."

Eddie said, "I'll see him in the morning. It would be good if you were there too. Can you do it?"

"Classes in the morning. Instead, let's have dinner. That way you and I can fill in each other's gaps. I'll set it up. We probably should invite Margaux."

They parted when the train pulled into Gare Montparnasse. Eddie and Paul went separately to the Luxor to make plans for the next day.

"Aurélie's going to set up a dinner so we can brief Philippe together. In the meantime, we need to find out how Erich gets messages at the number Jacques gave us."

Paul replied, "That won't be the last number in the loop. Either it will be forwarded somewhere else, or the person who answers it calls another number. Either way, we have to start with what we have. I'll find out."

The number started with 01, which meant it was a Paris landline. Eddie went down the hall to the bathroom while Paul used the reverse directory on his iPhone to find out where it was installed. When he returned Paul had just finished writing the address in his small pocket Moleskine notebook.

"Sort of what I thought. It's an Internet cafe on Rue Montparnasse, just down the street from the gare. I've passed it dozens of times, and I know you have, too."

"Should we pay them a visit? Like right now?"

"Why not? If we hurry we might catch the owner, rather than a night clerk."

"I'll have the desk get a cab."

The cab dropped them at the corner of Boulevard Montparnasse and Rue Montparnasse. They walked up the one-way street looking for the Internet café on their left. They passed a crêperie, then a second, and Paul said, "If you like crêpes this is the place. Thousands of ironworkers from Brittany lived in this area while they were building the Eiffel Tower and the rest of the 1889 exposition, and they brought their food with them."

His wife was a Breton, and proud of it. She was one of just a few hundred thousand people still able to speak Breton, a celtic language imported from Cornwall and Wales that had little or nothing in common with French. Although she was a long-lapsed Catholic, she still reserved one Sunday every month or two for services at Notre-Dame du Travail, whose exposed armature, it was said, had been constructed with iron left over from the tower. There were differing opinions about whether M. Eiffel knew about his gift.

"We come over here at least every couple of weeks, mainly for the crêpes. The cider, too." Breton restaurants were famous for their hard cider. "I've seen this Internet café and it seems less seedy than most."

"It's probably offering this message service as a moneymaker and doesn't ask if all its customers are legal," Eddie said. "We'll have to pay for the information we need."

They agreed Eddie would do the talking, as Paul's accent would immediately mark him as American. "I'll stand in the background and look menacing," he said.

Three phone booths stood inside the door on the left and a dozen computers stretched along three counters on the right. A bored-looking man, paunchy and balding, stood behind a counter near the phone booths, looking warily at two strangers better dressed than most of his clients, who tended to be young or foreign or both, but not affluent.

Eddie pushed open the glass door and stepped inside the store. A middle-aged man with a mustache looked at him from one of the phone booths with interest but not hostility. The three young men at computers did not look up from their video games.

The man behind the counter shifted from foot to foot as he eyed them warily. He thinks we're the police, Eddie thought. Let's let him keep thinking that.

"Excuse me for disturbing you, sir," Eddie said, his tone colder than his words. "Your telephone number has come up in a search for a man we must find, and we are here to ask for your help." He had written the number in his Moleskine notebook, and laid it on the counter. "Is this the telephone number of this establishment?"

The man was growing more nervous by the minute. He pulled the notebook toward him and adjusted his glasses. "Yes, that is my number." Two paces behind Eddie, Paul looked directly at the man, his face closed.

"And may I know your name, please? Write it in the book below the number." Unwillingly, the man did so. "Now write for me your home address, please."

When he had finished Eddie took the book back and looked at the page. "Monsieur" — he looked at the name — "Arobas. This is a confidential investigation and you must not repeat to anyone what we ask you or what you have told us. Do you understand that?" The man gulped and nodded.

Eddie turned to Paul and held out the notebook. Paul ostentatiously copied the page into his own. Then Eddie turned back to M. Arobas.

"You receive from time to time telephone messages at this number from a man you know as Erich. I must know what you do with those messages."

The man immediately relaxed, overjoyed to learn they were only after one of his customers. He'd been afraid they were, the dreaded tax police, for whom almost any tax evasion merits time in prison.

"Oui," he said, looking first at Eddie and then at Paul. "I receive calls from time to time for Monsieur Erich. His instructions to me are to immediately call another number and pass the message on to the person at that number. He does not receive many calls."

Eddie opened his book again and said, "Please write that number in my book." The man reached under the counter for a small file box and extracted an index card, which he consulted before writing a number in the book. Then he slid it back over the counter to Eddie. He displayed the card, which contained only the name Erich and a Parisian 01 telephone number. Paul again duplicated the information.

"Thank you for your cooperation," Eddie told him. "If all you have told us is accurate and you do not tell anyone else of our visit, you will not see us again."

Back on Rue Montparnasse they walked toward the Gaîté métro station, where both could catch trains home.

Paul asked tentatively, "How much do you want to tell Philippe?"

"Ultimately, everything. The question is, How much do we want to tell Philippe before dinner tomorrow? The answer to that is, not much. I'd like to find Erich first, because Philippe is going to lock him away and keep him from the Sarasota prosecutors just the way they've kept him from Al Sommers and Sonny Perry.

"How would you feel about trying to get him tomorrow?"

"Great, but time is pretty short."

Eddie thought a minute, then said, "We could set up a fake meeting with Jacques, but Jacques would have to be in on the planning because Erich's likely to call him for a confirmation. Let's take a chance that he checks the message drop every day and go watch it. Can you find out where the number is installed?"

"Easy." Paul went to the Pages Jaunes site on his iPhone and typed the number into the reverse directory. In a minute he looked up and said, "A place called Café Stop, in the 18th not too far from

Barbés-Rochechouart. It's probably one of the many workers' cafés in the neighborhood. Let's go take a look at it."

They stood under the elevated track of the 2 train to get their bearings.

"It's a few hundred yards north," Paul said, leading Eddie up the busy Boulevard Barbés. At sunset, its sidewalk cafés were crowded, many with North African men having coffee or a drink before going up to their tight apartments in the buildings looming over them. A satellite dish hung on each balcony next to the laundry.

Idly, Eddie asked, "Do you think the Muslims would integrate better if they didn't watch the foreign TV channels?"

"Probably," Paul said. "My wife thinks so, and she has some Arab blood from several generations ago. But most of them don't speak French. Almost none of the women do, so they'd have to work at it, and their husbands want them at home. Look at me — I learned French late, and it was rough."

They turned right on Rue Suez, a narrow one-way street of plain-front apartment buildings with North African hair salons and small groceries specializing in vegetables and fish on their ground floors. Halfway down the block they saw Le Stop, its name emblazoned in fading gold on a blue awning that protected a half-dozen men drinking small cups of black coffee.

"If he comes by now we're screwed," Paul said. "But I suggest we just walk into that hotel across the street from it and rent a room on the front."

"OK with me. The desk clerk'll just think we're a couple of foreign perverts."

Paul paid cash for a double room on the second floor. Its single window was covered by a sagging once-white shade that slapped in the light breeze. Le Stop was directly across the street, but its awning prevented them from seeing most of the coffee drinkers. They would have two chances to spot Erich — once as he went under the awning and once when he emerged from its cover. A weak street light bolted to the hotel wall above their window cast a violet shadow on the curb in front of Le Stop. It darkened as the sun fell steadily toward the horizon, deepening the shadows filling the narrow cavern of Rue

Suez. By eleven o'clock there would be only the street lights and a few lighted shop windows and bars for illumination.

Paul sat on the edge of the double bed while Eddie took up his position in a folding chair. They raised the window as far as it would go to get more air, then checked to be certain they were in the shadows and couldn't be seen from the street.

"At least it was cheap," Paul said.

"Hotels get stars based mainly on the size of their rooms, plus amenities," Eddie responded. "This is a no-star, and always will be."

A couple walked arm in arm under the awning from the left and a few seconds later emerged from the other side.

Every fifteen minutes or so a single man would leave, but replacements came only half as often and most of those stayed less than a half hour. At eleven-thirty a thin man wearing a white taguiya came out from under the awning and began to raise it, using a crank he fitted into a socket in the wall. As it rose, they saw the tables and chairs under it were empty, except for one against the wall next to the entrance. Two bearded men sat talking, one with a wine glass of the distinctive balloon shape used for Bordeaux, the other — also wearing a white lace prayer cap — with a small coffee cup.

The two stood, then went into the restaurant. Seconds later, a light came on in the window above the awning. Paul and Eddie ducked instinctively until they realized at the same time that their window would be just another dark rectangle viewed from a lighted room across the street. "Jumpy, aren't we?" Eddie said with a chuckle.

The men came into view as they walked across the room, then sat down at a table in the center of the room under a bare bulb. The man wearing the taguiya carefully counted ten green 100-Euro notes, then picked up the stack and handed it across the table. The other man counted them again carefully before putting them into a wallet he extracted from the pocket of a brown jacket. He extended his hand across the table for a perfunctory shake, then rose to leave. As he turned away from the window they saw the notch prominently missing from his right ear, starkly silhouetted against the white wall.

"Now's the time. We'll never have a better chance," Eddie said. His voice was as calm and cold as Paul remembered it in Kuwait. "We'll watch from the lobby to see which way he goes, then take him at the corner. If he goes to the right all the scaffolding around the building down the street will be the perfect place." A large apartment building fifty yards away was shrouded in scaffolding and netting for the cleaning and surface repairs the city mandates every ten years.

They watched Erich leave the café and turn to their right. He moved without haste, seemingly satisfied with his money and the wine. When he was thirty paces away they left. Eddie crossed the street to come up directly behind him while Paul stayed to provide cover from the other side. He walked fast, a man on his way to an important rendezvous, and quickly pulled abreast of Erich, who glanced at him once and then ignored him as he moved away.

Eddie's rubber-soled shoes enabled him to catch up with Erich almost silently, so by the time he reached the corner opposite the scaffolding Eddie was only ten yards behind, then five, as Erich headed for the covered sidewalk beneath the scaffolding. He became alarmed when Paul began to cross toward him, and as he put his hand into the right pocket of his trousers Eddie's hand gripped his wrist like a vise. Paul immediately grabbed his other arm and together they hustled him into the inky shadow of the scaffolding.

"And now we meet the famous Erich Kraft. Or Erich Wetzmuller. Or is it something else?" Eddie asked in English, tightening his grip on Erich's right arm.

"Fuck you."

Eddie's voice dropped an octave to a menacing growl. "Understand this," he said. "This is not about me. This is about the people you've killed and injured. Roy Castor, most recently. My father. My wife and son. The innocent desk clerk at the Hôtel Chopin. God knows who else."

"I don't know anything about any of that."

"Think about something before you take that line. Did you know I killed Dmitri? With my hands? I could do the same to you and sleep like a baby.

"I could turn you over to the Paris police and you'd spend forever in their rat-infested prison system. Or I could take you back to Florida and turn you over to the Sarasota police. That might be the best. Florida still has the electric chair, and I understand they like to use it. Or you can answer my questions and walk away and deal with your own nightmares in your own way. Which will it be?"

Erich sat silently.

"What do you want to know?" he finally asked.

"Everything, from the first time you met Albert Sommers."

He thought again. "And you mean you'll let me go? I can look out for myself."

"You can walk down this street, go back to Germany, wherever."

Then, without prompting, Erich confirmed most of what Eddie had picked up from Philippe and Carole Westin. He told how a man in Paris, whom he wouldn't name, had told him that Al Sommers had a lead on some leftover Nazi treasure and was looking for help in finding it. He knew Erich had an American green card and offered him expenses plus wages and part of the profits for finding out what Sommers wanted and leading the project.

"I thought Sommers was nuts, but he did seem to have some good information. He knew about this old fellow in Paris who knew about the painting, and he knew how the top Nazis had thought, so he was pretty sure there would be hard goods with it, maybe even gold bullion. Al told me his friends Sonny and Dmitri would help me when the time came.

"While I was there I got Jennifer to vouch for me and help me get citizenship. She was pissed that I took her name, but I didn't have much choice. The Krafts were too well known to Interpol. I'd been visited once or twice by German intelligence. They were trying to make sure I hadn't linked up with any of the guys my father had run in his Stasi days."

"Is she part of the gang?" Eddie asked.

"Her? She's just a woman. She just wanted the money. Al told her he'd give her $100,000 of the proceeds if she'd help with my citizenship and a few other errands. I never knew exactly what. And she liked what I had to give her, too."

He told of returning to Paris and telling his boss he needed a safe house to question the man Sommers wanted targeted. "He was old, so we figured he wouldn't put up much of a fight. My boss gave us part of a warehouse he rented in Rennes. That's after I found out this Mr. Grant went out there every month. Was he your father?"

"He was."

"I'm sorry he died. It shouldn't have happened that way. We took him at the Rennes station, in the car rental parking lot, and tied him up in this warehouse. We'd lined the floor and walls with plastic just in case. He just wouldn't talk. He wouldn't tell us anything. We questioned him a couple of hours until he passed out. Then I went outside for a smoke and to figure out the next step. I told Dmitri and Sonny to watch him, but he waked up and that Russian idiot decided he'd scare him by putting a plastic bag over his head. The idea was to threaten to suffocate him. But just after I got back he had a heart attack and died. We ran his car into a tree in a park nearby and burned it."

Erich told how he'd reported the death back to his boss, who was furious about it. He was angriest at Dmitri and Sonny, whom he hadn't wanted to use at all, preferring his own Russian or German muscle, but he was also furious at Erich for leaving the room.

He told Erich that when he reported Artie's death Sommers already knew about it from Sonny's telephone call.

"He called the whole deal off. I didn't hear another word about it until my boss sent me to Sarasota to snatch Roy Castor. But this time our men went with me. He wasn't about to take the risk of Al's amateur hour again, and told him so."

Eddie asked, "Then tell me about my wife and son."

"I knew it happened after, but I wasn't involved in it, God help me. I'd never even heard of you until Al called me a couple of weeks ago. All I knew was when my boss told me he'd had a couple of noirs killed. It wasn't nothing to me."

Before the sentence ended, Eddie struck him violently with the back of his left hand, breaking his nose, which bled copiously through his beard and down the front of his shirt. Erich didn't flinch or complain.

"Now tell us about Roy Castor."

"Al called my boss and said he wanted to try again on another old geezer who'd worked with your father. He told us where to be and called when the mark was on the way. I didn't figure he'd be strong enough to get loose, much less that he'd run straight into the car and get killed. We got out of town as soon as Sonny could take us to the airport."

"And the next step?" Eddie asked.

"Pick up that semi-sister of mine in Paris, and you as well if we could. The idiots working for me reached for the wrong woman and got the timing all off, and they sure didn't count on you knowing hand-to-hand like that." He looked up with grudging admiration.

"Why did you have to stab the hotel clerk?"

"He tried to stop me. I was following my guys until that happened, but I knew the cops would be there soon so I just left the car. Some of the Frogs beat me up pretty good but I finally managed to get away before the police got there. I know they're still looking for me, which is why I'm in this part of town. Don't worry — I'll be somewhere else tomorrow."

"One more question. Who's your boss?"

"That's the one thing I'll never tell you. I don't think you'll kill me, but he would if I told you anything that could lead back to him. I won't tell you."

Eddie thought for a moment, then said, "That's all, then. Walk north up this street and we'll go the other way. Before you leave, give me one of those 100-euro notes you got back above Le Stop."

"Why would I do that?"

"Because if you don't I'll hogtie you with your own belt and carry you to the police myself. And if you do I'll give you the 100 euros back. I just want one of those bills.

"Paul, can you give him the cash?"

"Sure." Paul reached into his wallet to extract two orange Euro notes and held them out to Erich, who pulled one of the 100s carefully from his pocket. Eddie kept his grip on Erich, but with his other hand reached for his own handkerchief, which he folded around the note without touching it and carefully returned to his pocket.

Then he pushed Erich away from him just strongly enough to keep him from pulling the knife in his pocket. Paul stepped aside as Erich staggered past.

"You should hope you never see me again," Eddie told him in a level voice.

They waited until Erich was 50 yards away, then started back down Rue Suez toward Le Stop.

"I'm going in to see the owner," Eddie said to Paul. "You wait on the street just in case. It won't take long."

The bearded man in the prayer cap was sweeping the floor when they arrived. Most of the lights were off but the door opened to Eddie's push.

"We are closed, monsieur," the owner said.

"I have something to show you."

He reached into his pocket and pulled out the handkerchief, opening it so the man could see the banknote.

"You gave this note less than an hour ago, in the room directly above us, to a man with the first name of Erich, and several last names, and he gave it to me. It has both his fingerprints and yours. In fifteen minutes it will be in the hands of the security police. That is all I wish to say to you, other than good night." He backed away from the shocked owner, pulled open the door, and walked into the night. At the métro he bade Paul good night and picked up his iPhone to call Philippe who, he suspected, would not be pleased.

Philippe exploded. "You let him get away? What kind of idiotic thinking was that?"

"Before he got away I was able to get from him a 100-euro note with his fingerprints and the prints of the man who gave it to him, the owner of a café called Le Stop on Rue Suez. I suspect they will lead you where you want to go. Would you like me to bring the banknote to you now? It's pretty new, so you should be able to find the prints easily."

"No. Take it to the prefecture. I'll call them about it. I'm sorry he got away. I'm sure you are, too."

"I hope you can catch him. He deserves even more than you can do to him."

"We can do a lot to his type, but the fingerprints are all we can do tonight, I suppose. Take the note to the prefecture right away, and

I'll see you at dinner tomorrow night. Margaux will decide where we go. Check with her."

He took the métro to Châtelet then walked the two blocks to the prefecture. At the door two uniformed policemen stood guard. He approached the older one.

"M. l'agent," he began politely. "I have just spoken to Commissioner Cabillaud and he has asked me to bring this evidence to you. He will call the appropriate officer with instructions." He held out his handkerchief and the 100-euro note so the befuddled policeman could see it. "He has asked that I meet him immediately, so may I ask you to deliver this to the senior officer on duty tonight?"

The policeman was suspicious that Eddie could not deliver the note himself and resisted, but his younger colleague finally said, "I'll take it in." He held out his hand for the handkerchief, then turned and went into the building.

Eddie turned and left, relieved. He did not think Philippe would order him questioned but he didn't want to take any chances, so he went home as quickly as he could.

Jacques had hinted strongly that the treasure might never have left the Count's house, that the SS contact was imaginary. Even though he was an enthusiastic and well-known collaborator he would have been suspect, especially among the anti-Frank contingent in the German Army, which was strong. And the Germans were scrambling like rats trying to find a way off their sinking ship. The odds were high that he had never called the SS.

Aurélie found that the house had been sold in 1979, then almost immediately torn down and replaced with an apartment building. But the new building was built on only part of the property. The Count's ancestors had assembled several parcels between 1770 and 1775 and added more just as the legal system was changing to the Code Napoléon. In 1865 a strip of the property was sold to the French government for installation of new tracks into Gare Saint-Lazare. As a result of all the purchases and sales, title to part of the lot was no longer clear. An additional disadvantage was that the grand townhouse overlooked the deep trench housing the railroad tracks.

The buyer decided to build the new apartment building on the part to which he had unquestioned title, which happened to coincide with the cellar, so he built the building over the existing two-story basement, reducing his construction costs substantially. The upper level he subdivided into storage for his tenants, the second he held in reserve. He had planned to build a restaurant on the other part of his land as soon as he received clear title, but by the time that happened France was deep in the recession of the 1980s and there was no appetite for financing a restaurant. Before the recession ended he died and his widow rented the lot to a restaurant across the street, which paved it for parking.

"And you got all this information where?" Eddie asked as he carried two espressos from the kitchen into his study, where they had spread their papers on the desk. They had just finished their lunch of fritto misto, small fried fish, with a cucumber salad and a glass each of Pinot Noir.

"From city hall. An old friend of Philippe's works in the office that issues building permits. Actually, I guess he runs it. His name is Jerôme Fontainbleu. I called him before class this morning, and by the time the class was over he had found the old construction plans from 1980 and described them to me. To get a building permit you have to write an essay about what you're doing and why, so that's the most likely source of the background. Plus the fact that he was a young inspector at the time and saw the building go up."

"Damn, you're good," he said in admiration.

Eddie had spent the morning at his language school reviewing the last month's results with his accountant. Aurélie taught a long seminar on Louis XIV. They had agreed they would meet at his apartment at 1 p.m. to organize their findings and decide what action they would request of Philippe at dinner that night. Eddie would bring in lunch.

"Good job picking out lunch, by the way," Aurélie said. "A lot of the stuff the Italian carryout places sell is too heavy."

With a smile, he reached out to touch the back of her hand softly. "Where do you think this leaves us?"

"Hard to say, but I told Jerôme what we're looking for and he'd put money on the lower level of that cellar. He never knew the old

Count or the daughter but he thinks the same thing Jacques seemed to believe, that the Count would keep the treasure under his own control. And then he was arrested, then died a few months later. He may not have told anyone what he had. What good would it be to the Fourth Reich if the new Hitler didn't know about it, whoever he turned out to be?"

"Maybe it wasn't for the Fourth Reich after all. Maybe it was Hans Frank's own golden parachute. When he got away from the Russians he must have thought he was home free. I know from my father's interview notes that his death sentence was a big shock to him."

"Any of that could be true," Aurélie said. "Maybe he figured Eric Kraft was enough. After all, he was the son of his own sister. Things get very confused in wartime, loyalties get switched around or forgotten. We may be searching for an answer that doesn't exist. In any case, we probably need to look at that cellar. The question is, do we go there on our own and try to talk our way in, or do it with the backing of the French police?"

"In this case I think we need to get the police involved. I've pissed off Philippe more than enough for one day." He explained his and Paul's meeting with Erich the night before.

"So you just let him go?"

"Well, I got his fingerprints and the identity of his contact. I suspect they're both already in custody by now, if one of them hasn't taken things into his own hands."

"You mean … "

"Let's just see what happens."

She turned away from him for a moment. "Then you think we should bring this up with Philippe tonight?"

"That's certainly one approach. How does it strike you?"

"Good. It's the right way."

"Then let's do it that way."

Eddie and Aurélie walked arm in arm from Rue Saint-Roch across the river to Les Ministères, a favorite. "I seem to spend a lot of time walking down this street," he said.

"Is this how you used to come to meet me at la Sorbonne?" she asked.

"Almost every time. It's one of my favorite walks."

"Maybe we can start that up again."

At precisely nine o'clock he pushed open the door and waited for her to enter. The waiter recognized both of them and was surprised and pleased to see them together. He led them immediately to a banquette off to one side, where Margaux and Paul were already seated, a bottle of champagne open between them.

Eddie stooped to buss his mother, followed by Aurélie. Margaux noticed immediately that she was wearing almost no makeup and jumped to the conclusion that she and Eddie were a couple again. "Bon!" she said softly, just to Aurélie.

"I'm glad you're here," Margaux said to the group. "Philippe said he'd have to be about a half-hour late because something came up. Aurélie, he said he tried to call to tell you."

"Sorry. I've had the phone turned off while Édouard and I went over all the things we need to discuss with Philippe." She reached into her purse to turn it back on and glanced guiltily at Eddie.

Margaux had told the waiter Philippe would be late so he brought small plates of cheese pastries for them to snack on. The bottle of champagne quickly disappeared, and by the time the second was half finished Philippe sat down next to Margaux and immediately began talking.

"I hate to be late like this, especially for a table of beautiful women, but I thought you'd want to know what's happened. Eddie, you will be especially interested." Eddie looked at Aurélie and raised his eyebrows in interrogation but she shrugged to say she had no more information than he.

"Everyone, last night Eddie and Paul…" He looked meaningfully toward Paul, who didn't blink. "Eddie and Paul had a chance to talk to Erich Kraft. Erich got away, but they were alert enough to get his fingerprints on a 100-euro note as well as the fingerprints of the owner of a little restaurant in the 18th who gave it to him.

"Eddie took the note to the préfecture last night and I had them analyze the fingerprints immediately. Erich was indeed who we thought he was, but the restaurant owner turned out to be a terrorist named Hamid we've been looking for since the 90s. He'd been hiding in plain sight. To the public he was an upstanding citizen running a small business and keeping his nose clean.

"Except that he wasn't. We don't know yet who he was fronting for, but he was running some of Erich's activities on behalf of a third party. Not very often, but he did pay out a thousand euros last night.

"But that's all just a sidebar to the story. As soon as we identified his fingerprints we put watchers on his café. We used the hotel across the street — was that the one you used?" Eddie shrugged noncommittally. "We also tapped his phone."

"Early this morning he made a phone call to an anonymous cell number, which connected somewhere in the Gulf states — we'll know more about that tomorrow. A few hours later he received a call back from the same number, then he called a cell number, owner also unknown, and after that he left the café. He took the Line 4 and the tram all the way across town to Parc Montsouris. It's green and beautiful this time of year — Aurélie and her mother and I used to picnic there long ago — but he was all business. No waiting around, no admiring the scenery or the girls, no looking for a tail. He went straight to the old railroad track that runs across the park.

He turned to Paul. "I think everyone here knows about it, but just in case, there used to be a circle line around most of Paris called the petite ceinture, or little belt, much of it in a cut well below surface level. It couldn't run entirely in tunnels because it used steam engines, but it was deep enough not to be much of a bother to the residents around it. Its route was a short distance inside the path of the modern beltway."

Aurélie interrupted. "Aren't there openings to the catacombs in the tunnels of the petite ceinture in the 14th?"

"There are," Philippe replied. "But they don't make for easy access and our man is my age, so he'd have a hard time getting through them. Nevertheless we had the catacombs police on alert.

"Hamid found an access ladder where the security fence had already been breached. It's very overgrown along the track and it was too early for picnickers, so he had cover. He climbed down the ladder to the track level, then disappeared into the tunnel. We couldn't follow him down because there's nowhere in there to hide.

"We heard a loud scream, which ended suddenly, and after a few minutes he came walking back down the tracks. We waited until he'd got back to the surface and arrested him. At that moment we weren't quite sure what the charges would be, although he did have a lot of blood on him. Then some of us went back down the ladder."

Margaux smiled and said, "Must have been quite a climb for such an old man."

"You do what you have to do," he said, returning the smile.

"We walked down the tracks into the tunnel and about thirty yards in we found a body. Not an ordinary body, mind you. A body in two parts, a decapitated body. The head was on one side of the tracks, the torso on the other. There were no other injuries, so the victim must have been alive when his throat was cut."

"How awful," Aurélie said, covering her mouth with her hand.

"Awful for him, but there's more.

"Both ears and all the fingers had been cut off. Hamid obviously hadn't thought far enough ahead, because we found them in his pockets. I was late because I was waiting for the report from the fingerprint department. The head and the body belonged to Eric Kraft. There's no doubt about it."

Everyone at the table sat silently while the news sank in, then Philippe broke the silence.

"Eddie, is this the way you thought it would work out?"

"I'm not unhappy about it. It's no less than he deserved."

Dinner arrived and they turned their attention unenthusiastically to the lamb chops Margaux had ordered for everyone. In twenty minutes they began to share a plate of cheese and Philippe picked up the story again.

"As you can imagine, the café owner would tell us precisely nothing. He will go to jail for life for the murder but we won't learn anything more about it. Eddie, maybe you've had better luck. Did you learn anything from old Jacques?"

"Quite a lot," Eddie said. "We know now that Erich's father brought the painting and six wooden cases of gold bars from Krakow to Paris on behalf of Hans Frank, and that he delivered five of them plus the painting to a collaborator, an old Count who lived in the seventeenth. Getting that much took quite a long time and quite a lot of persuasion, mainly on Aurélie's part.

"But the most significant followup information came just today. Aurélie, why don't you explain what you found."

She detailed her conversation with Jerôme Fontainbleu, including his view that the treasure was probably hidden in the abandoned second basement under the apartment building.

"I know Jerôme, or at least I did once, and as I recall he was always pretty straight. But some of his co-workers aren't, so we'd better act quickly just in case they get wind of what might be there," Philippe said.

The plan he outlined was elegant in its simplicity. "If I go up the chain of command and tell them we think we've found millions of Euros worth of Nazi treasure the bureaucracy will be all over us and there's a huge chance the delay will let someone get ahead of us. On the other hand, if we go into the building using a slightly misleading but not illegal subterfuge, we can find out if the treasure is there for someone to take. If it is, I'll have uniformed officers secure the building and let the bureaucracy do its work. If it's not, we won't have raised any unreasonable hopes."

He proposed to contact his friend the chief fire inspector and ask that an inspector go to the apartment building the next day for a safety inspection. He would have a larger entourage than usual, but it shouldn't raise suspicions too much.

"Most people have no idea how much power the fire inspectors have in a city like Paris," he said. "Basically, they can go anywhere for any reason so long as there's a reasonable concern about public safety. We have so many people crowded together that, otherwise, we'd have a terrible risk of fire deaths. They are bad enough as it is.

"Is that OK with everyone?" No one disagreed.

"Good. Then let's have our dessert and coffee, and plan to meet at the Rome métro station at ten o'clock tomorrow morning. Aurélie, can you make it?"

"I'll have to reschedule, but a colleague owes me a class anyway. I'll be there."

Margaux said, "I think I'll wait for you to tell me the results. I couldn't add anything and would just get in the way."

She had ordered a light and soft chocolate mousse with fruit sauce for everyone but Eddie. "I knew you'd want the café gourmand."

"Right as always," he said. "Thanks."

Eddie paid the check — "You got the last one," he told Margaux sternly when she reached for it — and walked out onto Rue du Bac, the elegant seventh-arrondissement street connecting the Seine to Boulevard Raspail and the grand department store Bon Marché.

Eddie and Aurélie were the last to leave. On the sidewalk he looked at her and said, "Well?"

"I thought we settled that today, Édouard. Let's walk up to my place so I can pick up some things, then we'll go to the Luxor. You know my concerns, but I'm much more comfortable having seen how you handled Erich. Five years ago you'd either have called the police or killed him yourself and got in trouble. This was much more subtle. It took confidence. I like that. I think Philippe did, too, but he'll never tell you."

CHAPTER EIGHTEEN

Treasure of Saint-Lazare

Paris

Aurélie stood impatiently inside the door, bag in hand, dressed in slacks and walking shoes for what she expected to be a dirty visit to the past.

"Édouard," she called down the hall toward the bedroom. "We need to go now if you want to look at the tracks first."

"Call the elevator. I nearly forgot my camera." He came through the door, buckling a small leather camera bag on his belt. "I also had to change the flash battery."

The half-hour walk took them around the grand and gilded old opera, then down gritty Rue de Rome next to Gare Saint-Lazare.

The station, the second-busiest in Paris, was alive with activity. As always, the street was clogged with distinctive blue-green and white city buses and pedestrians crisscrossed the plaza in front of the nineteenth-century building, which was in the process of major renovation.

The entrance to the Rome métro station sits a few blocks behind the railroad station at the center of a small park dividing Boulevard des Batignoles. The Boulevard is one of the spokes radiating from Place de Clichy, where tourists and immigrants pass briefly through each other's lives on their way to or from the Butte Montmartre, the romantic home of painters and writers and Sacre-Coeur Basilica, or the immigrant areas beyond the Montmartre Cemetery.

Rather than turn right toward the Rome station, Eddie and Aurélie continued along the deep trench. They peered across it, looking for the apartment building constructed on the site of the Count's grand townhouse, and the parking lot next to it.

"That must be it," Eddie said, pointing to a seven-story building perched precisely on the edge of the trench.

"Deep," Aurélie said. "I never looked at it from this angle. The whole building would fit in the trench."

"The top floor or two might stick up, but that's about it."

Below them a steel catwalk extended across the nine tracks to a narrow fenced ledge that ran down the other side to the next catwalk. The walls had been carefully faced with stone cut and laid like bricks. Below the catwalks the stones were larger, and all bore the faded work of taggers of years past. The graffiti stretched along the length of the tracks as far as they could see and as high as a man — or a teenager — could reach from the ground and from the maintenance walkway above.

"Do you think they had those catwalks during the war?" she asked as he leaned over the fence to photograph the wall below them.

"Something like them. The tracks into Paris were partially electrified in the 20s, so they would have needed something to support the catenaries. After the war it was all rebuilt when the power system was upgraded from 1,500 volts DC to 25,000 volts AC. So these were probably added in the fifties but there would have been something there before that.

Aurélie asked, "Do you think the painting could be behind that stone wall?"

"Based on what Jerôme told you, it seems possible. My big concern is water. The water table is pretty high on the Right Bank. That's why the Catacombs and most of the old quarries are on the Left. More water is one of the reasons the Right Bank developed faster. You can't have a city without water.

"But if the lower basement is 15 or 20 feet below the surface and there's drainage to the tracks, the painting might be OK. It's on a wood panel and wood doesn't like moisture, so if the drainage is poor it could be damaged or even destroyed."

They turned back toward Rome, arriving just seconds before Philippe walked up the stairs accompanied by a short, round-faced man with a salt-and-pepper walrus mustache. Paul leaned against the métro entrance railing reading the International Herald Tribune.

"This is Jerôme Fontainebleu," Philippe announced. "Jerôme, you've talked on the phone to my daughter Aurélie. You helped her greatly with the plans for the building. And M. Grant and M. Fitzhugh, his associate."

Jerôme was tongue-tied. Aurélie did not fit the mental picture he'd drawn of the Sorbonne professor curious about an abandoned basement.

"Enchanted," he said after a pause. "And M. Grant. I know your family name well, and once I had the pleasure of meeting your father."

Jerôme took charge. "Philippe and I discussed having a fire inspector go with us but we ultimately decided it would not be necessary. I believe I can make this inspection as building inspector, and fewer people will therefore be involved. If we ultimately need a fire inspector I can arrange for one very quickly.

"In fact, I spoke this morning with the building inspector for the district and he told me the gardien, Mme Tuelle, is very accommodating, at least by the standards of her tribe. I suggest we go see her now."

They walked the hundred yards to the front door. Jerôme consulted an orange notebook, then keyed in the digicode another inspector had given him that morning. The door buzzed then slowly pulled itself open, allowing them to step into a small lobby with mailboxes along the right wall. A glass door would normally have blocked their way into the rest of the building, but today it was held open by a bucket of soapy water, with which Mme Tuelle energetically mopped the marble floor and stairs.

"Excuse me for disturbing you, Madame," he said politely to get her attention. "I am the building inspector and it is important that we go quickly into your basement." He held his identity card so she could see it. She touched one corner with her hand and suspiciously compared his face to the picture.

"I was younger when that was taken, but I assure you I am the same person. And I believe you are Mme Tuelle? My district inspector speaks highly of the care with which you keep your building."

All resistance vanished. "And your friends also?"

"They are all intimately concerned with the matter at hand."

"Of course." She pulled a ring of keys from her apron pocket and led them to a door under the stairway opposite the elevator, unlocked it, then reached through the door to turn on a weak yellow light that barely illuminated the concrete stairs.

"And, Madame, we will also require the key to the second basement," Jerôme said.

"I myself have never been there. But you will find the key in a small recess just above the door, which is next to cave number 6. Beware of spiders."

Philippe led the way down the narrow staircase. "You couldn't store much down here. Stairway is too narrow to get it in and out," he said.

The basement was divided into two long bays with a row of storage rooms on each side. Philippe took a small flashlight from his pocket and pointed it at the closest door. "Twelve," he said. "And its neighbor is eleven, so six must be straight ahead. Watch your heads."

Jerôme turned on his large inspector's lantern, brightening the gloomy space considerably. He walked ahead of Philippe to the end of the corridor and stopped, shining his light to the left.

"Here is number six, and next to it an unmarked door. This must be the one we require."

He pointed the light down toward his feet and looked around until he found a narrow piece of wood a foot long. He picked it up, then looked above the door for the niche Mme Tuelle had mentioned. When he had found it he put the end of the stick in it and, as she had warned, two spiders came scurrying out. He moved the point of the stick around until a key clattered onto the floor.

"That must be what we're looking for," he said jovially as he bent to pick it up. He inserted it carefully in the lock, pausing only long enough to say, “We’re not the first people in here. This lock was changed no more than ten years ago.”

The door swung open, its hinges complaining. Jerôme looked through and pointed his light to the left and followed it down the stone staircase, which was decades older than the one leading from the lobby.

The room was as large as the building, interrupted at intervals by stone columns that had been the main support of the old townhouse. Concrete pilings driven into the earth to support the added weight of the apartment building were spaced evenly.

“I hope they didn’t drive any of those through the painting,” Eddie said quietly to Philippe as he used his flashlight beam to pick out the pilings.

“I propose that all of us walk together around the walls,” Jerôme said. “There’s no substitute for more than one set of eyes.” They agreed and followed him as he began to move slowly around the wall, shining his light carefully on every square inch.

“We are looking for any disturbance in the old stone foundation,” he told them. “It’s possible that the treasure was buried below the floor, but that would pose greater risk of water damage because it would be closer to the water table. Therefore I believe it’s likely the treasure chamber will be reached through a wall.”

The wall looked impossibly ancient. It was built of rough-hewn stones mortared together into a foundation strong enough to support the townhouse. Eddie had seen a similar wall in the basement of his hotel building, and he suspected that behind the stones was a wall made up of even larger stones, which carried most of the weight.

Two-thirds of the way around they found a closed room built into a corner. A steel door stood slightly ajar in the solid concrete wall.

“Maybe we have something here,” Aurélie said.

“Or perhaps not,” Jerôme replied. “We shall see.” The door yielded slowly as he pushed until it was half open. Inside, the room was bare but for a rusted pail standing in the corner, half full of concrete. Jerôme bent to look at it as Eddie held it for his inspection.

“Ah! Now we’re getting somewhere. This is a Wehrmacht bucket, and was probably used to build these walls.” He turned to Aurélie and Eddie.

"Your friend the old art dealer was telling you the truth, or at least most of it. This basement was definitely used for some military purpose during the war. We will find something here. I'm certain of it!"

A half-hour later the group sat in front of the Café Normandie waiting for expresso. As they left the building Philippe introduced himself to Mme Tuelle as a commissaire de la Police and complimented her on the condition of her building. Then he asked if there were any other keys to the sub-basement. She produced one from a peg in her apartment and he put both in his pocket.

"Madame, it is very important that no one go into the second basement until we return. We are not investigating a crime but the history of a crime that long predates your building." She assured him she knew of no other keys and would guard the door carefully.

"Jerôme, what do you think that room was used for?" he asked as the waiter brought their coffee.

"We've seen others around the city, but almost all were empty like this one. In one or two we found a little loot, but that was years ago. If you think about it, an honest German wouldn't have hidden anything in the home of a Frenchman, even one as politically reliable as the Count.

"If the Count hadn't been sent to jail right after the Liberation and died soon after he got out of jail, I'd guess that he had moved the treasure somewhere else and we'll never find it. But he wouldn't have told his daughter about it. She was a Résistante and a patriot and would have turned it over to the government, especially since she had enough money from his estate. So that means either that the Count told Jacques the truth and he did give it to the SS, or it's still here."

Eddie interjected, "I remember my father telling me the Monuments Men found art objects of all types hidden in all sort of places, from cemeteries to barns."

"We will know tomorrow," Jerôme responded. "Or at least we'll know that we have more to learn.

"Philippe, can we come back at the same time? I'll need to organize some technical help."

"Sure. But what kind of help? Are we going to tear down the building?"

"Nothing like that. We'll use radar just like we do to look under roads and bridges."

Eddie and Aurélie looked at each other. "We wouldn't miss it for anything," he said. "We'll be here early." She nodded in agreement.

At ten o'clock the next morning Jerôme drove up in a blue city car, followed by a small white van with the name of an engineering firm painted on the side. A burly North African man wearing an incongruously lacy white taguiya stepped out of the driver's seat at the same time his assistant, thin and nervous, opened the right-hand door.

Jerôme met them at the rear of the van and watched as they carefully unloaded what looked like a lawn mower, an aluminum box painted bright yellow fastened to a low four-wheel cart with a push handle. The assistant set it carefully on the sidewalk, first checking carefully for dog droppings, and went back for a long extension cord. The senior technician took out a computer case, carefully closed and locked the door, then walked around to check that both front doors were locked.

"Are we ready, Monsieur?" Jerôme asked the North African man.

"We are ready, Monsieur Jerôme. We will need only power, and as you see we have a long cord."

Mme Tuelle had come to the sidewalk to determine who had the effrontery to block her door, only to find a smiling Jerôme waiting.

"Bonjour, Madame," he said cheerfully. "Please admit us to your basement. And our friends here will need electricity for their machine, and they have a long wire."

The gardien thought a minute and said, "There is a point in the cave not too far from the stairs. They may use that."

The two radar technicians muscled their machine down both sets of stairs to the lower basement. The younger one went back to find the electrical outlet on the floor above and plugged it in, while his older colleague took an HP laptop from its case and locked it into a bracket on the handle. The radar device, which looked much like a metal carryon suitcase painted bright yellow, hummed as the computer booted.

As he waited for the machine, he explained that the radar signal it generated would penetrate up to 20 meters into the earth below it. "Sometimes to look behind walls we bring a special frame that holds it up sideways, but this is a small space so we'll just hold it," he said. He rolled the transmitter slowly across the floor. They saw a baffling array of squiggles and curves that meant nothing to them.

"See, this shows a layer of packed stones just a few centimeters below the earthen surface, and then more than a meter of crushed rock. Below that there is undisturbed earth as far as the signal can penetrate."

Eddie knelt down to scrape at the floor with a stone. About three inches below the surface he found a smooth layer of small gravel.

"Jerôme, what were the sub-basement floors of buildings this old? This layer of rock looks like it might have been the floor at one time."

"Packed stone would have been usual for a second basement." Jerôme bent over to look closely at the small excavation Eddie had made. "This top layer is much looser than I would expect. We'll know shortly, but if I had to guess I would say that this was the dirt taken out of a room hidden somewhere behind these stone walls.

"That tells us pretty much all we need to know. Let's get started. We'll begin at the stairway."

Philippe interjected, "Perhaps we should try inside the little room first. It might have been built so they could close up the work while the digging went on." Jerôme agreed.

"After everything that's happened maybe we'll get some good luck," Aurélie said to no one in particular.

They all crowded into the small room. The older technician told his assistant to remove the handle and give him the computer. The slightly built young man proved stronger than he looked as he picked up the cumbersome machine and placed it against the rough wall. Jerôme held his bright lantern as the humming machine slowly made its way down the ten feet of the wall.

The man with the computer looked up. “Wrong wall,” he said with disappointment. “This is the one facing the tracks. After three meters it’s showing me air.”

They turned 90 degrees to try the other wall. The young technician set the machine carefully against it and began to push it toward the corner. “Slower,” his boss said. “There’s something there.”

“Look at this,” he said excitedly, holding the laptop screen out to the others. To them it looked different from the demonstration they’d seen earlier, but there was no detail they recognized.

“Look,” he said again, pointing toward the left edge of the screen. “This is the wall where we started. After about 30 centimeters we see an opening just behind the wall, here. Then after another meter we see this heavy solid object, which completely blocks the signal, and then more open space.

“Ladies and gentlemen, we have discovered your hidden room.” He took a pencil and made a faint mark on the wall, then another almost a meter to its right.

“The stones you see between these marks are just decoration. Behind them is a solid steel door, and behind that there is an open room that appears to be about three meters by three meters, a small bedroom. I cannot tell how high it is, but it will not be large. There are some odd reflections from within the room but my machine cannot resolve them well enough to tell what they are.”

Jerôme asked the radar technicians to survey the entire wall just in case there was more than one hidden chamber. He gave them his light and as they moved away he huddled with the others.

“Well, mes amis, we have definitely found something. When we get through that door we will probably find at least five cases of gold and one old painting, but there could be other treasures as well. On the other hand, there could be nothing.

“Do we report this to our bosses and go through a lot of bureaucracy or do we find out first what lies there?”

It would be Philippe’s decision, although there would certainly be differences of opinion between the police and the building department.

"If we go through the proper channels it will take weeks and become a complete circus. Then if the room is empty it will be more than a disappointment, it will make us all look like fools. I believe we need to find out what is there, but not move it."

"Good!" Jerôme responded. My view exactly." He lowered his voice to a whisper. "When the radar men are finishcd I will swear them to secrecy. I brought some tools with me today. I will get them and we will find out now what is there."

They waited a half-hour while the radar crew circled the room.

"Nothing," the senior man said. "I hoped there might be a second room."

"You have done well. Thank you for your work," Jerôme told them. "And please remember that you must not speak of this to anyone. When you prepare your report for billing, simply refer to a survey and not to the results." They agreed.

Jerôme saw the radar technicians off and returned with a heavy canvas tool bag. "I was a carpenter before I became an inspector, but I did a little masonry on the side. In Paris, every tradesman has to do that. So let's find out what's behind the wall."

Philippe added, "Let's just remove the stone, then we'll consider what to do about the steel door."

"This will probably do the job," Jerôme said as he pulled a heavy bricklayer's hammer from the sack. "With the pick end I can pull out the stones and with the hammer end I can use a chisel if they don't yield immediately. This can be dangerous work, so you'll need these." He pulled out four pairs of protective goggles and handed them around. "Who will hold the light?"

"I'll do it," Aurélie said quickly. She stepped to Jerôme's left and pointed the heavy lantern at the pencil marks on the stone. "Will you start with this one?"

Jerôme carefully inserted the pick end of his hammer into the crack between the marked stone and its neighbor to the left and pried. It moved but would not come loose, so he tapped all the way around to loosen the mortar. This time it came free and he caught it as it fell.

"The light?" He took the lantern back from Aurélie and held it close to the opening he had made. Then he struck the back of the hole with his hammer. It responded with a dull thud.

"Wood. They faced the steel door with wood to make a level surface, then mortared this wall on it. They probably used the rocks they'd removed earlier. One good thing is we won't have to worry about supporting the top of the doorway, assuming the steel looks strong. The last thing we want is for the building to sag."

In an hour he pried fifty stones from their wooden backing. Paul, Eddie and Philippe had stacked them neatly outside the small room, and a solid wall of old wood planks now faced them.

"Take it down," Philippe said.

Jerôme had to remove another twenty stones to find the edges of the false wall, but then it pulled away effortlessly to reveal an opening made by removing stones from the foundation. Behind it, cemented to the remaining foundation stones, was the steel door they'd expected. "It looks like a cell door from some Berlin basement," Philippe said. "And that's probably exactly what it is."

The door was the width of a normal door but short, about five feet from the floor to the top. It appeared to have been cut off at the bottom with a torch.

Philippe pulled on it but it refused to yield. "Smart of them to put the hinges inside so we can't cut through them. But this lock shouldn't be hard to pick. It looks like something from the 30s. I think we'll have to stop here and get help."

Jerôme said, "I don't really think we should stop. I know the radar men said they'd keep quiet, but they won't, and by tomorrow this will be common knowledge around the building department and maybe the police. Could you get a police lock specialist over here this afternoon?"

"I suppose so." Philippe went to the street to find a cell signal and called the préfecture. Within a few minutes he had a promise of a locksmith, two photographers, and two uniformed officers to provide security. Worse, the Préfet de Police himself said he would be there for the opening, and they were not to proceed without him.

An hour later the police photographers and the locksmith had arrived. Philippe had the entire basement carefully photographed and narrated a brief video explaining how radar had been used to see through the walls. The photographers had brought lights, which brightened the dim space considerably. The lock itself, which the locksmith was inspecting carefully with a magnifying glass, was mounted in a six-inch-square steel box welded securely to the door.

"There are still some cylinders like this around Paris," hc said. "It's a 1930s German model. It will take a few minutes but I can open it. My big concern is that the door may be rusted into the frame."

"Don't just stand there, man. Get on with it," the police chief said, not unkindly.

"Yes, Monsieur le Préfet." The locksmith asked everyone to leave the room and turned to his work.

"So you are the man who untangled this old knot?" the préfet asked Eddie. "We have not met but of course I know of you. This doesn't seem the sort of thing an English teacher would do."

"I had a lot of help…" Eddie started to talk but Aurélie cut him off.

"Monsieur le Préfet, I found the outstanding detective work Édouard did to be entirely consistent with his background as a decorated officer of the American Special Forces," she said. Philippe stood in the background and smiled.

"Is that true?" the chief asked. "I had no idea."

"Sir, this was a team effort and I am part of that team. I became involved because my father and his old friend were murdered by the people seeking this treasure. When this door is open I hope my brief career as a detective will be over," Eddie said.

The locksmith shouted, "I got it." Everyone moved back into the small room as he tried without success to pull the door open.

"Let me try," Jerôme said, moving up with his bricklayer's hammer. He inserted the pick end between the lock and the stone and began to pull on the handle. At first there was no movement, but then the hidden hinges emitted a high-pitched shriek and it budged a quarter of an inch. After ten minutes he had it open by an inch.

"Time for new manpower," Philippe said. "Eddie, would you give it a try? Still lifting weights?"

Eddie put both hands on the handle and one foot on the wall and pulled as hard as he could. The door suddenly moved another inch and the hammer came loose. He stumbled backward into the arms of the police chief, who caught him deftly and put him back on his feet while telling him, "Keep going. You're going to get it done. It should be your privilege, in any case."

With another minute of tugging on the hammer handle Eddie opened the door enough to get both hands around it. Philippe joined him and together they opened the door halfway, enough to gain access.

"You do the honors, M. Grant," the préfet said, handing Eddie the inspector's flashlight.

He stepped carefully to the door frame and pointed the light in — and whistled. "We've found most of what we've been looking for and I don't see any nasty animals, so we can go in. Be careful because the ceiling is only five feet high, and it's rough.

The préfet stooped to enter behind him, followed by Philippe, Paul and Aurélie. On the opposite wall a rack of three rough wooden shelves had rotted away and spilled their contents on the rough concrete floor. At their feet lay a pile of pristine gold bars mixed with the decomposing wood of the crates, plus several moldering leather suitcases marked with SS runes.

"Those valises probably have jewelry taken from concentration camp prisoners," the préfet said. "But there must be at least twenty of the wooden crates. I thought there were only five."

"Five is all Eric Kraft brought," Aurélie told him. "What this tells us is that Hans Frank sent much more than one shipment. I just wonder how many other Erics were out there, and if any of them had nasty sons.

"Édouard, what about the painting?"

"There seem to be several, all wrapped in canvas. I suggest we leave them to the experts. It's not as damp in here as I feared, but they may have been damaged already and we could do more damage by moving them. The Raphael is on a wooden panel, and we can see what's happened to the wood in here."

Philippe said, “Sound thinking. What do you think, M. le préfet?”

“We need to call in the experts from the Louvre right away, to take the paintings to their laboratory. We’ll seal this basement and leave two officers on guard but out of sight, and tomorrow we’ll have it all cleared out.

“M. Grant, you have done a great service. I will see it is not forgotten.”

Aurélie turned to Eddie, her eyes shining in the light of Jerôme’s lantern.

“It never would have happened if you hadn’t been so persistent. Thank you a thousand times.

“And welcome back.”

A REQUEST FROM THE AUTHOR —

If you enjoyed *Treasure of Saint-Lazare,* please consider posting a review on Amazon.com so other readers will learn about it.

The link is:
Amazon.com: http://j.mp/ReviewTreasureOfSaintLazare

I also invite you to subscribe to my blog, Part-Time Parisian
http://www.parttimeparisian.com

The sequel, *Last Stop: Paris* will be issued soon. Please stay in touch by joining my blog.

I hope you enjoyed my novel of Paris.

John Pearce

Made in the USA
Lexington, KY
30 October 2017